Emma's Gossamer

Dreams

Nurse Hal Among The Amish Series
Book Five

Fay Risner

1

ISBN-10 0982459556
ISBN – 13 9780982459553

Booksbyfay Publisher
fayrisner@netins.net
author website: http://www.writersownwords.com/booksbyfay
author bookstore http://www.booksbyfaybookstore.weebly.com

Gossamer dreams tangle in the mind like finely woven spider webs floating in the air. Thin and filmy objects they are that move about like strong transparent gauze in a gentle breeze. In the dark of night they are seemingly so very real, but the break of day leaves room for doubt and disappointment.

Look for all of Fay Risner's books in her book store
Http:www.booksbyfaybookstore.weebly.com

Nurse Hal Among The Amish series

Promise is a Promise – book one
The Rainbow's End – book two
Hal's Worldly Temptations – book three
As Her Name Is So Is Redbird – book four
Christmas Traditions – Margaret Yoder's story before she moved to Wickenburg
Amazing Gracie Mystery Series

Neighbor Watchers - book one
Specious Nephew – book two
The County Seat Killer – book three
The Chance Of A Sparrow – book four
Moser Mansion Ghosts – book five
Locket Rock, Iowa's Hatchet Murders – book six
and coming soon book seven – Poor Defenseless Addie

Stringbean Hooper Westerns

The Dark Wind Howls Over Mary – book one
Small Feet's Many Moon Journey – book two

Civil War story

Ella Mayfield's Pawpaw Militia-A Civil War Saga in Vernon Co. Mo.
Tread Lightly Sibby – Serbina Ellen Monroe Story in Texas Co. Mo.

Non fiction
Open A Window-Alzheimer's Caregivers Handbook
Hello Alzheimer's Good Bye Dad – A daughter's Journal

Chapter 1

"What was I thinking when I agreed to teach school?" Emma Lapp grumped as she threw quartered apple pieces into a bowl of water on the table. The water splashed her face. "That was not gute," she mumbled. She laid her paring knife down, grabbed the tail of her apron and wiped the water off. While she was at it, she scooted her prayer cap back where it belonged and wiped her sweaty forehead.

Hal rubbed the insides of a glass quart canning jar with a knife wrapped in the dish cloth as she twisted to look over her shoulder. She giggled. "That must have felt gute. It's hot in here. How about I stand close to the bowl, and you throw an apple in for me?"

Emma couldn't help smiling. "Ach, Hallie!"

"I knew you were too quiet. Now that you're in a better mood how about telling me what's wrong," Hal suggested.

Emma sucked in her cheeks and concentrated on peeling another apple. Finally, she stated emphatically, "I decided I am going to tell Bishop Bontrager I changed my mind. I do not want the teaching job."

"Ach fudge! That's nervous jitters talking. You're just worried, because this is something you've never done before," Hal reasoned as she placed the canning jar in the rinse pan with half a dozen others.

"You have that part right. I have never been a teacher before. I am not sure I will be gute at it," Emma said truthfully. Her gray green eyes sparked at the thought of becoming a teacher.

Hal rolled each jar in the rinse water and placed them upside down to air on a dish towel beside other jars she'd washed.

1.

"Take it from me, you will do just fine. Besides, you can't back out now. It wouldn't be fair to the bishop. At this late date, you should teach at least long enough for Bishop Bontrager to find another teacher to replace you. Just where do you think Elton would find someone now?"

"I reckon you are recht," Emma agreed reluctantly. "It is just I am not so sure I will be gute at teaching."

"I'm sure enough for both of us. You will do a gute job so go for it. This is just a year to year job. Everyone should try a new experience once in awhile. Make it through this year. See how you like it before you say jah again," Hal encouraged as she draped the dish cloth on the wire line behind the cookstove.

Emma looked troubled. "I always thought I wanted to learn more about nursing so I can help you in the clinic. I thought that was what you wanted, Hallie."

"Oh my, is that what is bothering you? You do a gute job of assisting me when I need you. As far as that goes, you will still help me when you're home. I repeat. Everyone should be able to have a new experience, and teaching is going to be it for you. You can learn nursing from me and still teach.

Now we have to get that kettle of apples on the stove along side the other two if we're going to get all the applesauce cooked and canned before we start supper."

"We did not make a dint in the baskets in the mud room," Emma said, transferring the apple pieces to the kettle.

"Nah, but once a bunch of us gets together at Freda Mullet's house the first of the week we'll make short work of all our apples," Hal assured her.

Emma giggled. "I wonder if Freda will be giving her broom a workout on the front porch when we arrive."

Hal smiled. "I expect so. You'd think Freda would have that porch floor clean by now. She sure works at it hard enough when company is around."

"Jah, and the rest of the time we are working, she is busy trying to make us do everything her way," complained Emma, placing the lid on the kettle.

Hal nodded agreement. "That's one bossy woman all recht,

but she knows how to organize to get the most work out of the rest of us. Got to give her credit for that, Emma. Speaking of organizing. It's our turn to have the worship service. We've got house cleaning to do before next Sunday."

"Jah, we must get redded for that," Emma agreed.

The back door slammed. Hal and Emma flinched as Noah and Daniel burst into the kitchen from the mud room.

The loud noise woke Redbird and Beth in their infant seats on the end of the table. They let out startled squeals.

Hal scolded, "Daniel, are you ever going to learn to come in quietly when the babies are sleep ----?"

Grinning from ear to ear, Daniel held his hands out with a new find to show them. A squirming baby raccoon that he had a tight grip on. The frightened creature was trying to claw its way out of Daniel's gloved hands as the boy walked toward Hal. "Look at what I found in the timber."

"Stop recht where you are. I see it fine from here. Daniel, be careful with that animal. It will scratch you," Hal scolded, backing up until she felt the counter stop her. "That wild animal wants to be turned loose. Those claws are sharp and ---- and ---- germy. Please, back away from the babies with it."

Emma looked scornfully at the raccoon. "Why do you have that nasty thing in the house anyway?"

Two years older and a head taller than his eleven years old brother, Noah gave Daniel a knowing look as he leaned down to say in his brother's ear, "I told you the women would not like your coon."

Daniel's face took on exasperation that widened his large dark eyes. "I just wanted to show you I caught it."

"That animal must be sick," worried Hal, staring at what at the moment seemed to be all legs and a long snout. "Otherwise, you wouldn't have been able to catch a wild animal in broad daylight and out by himself alone like that."

"He is not sick, and he was not alone," Daniel defended. "The rest of the babies in the litter were hidden in a hollow log with him. I heard them tweeting for their mother and thought it was baby birds. I got down to look in the log, and there they

3

were. Five of them. I grabbed the closest one and left the others. Noah said he didn't want one." Thinking that answered Hal's worries, Daniel held the raccoon up again for inspection.

Hal rolled her eyes toward the ceiling. "Denki for small favors. Daniel, why did you bring him home?"

"He is going to be my new pet." The boy held the struggling animal toward Hal and Emma for closer inspection. "Now you want to see? He is cute, ain't so?"

"We can see that coon just fine from here. Keep him away from us," Emma snapped as her face reddened enough to highlight her freckles. "Daed was all recht with you bringing that thing home?"

Daniel shrugged his shoulders. "Jah, he must have been. He did not say anything when he saw I had the coon."

"A raccoon may not be a gute idea. Won't Tom Turkey be upset to see you replaced him with a new pet?" Hal asked, trying to come up with a reason to get rid of the raccoon.

Emma agreed, "Jah, I would be if I were Tom. That is the worse pet you can have around him. That coon will eat Tom when he grows up, and you will have to get rid of him. Then you will be out of pets."

"Nah, do not worry. He will not eat Tom. I will not let him," insisted Daniel.

"I worry you will not be able to stop the coon from eating my chickens. When you are in school, you will not be able to watch him all the time. Where are you going to keep him?" Emma asked heatedly.

"In that wire cage in the barn," Daniel retorted.

"I use that cage to put setting hens in to break them up," Emma shrilled.

"How did wood cutting go?" Hal interrupted quickly. It was time to change the subject.

"We brought in a wagon load Daed parked by the chicken house. Daniel and me are going to rick it up along the back wall while Daed starts milking," Noah told her.

"You two better put that raccoon in the cage before he gets away from you in here. You need to get busy stacking wood. It will be supper time before you know it," Hal told them, flipping her apron tail at the boys as if she was shooing hens out of the garden.

"Can I have some milk for the coon? He is still small enough to need milk, and he must be hungry by now," Daniel worried.

"Sure. Noah, get some milk for Daniel out of the supply tank," Hal said, thrusting a cool whip bowl into Noah's hands.

"Quickly, Noah, get the milk." Emma voice held urgency, trying to get her brothers out of the house. "Daniel, the coon can drink it in the cage."

Hal and Emma stood at the open window, watching the boys walk across the front yard. The curtain swayed gently as the hot breeze carried the smell of cows from the barn into the kitchen.

Emma said, "That was the homeliest baby animal I ever saw."

Hal nodded. "Englishers have a saying. That baby was one only a mother could love."

"Jah, I agree," Emma said seriously.

"What creature will they try to make a pet out of next?" Hal asked, shaking her head. "First, a duck, a turkey and now a raccoon.

"We better get the boys a dog, before Daniel captures anything else strange."

"Jah, that's a gute idea," Hal agreed.

"The sooner the better," Emma said with certainty. She turned and saw the apple peelings. "Ach, nah! I should have told Noah to take the apple scraps to the hog pen." She rushed into the living room, opened the screen door and shouted over the hum of the milk generator, "Noah!

The boys turned.

"After you help Daniel get the milk come back for a bucket of apple scraps in the kitchen. Give it to the hogs."

"Jah, I will," Noah assured her.

In a short time, he was back for the bucket. As he picked it up, Emma asked, "While you were catching that coon, did you take the time to check out the walnut trees in the timber like you were supposed to do?"

"Jah, looks like there will be a gute crop this fall. We just have to wait for the nuts to drop and get to them before the squirrels carry them all off," Noah replied, headed out the mud room door.

In a minute, Hal glanced out the window toward the barn. "Noah isn't going to the pig pen with the bucket."

"Where is he headed?" Emma asked in exasperation, joining Hal at the window.

Noah met Daniel by the horse pen fence. Noah whistled shrilly. Six horses, in various shades of red, raced across the pen and lined up at the fence. He rifled through the peelings in the bucket and came out with an apple core. Daniel did the same. They held the cores at arm's length. Two of the horses curled their lips back and bared their teeth as their long tongues wrapped around the cores.

"That is not gute." Emma rushed for the front door and yelled through the screen, "You two stop feeding the horses those apple scraps. They will get colic if they eat too much."

"Ach! We did not mean to give them but only a treat," Noah called back.

Daniel held a core out to a bright red mare. She stretched her long neck over the fence and lapped up the core. "See how Molly likes apples," he shouted toward the screen door.

Emma walked out on the porch and planted her hands on her hips to reinforce her order. "I see just fine. Give the rest to the hogs. They like apples, too."

John Lapp peered over the barn door. "Boys, stop rutsching around. Get that wood unloaded, and help me milk."

Noah picked up the bucket, and hustled to the pig pen. Daniel headed for the wagon load of wood.

During supper, all the boys could talk about was Daniel's new pet. After devotions, the family settled down in the living room. John sat in his rocker, reading the latest issue of *Family Life*. Emma pulled the treadle sewing machine away from the wall and sewed on a dress for Redbird. As soon as she finished that dress, she'd sew another one for Beth. Hal carried the mending basket over by the couch and picked up one of Noah's pants that needed the leg hems let down. The boys turned out the Scrabble game on the table by the window and set it up.

"Did you hear the coon chattered after we left the barn tonight?" Daniel asked Noah. "He misses us when we are not with him."

"Jah, he does get noisy," Noah agreed.

John laid the magazine in his lap. "The coon is missing his mother. It was not a gute thing, taking him away from his family."

Daniel put down a letter tile. "I take gute care of my coon."

"Jah, we both are," Noah agreed.

John nodded. "Keep in mind he wild, and he grows fast. He will always have a wild nature. You can not take that out of him. How long are you going to keep him?"

"We did not think about how long," Daniel said, looking at Noah for an answer. His brother shrugged his shoulders.

John urged, "You should think about it. Early spring is mating season. Coons are set on finding a mate at that time. This one will not be any different. He can not be trusted, and he is very strong. He will attack you when he smells a female coon around. You need to turn him loose before then."

Daniel saddened at the idea. "All recht, we will." With a new thought, he brightened up. "Until then we need a name for our coon. Any ideas?"

"How about Barnabas?" Hal suggested.

Emma spoke up. "Nah, the best name is Barabbas."

John grinned at the significant of that name for a raccoon.

"I like Barabbas. How about you, Noah?" Daniel asked.

"Has a gute ring to it," Noah agreed, thinking they could appease Emma by allowing her to name the raccoon.

At bedtime, Emma knelt by her bed to pray. She felt as if she'd boxed herself into a worrisome corner. School would start soon, and she was so very afraid she wouldn't make a good teacher. What if she should fail? She always attempted to be the best at everything she did. She wondered what the People would think if they knew about her intense need to do her best. They might say she wasn't being a humble servant. They might call her prideful instead.

In her opinion, Emma didn't see a sin in wanting to do a good job no matter how great or small the task. She reasoned she wasn't trying to be perfect to show off or stand out from everyone else in the community. She couldn't help it if she felt the need to do only her best at everything she tried her hand at. She clasped her hands together and bowed her head.

"Lord, I need you to guide me. I can not do this job as school teacher on my own. This will be a long school year for me if I can not do a gute job. You are the one who measures how we do in life and determines if we have been successful at living our life. Help me keep my focus on you." As an after thought she added, *"Even if I am a disappointment as a teacher. Amen."*

Chapter 2

The first August worship service was in the basement at the Lapp farm. The humidity was stifling no matter where they congregated, but it was just a tad cooler in the basement.

At the end of the service, Bishop Elton Bontrager finished his portion of the sermon a few minutes before noon. Next he made the announcements. "I am sure everyone has heard by now Emma Lapp is the school teacher this term.

Parents need to meet on a week from Thursday morning for school clean up day. Everyone is to bring food for lunch and the necessary tools. As usual, you stay until the job is done.

Bill Boxholder is the school caretaker this term. Some of you men should make a trip to the school ahead of time to see what needs repaired. Give Bill a list so he can buy supplies needed for clean up day."

That afternoon, the younger children played a noisy game of volleyball in the back yard. Emma and the teenage girls sat on the shady end of the porch and in the grass.

Dangling her bare feet off the end of the porch, Emma said, "While we are together, anyone have a report about what you have done as our Young Mothers Secret Pals this two weeks?"

Fair haired Katie Yost, sitting next to Emma, perked up and swung her feet back and forth. "One afternoon the first of the week, I drove by the home of my secret pal, Marie Zook. Her laundry was still on the line. I knew she was spending the day at her mother's house. I stopped and gathered the laundry, took it in and folded it so all Marie had to do was put the clothes and linens away when she came home.

Katie giggled behind her hand. "My mother went over to see

the new Zook baby the last of the week." Her big blue eyes twinkled and her pale cheeks flushed pink with pleasure as she continued, "Marie was going on about how her clothes had been mysteriously taken off the line for her. She could not imagine who would do that, but she told Mama she sure did appreciate the help. Her baby had colic. She had been up all night walking the floor so she went to her mother's to get her to take care of the baby while Marie rested."

"I made two loaves of bread for Jennie Hoft while I was baking and slipped them onto her kitchen table while she was working in her garden," Emma told the group. "She has such a sweet baby. It was sleeping away in its carrier at the end of the garden while Jennie gathered tomatoes. The other children must have been with their father so I did not get caught."

"Same here." Priscilla Tefertiller leaned back with her hands behind her as she crossed her long, thin legs at the ankles and wiggled her toes. "We had so many odds and end vegetables at the tail-end of harvest. I put together an extra casserole and took it over to the Briskey place. Isaac and Molly Briskey's twins are at just the right age to be a handful now that they are walking. Molly took the twins with her to the hen house to gather eggs. She did not know I slipped in and left the casserole on the table."

"How will you get your dish back if she does not know who left it?" Emma asked.

"I bought some tinfoil pans that can be thrown away," Priscilla shared.

"That is a gute idea we can all use," Emma said. "I have one more request for a secret pal. Is there someone that can help out Hallie? I will be gone, and with two babies to care for, I am afraid Hallie is going to be snowed under with work since she is not used to working alone."

"I can stop by," Priscilla offered.

"So could I," Edna Stolfus said bashfully, ducking her head.

"Des gute. Denki to both of you. It takes a big load off my mind to know someone is checking on Hallie. The mothers will all be surprised later on when they find out which secret pal they had, ain't so?"

While they talked, the girls darted looks toward the barn at the teenage boys grouped in the shade of the lean-to. The one that really caught their eyes was Eli Yutzy, Deacon Enos Yutzy's son. He leaned against the barn in a slouchy way with his hands in his pants pockets. He wore a bright blue T shirt, with a Harley Davidson motorcycle plastered across the front, and blue jeans which created a curiosity among all the girls.

Katie spoke softly, "Do you think Eli is serious enough about rumspringa that he might turn English?"

Emma glanced toward the barn. Just her luck, Eli caught her checking him out. He gave her a smirky smile. Her face reddened as she quickly turned back to the girls. "Who knows about that one."

Priscilla sighed. "I wish Eli would look my direction."

All eyes were suddenly on her. It was clear the girl was enjoying rumspringa, too. Priscilla wore a handmade pink striped, tan dress with the hem way above the legal Amish dress code limit and no prayer cap. Her dark brown hair was in a pony tail. She looked defensively from one to the other of the girls that frowned at her. "What is wrong with all of you? It does not hurt anything to just look. If Eli was to take a liking to me and wanted me to go English with him I just might do it."

That brought gasps from among the group as Katie uttered timidly, "I hope you stay one of us. We would miss you."

Through the whole conversation, Diana Kingman sat next to Priscilla without talking. Emma inwardly groaned when she surveyed that girl's clothes. She wore a yellow dress, covered with tiny blue for-get-me-nots, and a prayer cap. At least her dress was as long as it should be.

Diana half heartedly experienced rumspringa. Her prayer cap was a way to keep one foot in the Amish world while she explored her options. Emma understood how the timid girl felt. Rumspringa brought many uncertainties into the lives of teenagers that they couldn't imagine until they went too far toward the English world. Often by the time that happened it was too late to turn back.

Diana was a plain girl with a long face and a nose to match. When she attempted a rare grin, her uneven teeth were the first thing to catch the eyes.

While the other girls risked a glance at Eli Yutzy, her gaze stayed on Jason Fisher, a friend of Eli's. The tall gangly boy dressed like Eli, but he didn't have Eli's easy going way with the girls. From what Emma had heard lately, Jason wasn't living very close to an exemplary Plain life. It didn't matter now during Jason's rumspringa that his parents had been very strict about their children's upbringing. Before rumspringa, Jason toed the line. Now that his parents wouldn't say anything about his behavior, he did anything he wanted. Most of it wasn't good.

Emma decided it was time to change the subject away from the boys. She invited the girls for a picnic in the walnut grove that evening and told them to help her spread the word to the others. They would have their youth group singing around a bonfire after they ate.

Soon Daniel, Noah and the other boys their age grew tired of the volleyball game. They trouped across the yard to join the older boys. At the sound of Daniel's voice, a loud chatter commenced in the barn.

Katie Yoder asked, "What is making that noise in your barn, Emma?"

"Daniel brought home a baby coon. When it hears his voice, the coon makes loud rackets," Emma explained, standing up when she saw people come out of the house. "We better make sure the rest of the youth group knows about the picnic before they leave."

Emma caught up to Eli Yutzy and Jason Fisher. They were headed for their buggies tied to the fence at the end of the driveway. "Hold up a minute, Eli and Jason. Did not know if you heard, but I am having a supper picnic in our grove and fishing in the pond if you want to bring a pole back with you. We will have the singing after supper around a bonfire."

Jason said, "I can not come back. I have a date so I have to get my folks home and get the chores done. Maybe next time,

Emma." He held his hand up. "See you around, Eli."

"See you around." Eli swaggered over to the fence post his horse was tied to and leaned against it, watching while Jason backed his buggy into the driveway. He gave Emma a crooked grin. "Sounds like a gute time tonight. You figure on slipping in anything stronger to drink than root beer cause I could help with that."

Emma frowned as she scolded, "Nah! I just made a fresh batch of root beer so we have plenty. Just because you are in rumspringa does not mean the others in our youth group practice it the way you do including myself."

Eli held up both hands in surrender. "Hey, I was just asking." He paused a long moment, studying her. "How come you do not take advantage of rumspringa now that you are of age? You should try something different while you have the chance."

"I already know what I want to do with my life. Besides, I would not make a very gute role model as a teacher if I showed a wild side," Emma explained.

Giving her that crooked grin again that made the girls take notice of him, Eli agreed, "Reckon not, but you should have some fun anyway while you can. That is what I am doing, and I like it." He asked, "How long has it been since you went for a horse ride?"

Emma shrugged. "Long enough I can not remember when."

"How about going for a ride with me? Say on next Wednesday afternoon after I get my chores done. We can ride in your pasture. How does that sound?"

"It sounds like fun. Denki for asking me," Emma said.

"As long as I am in an asking mood, the next preaching is at Abram Beiler's farm. How about I pick you up for the meeting. We can stay for the youth group singing that evening, and I will bring you home," Eli suggested.

The invitation surprised Emma. She twisted on her prayer cap strings, giving him an appraising look. While she wondered if he was serious about dating her, she took her time to answer.

Eli shrugged his shoulders and turned his back to untie the

horse lines. "That is if you would like to."

"I would like to," she said swiftly to his back, suddenly afraid he might change his mind. "I better help Hallie get our picnic supplies laid out while my brothers are helping Daed load the benches on the pew wagon. See you later."

As Emma walked up the driveway, she met Levi Yoder going after his family's enclosed buggy.

"Coming back for the picnic and singing?" Emma asked.

"Sure I am after I go home with my family and help do chores. A picnic will be fun. I am glad you thought of it. In a few weeks, we start harvest. Picnic weather will be gone before we finish with our work," Levi said with a twinkle of anticipation in his blue eyes.

Emma smiled. "I am glad I thought of it myself. We could have had the singing in the basement. It is only some cooler in the trees than the house, but the picnic grove is more pleasant than the basement on such a hot day."

Levi walked around her then turned back. "Ach, Emma, the next youth group singing is at the Beiler farm. You come to my house, and I'll drive the rest of the way."

Emma looked at the ground and blushed. "Ach."

"Was ist letz?"

"Nothing is really the matter. It is just you will not have to take me. Eli Yutzy is taking me to the singing," Emma said.

"I will see you there then." Levi quickly walked away.

Emma hadn't expected him to look and sound so bothered about her not going with him. It puzzled her that he did. Since they were old enough go out alone they went to the singings together. Matter of fact, they grew up together. She thought of Levi as a brother. She always felt he thought of her as his sister. She didn't understand why he'd be upset if she went to the singing with Eli instead of him.

Later, the youth group gathered around the pond and in the picnic grove. Emma and the other girls worked near the bonfire, laying out the meal. A fly buzzed past Emma's face. She swatted at it and felt a trickle of sweat run down her cheek.

She brushed it away. She'd be glad when the sun went down. It was too hot to sit close to the fire until after dark, but they needed the fire to roast hot dogs and marshmallows.

Emma stretched patchwork quilts out in the grass while the other girls cut watermelons and stacked the slices in two large kettles. They laid out the hot dogs and marshmallows beside a large cooler of root beer, bags of chips, hot dog buns, ketchup, mustard, paper plates and glasses.

Once the meal was laid out, Emma walked to the pond bank. She knelt down beside Levi. "Catching any fish?"

"Nah. Looks like Daniel is having gute luck." Levi nodded across the pond in the boy's direction.

"I am glad someone is catching fish," Emma said wistfully as she watched Daniel reel in and wished she could have brought her pole.

Levi studied her a moment with a crooked grin. "Daniel is only lucky, because you are not fishing. You are the one that usually catches all the fish."

"I do not think that is always so." Emma had to try hard not to sound boastful. "We are ready to eat now so fishing is over." She stood up and yelled, "Time to eat."

After the hot dogs and chips were gone, Katie Yost and Emma came around with the watermelon. As they relaxed in the grass, the teens chomped on the slices, talking and laughing between bites and spitting seeds off to the side. As usual, Noah and Daniel started a contest to see who could spit seeds the farthest. Everyone cheered first Noah then Daniel.

The herd of Lapp horses ambled close to the grove, grazing now that the day had cooled off. One of the horses, named Molly, heard the good time the group was having and tromped into the grove to see what was going on.

The first Emma knew the bright red horse was headed at the group was when she heard the thrashing of dry grass and snapping of twigs. She jumped up and flapped her apron tail at the horse, yelling, "Molly, get out of here."

Molly kept coming. She lifted her nose high in the air and caught a whiff of sweet smelling watermelon. She bucked and

15

whinnied as she picked up speed.

The horse approached Levi Yoder. He waved his hand at her that gripped the watermelon slice and yelled, "Get!"

Molly opened her mouth wide and bit into the end of the watermelon offering that came at her. She jerked her head back and ripped the slice from Levi's hand. His mouth flew open as he looked at his empty hand and back at the horse.

Molly consumed the slice with a gulp on her way toward Eli Yutzy. He growled at her, but Molly ignored him. She stretched her long neck out and bit the end off his watermelon slice.

Everyone waved their hands and shouted, trying to keep Molly from coming their direction. Emma snapped at Noah and Daniel, "Help me turn that horse around and get her out of here before she bites someone's hand off."

The boys threw their arms around Molly's neck. She raised her head in protest and lifted the boys off the ground.

As Levi grabbed hold of Molly's mane in front of Noah, he asked amicably, "You two need help?"

Eli sprang up. "I will help, too." He got in front of Daniel and put his arm around the horse's neck.

The boys twisted Molly toward the path as Emma bemoaned to her brothers, "This is a gute reason you should not give Molly fruit. She has a sweet tooth. This is all your fault she is ruining our youth group picnic."

Emma followed along behind the horse, brushing her tail with a leafy limb to keep her moving. Now that she didn't have a choice, Molly walked out of the grove with the boys hanging onto each side of her neck. When the boys turned loose and got out of the way, Emma gave the horse a hardy swat with the limb. Molly whinnied shrilly, kicked high in the air with her back hooves and raced back to the other horses.

Embarrassed by the interruption, Emma said to the group, "I am sorry about that horse. She is the worse kind of nuisance. Des gute the pest is gone now. Levi and Eli, there are more watermelon slices. Help yourselves."

In the waning light, the group sat around the bonfire, ready to start the singing. Noah and Levi handed out the sticks they cut to use to roast marshmallows.

Eli and Levi managed to get on either side of Emma. Blushing, she ducked her head when she noted the curious glances from the other girls. If her friends were to bring it up, she'd tell them she was as baffled as they were by Eli and Levi's sudden attention.

Daniel sat down next to Eli. As he stared into the bonfire, the boy thought about how Molly invaded the party and helped herself to the watermelon. He said softly in wonderment, "Lapps may be the only Plain folks who own a watermelon eating horse." That silly thought caused him to chuckle.

Eli Yutzy heard Daniel. The chuckling was contagious. He burst into laughter at what Daniel just muttered. When Eli received curious looks, he repeated Daniel's words. Eli and Daniel's laughter was infectious. The rest of the evening in between singing hymns, the teenagers laughed and talked about the Lapp family's watermelon eating horse.

Emma was relieved at the way the group took Molly's interruption. She had to admit this had been one of the most unusual singings any of them had attended. Not that she intended to say that out loud where her brothers could hear it. They should have known better than to encourage Molly's bad habits. As it was, she had to worry about what would happen next. The others were encouraging Noah and Daniel by laughing with them. If her brothers thought there was more fun to be had, they would invite Molly to all the picnic singings. Or, come up with some equally embarrassing prank.

Chapter 3

Wednesday afternoon, Emma was impatient for Eli to arrive. She caught one of the mares and stood by the barn, holding the reins while she watched for him. Finally, she saw dust in the distance and made out Eli trotting his horse down the road. She put the reins in one hand, grabbed a handful of mane in the other and leaped onto her horse. Trying to look relaxed, she crooked her leg in front of her, waiting for Eli.

"Gute afternoon," Eli greeted. "I see you are ready."

"I am," Emma said, trying her best not to sound too eager. "I did not want you to wait for me to catch my horse."

Barabbas heard their voices. He put up a chattering fuss. Eli's black horse pranced back and forth, making it hard for Eli to constrain him. Not liking the wild animal noises, the horse held his head high and tail up as he snorted toward the barn.

"Is that Daniel's coon?" Eli asked.

"Jah, but he is in a cage. He always makes a racket when he hears someone talk," Emma said, pulling tightly on her mare's reins to keep her from dancing sideways. "Easy, Sugar. Come on, Eli. The coon is spooking the horses."

Eli and Emma walked their horses side by side. Midway down the lane on one side was the pumpkin patch in front of the cornfield. The green pumpkins, partly hidden in vines, had a splash of orange on them now. On the opposite side of the lane was the wooden gate to the pasture. Emma handed Eli her reins and slid off her horse. She opened the gate and waited for Eli to lead the horses through.

After she closed the gate, Eli handed Emma back her reins and watched admiringly as the girl vaulted back on her horse with the agility of a rider long familiar with horses.

"Your horse has lots of spirit. He wants to run," Emma said.

Eli arched his head to one side and grinned. "Du est recht, and he's gute at it. How long has it been since you were in a race?"

Emma paused to remember. "A long time."

Eli one fingered a black curl off his forehead as he eyed her pointedly. "If I remember recht, you always beat all the boys when we raced on Bender Creek Road."

"Du est recht," Emma acknowledged shamelessly. That wasn't being boastful. Just a fact.

Eli's mischievous dark eyes held a challenge. "Maybe we should race and see if you still can win."

Emma declined. "Nah, it is much more fun to ride slow so we can talk and enjoy what is left of the day."

"Ach, come on. How about a short race around the picnic grove and through the hayfield gate hole to just on the inside the hayfield," Eli wheedled.

Emma looked doubtful.

"You are scared you will lose," Eli provoked.

His words straightened Emma up. She did not like to be dared, and she intended to win if she raced him. "Nah, not so. I would not lose."

"Then race me," he dared. "We will see who wins."

"Jah, I will race," Emma decided against her better judgment.

Eli gave her a sly grin. "That es a voonderball gute thing! Now what do I get when I win?"

Emma's eyes narrowed. "It sounds to me like you gave this race some thought before you brought it up. What you want?"

Eli pulled his horse over close. "How about a kiss?"

Emma shook her head slowly as she stared at this brazen boy as cocky as her rooster, Abraham. How could Eli so quickly ignore what he'd been taught? He knew *special* friends were to abstain from any physical contact and that included kissing.

Suddenly, Emma's eyes sparkled. "All recht! I do not expect to lose. If I accept the challenge, you realize you have to do something for me when I win?"

Eli looked doubtful. He knew Emma well enough to know she always followed the Ordnung. It was out of character for her to give in so easily about the kiss. "What?"

"I expect a kiss from you," Emma baited.

Eli reared back in surprise as he eyed her. "You do?"

"Jah, I expect you to kiss your horse."

Eli's face scrunched up. "Does not sound like a gute deal."

"Take it or leave it," Emma said firmly.

"I will take it. This horse will not lose so be ready to pucker up, Emma Lapp." Eli kicked the horse in the sides. Over his shoulder, he called, "See you in the hayfield." The horse took off in long strides with his tail straight back, leaving Emma in a dust cloud.

She kicked her horse into motion, yelling, "You cheated, Eli Yutzy. That was not a fair start." A gust of wind lifted her prayer cap up. Emma patted it down on her head and wished she'd thought to tie the strings before the race.

Eli's horse surged forward with such a speedy burst of energy Emma didn't have any hope of catching up. The horse's muscles strained as his mane flew out in the breeze. Eli stretched out ahead and disappeared around the walnut grove. When Emma rounded the trees and caught sight of Eli, he was bent over his horse's neck, headed in the direction of the hayfield gate hole.

Too late, Emma noticed the wooden gate was closed. At breakfast, her father mentioned he was going shut the gate. How could she have forgotten that? She shouted, "Slow down, Eli."

Eli glanced over his shoulder and back ahead to where she pointed. He saw the closed gate and pulled back on the reins. It was too little too late.

The horse braced his hooves to stop and slid forward in the slick grass. His muscular chest rammed into the wooden gate, bowing it but not breaking the boards. Eli flew over the gate head first and dove into the knee high alfalfa. With the breath knocked out of him, the boy crumpled up in a ball.

Emma dismounted and vaulted over the gate. As she went to her knees, she cried, "How bad are you hurt?"

Eli's face was blue white. "The ground is hard," he groaned. "My head hurts."

"It should," Emma said, feeling panicky. "It is bleeding."

Eli struggled to sit up and fell back into the hay. He closed his eyes. "Everything is spinning upside down and right side up," he gasped. Slowly, he rose up on an elbow. "Give me a minute to catch my breath." He rubbed the fast growing, raw lump on his forehead that oozed blood. "Ouch!" His face filled with fresh pain as he grabbed his right wrist with his left hand. "I think my wrist is broken."

Emma gently took his arm and studied the wrist. A renewed feeling of guilt hit her in the gut. She should have remembered the hayfield gate would be closed. If she had, Eli wouldn't be flat on the ground in such pain. She said contritely, "I am so very sorry this happened to you." The way his wrist was swelling and his hand dangled, Eli was probably right about his wrist being broken. "Can you get back on your horse? We need to get you to the clinic so Hallie can check you out."

"I'll try." Eli undertook to stand up. His eyes rolled into his head as he flopped back to the ground, and passed out.

Emma opened the gate wide. She grabbed the black horse and tied him to the gate then hopped on her horse. She raced to the house, yelling for Hal before she reached the porch.

Hal rushed outside, drying her hands on her apron. "What's wrong?"

Tears ran down Emma's face as she explained, "Eli fell off his horse. His wrist is broken, and he has a lump on his forehead. I tried to help him up, but he fainted. He may be injured other ways."

"Hook up the wagon so we can bring Eli to the house. We shouldn't move him anymore than is necessary. I'll call for an ambulance." Hal jerked open the clinic door, ran to the table and rifled through her nursing bag for her cell phone.

It seemed like forever to Emma from the time she left Eli until they were back in the hayfield. Eli was still on the ground with his good arm over his eyes.

Hal slid her nursing bag strap over her shoulder as Emma drove along side Eli. When Emma stopped, Hal jumped off the wagon. She knelt beside the boy then noticed Emma was wringing her hands. Emma was usually calm under pressure. Hal decided the girl was really worried about her friend and picked up Eli's hand to feel for his pulse. "How you feeling?"

"I hurt all over," he said weakly.

"Can you see me?" Hal asked.

Eli opened his eyes. "Jah."

"Do you know me?" Hal asked as she counted his pulse.

"Jah, Nurse Hal."

"Who is this beside you?" Hal pointed to Emma.

"Emma." Eli looked puzzled by the silly questions.

"That's gute. Think you can stand long enough to help us get you into the wagon? An ambulance is coming to take you to the hospital to get you checked out," Hal explained.

"I'll try." He struggled to sit up.

"Emma, be careful of that wrist," Hal warned as Emma put her arm under Eli's right arm. Hal lifted the other side. Eli wasn't much help, sagging at the knees. The three steps he took to the back of the wagon were painful. He groaned as Hal and Emma boosted him up to sit on the wagon bed. Hal climbed in and gripped Eli from behind and scooted him back. After she eased him down, she laid his broken wrist gently on his chest. "Hold your arm with your good hand so it stays put."

Emma tied Eli's horse to the tailgate with hers while Hal rifled in her nursing bag for a gauze strip to tape over the wound on Eli's head to keep the dust out.

Emma scrambled to the wagon seat and clicked to the horse. Fearing Eli might have a concussion, Hal stared into the boy's eyes to see if his pupils were dilated. Eli's eyes rolled upward, and his eyelids flickered.

"Don't go to sleep. Talk to me. What is your name?" Hal asked, patting his cheek.

"Eli," he whispered softly.

"That's right. Stay with me," Hal insisted, patting his cheek again. "Did you think the ground was hard?"

"Jah, it was," Eli mumbled, coming back from the brink.

"Stay awake, Eli. It's important," Hal urged, pressing on the gauze on his forehead to slow down the bleeding. She kept talking to him until Emma stopped the wagon by the house. The ambulance screamed into the driveway.

As soon as the ambulance left, Emma and Hal followed in Hal's car. The ambulance was already pulling away from the hospital canopy as they parked.

Hearing the whoosh of the automatic doors, the evening nurse, Lucy Stineford, peeked over the nurse's station. "Hi, Hal. Haven't seen you for ages. You here for a patient?"

"The young Amish man that came in all banged up from a fall off his horse," Hal told her.

"Sure thing. He's in exam room four. We have a new doctor interning named Mike Jones. He's examining Mr. ----." She paused to look down at the admit sheet. "Eli Yutzy."

"That's him," Hal confirmed. "We'll be in the waiting room until the doctor let us know if we can take Eli home."

"Fine. What happened to the guy? I thought the Amish were good riders?" Lucy quipped.

"They are, but this one tried to race his horse through a wooden gate that was closed. The horse stopped, but Eli didn't. He landed on his head and right arm," Hal told her.

"Ah ha." Lucy tried to sound as if she understood.

Hal and Emma waited for some time. Finally, Doctor Jones rushed to them, carrying a clipboard. His words came out swiftly. "Nurse Stineford says you're here for Eli Yutzy. I examined him. Mike Jones is my name." He held out his hand.

"Nurse Hal Lapp from the Amish clinic," Hal introduced.

"I've heard of you and good things I might add," he said and focused on Emma's tear stained face and dusty dress.

"Thank you. This is my daughter, Emma. She's Eli's friend," Hal shared.

"Wie bist du beit, Dochtah. How is Eli?" Emma asked worriedly.

"I set his broken wrist. Other than that, he has a concussion.

He needs to rest for a few days. I'll take you to him."

Eli slumped on the exam table. His arm was in a black brace and sling. He held an ice pack on the lump on his forehead and down over the swollen shut black eye.

"Can he leave?" Hal asked.

"Yes, but he has to stay quiet for a few days. If he sees double or any other symptom occurs get him back in here." The doctor turned to leave and stopped in the door. "While you get him dressed, I'll go sign him out at the nurse's station."

Hal picked up the crumpled shirt on the bed and looked behind her for Emma. The red faced girl stared toward the far wall. Helping a special friend dress was more than Emma wanted to tackle even if she was willing to help Hal with nursing duties. Hal held the T shirt for Eli to run his left arm in. She pulled it over his head, taking note of the motorcycle on the front. "I'll slip the shirt down over the broken arm and sling. It will be easier for you to undress later."

Lucy brought a wheelchair for Eli to exit the hospital in. The nurse pushed the boy outside. Hal and Emma helped him into the back seat of the car.

By the time they reached the Lapp farm, the day had turned dusky. Hal said, "John and the boys will be done milking soon. I should start supper. Hitch up the covered carriage to take Eli home in. With all the pain meds in his system, he's groggy. He might fall out of the open buggy."

"I will," Emma said.

Eli protested as he opened the car door with his left hand and stiffly stood up. "I can ride my horse home on my own."

"I am sure you could try on your prancing horse with that concussion and broken wrist," Emma snapped at him. "But I would just have to follow along behind and pick you up off the road about half way home when you pass out from pain. You will be better off in the carriage with me and save me the trouble. I will tie your horse behind."

"If you say so," Eli conceded meekly. He grimaced from the pain of getting out of the car and realized Emma was right.

Hal took his good arm. "Come up and sit on the porch with

me while we wait for Emma to bring the carriage. We can try out the new porch swing John and Noah just put up."

Eli eased himself down and took a deep breath, trying to keep from gritting his teeth.

Hal listened to the hum of the generator. She wondered how much time she had to work on supper as she sat gently down beside him. Not that it mattered. She'd get done on time somehow. "You in very much pain?"

"Nah, I think the pills helped some. I just do not know which hurts worse. My forehead, my black eye, broken wrist or the rest of my bruised body."

Hal patted his arm reassuringly. "The pain will be less after a gute night's sleep. Have your mother give you Tylenol for pain when the meds the doctor gave you wears off." She paused, wrestled with her curiosity and lost." Maybe I shouldn't ask, but I've been curious. What happened to get you in this shape?"

Eli grimaced as he wiggled on the swing. "I dared Emma to race me. I was winning, but the hayfield gate was closed. I could not get stopped. Reckon Emma knew the gate was closed?"

"This morning at breakfast her father mentioned he was going to shut it. Was going into the hayfield part of the race?"

Eli nodded.

"You have a nice horse. Maybe Emma was trying to get an edge for herself. She doesn't like to lose at anything." Hal couldn't tell if Eli's expression was anger or pain. "Here she comes. You'll soon be home, resting. Remember you have to stay quiet for a few days until the concussion goes away. That means no chores or heavy work. Emma, you best explain the doctor's instructions to Eli's parents so Enos understands Eli is in no condition to work until he feels up to it." Hal stood up and took the boy by the arm. "Eli, come along, and we'll get you into the carriage."

John stepped from the barn as Hal and Emma helped Eli slide onto the front seat. Hal backed out of the way.

"What happened to Eli?" John asked, pushing his straw hat back from his forehead.

"He raced his horse against Emma. We had to send him to the hospital in an ambulance," Hal said causally.

"He looks like he lost for sure and certain. Emma all right?" John asked, worried.

"She's fine," Hal said, smiling. "I'll bet Eli will be too by the youth group singing he's taking her to in two weeks."

"Eli is taking Emma to the singing," John repeated slowly. He scratched the side of his beard, trying to let that idea sink in. "Are you sure it is Eli and not Levi Yoder? Levi always takes Emma."

Hal rolled her top lip over her bottom lip to suppress a grin. "That's what Emma told me while we were in the hospital waiting room. That's if Eli is up to going by then."

John watched their enclosed buggy fade into the distance. "I am not so sure I like my daughter going anywhere with Eli Yutzy. I do not care if his father is a deacon. Have you taken a gute look at that boy lately since he is in rumspringa?"

"Jah, but keep in mind your daughter has a very level head on her shoulders," Hal assured him.

John still worried. "Jah, I know, but where are they going this time of night?"

"Emma has to take Eli home. He can't ride his horse."

"He is in that bad a shape?"

"He has a black eye, a broken wrist, a concussion and stiff and sore. Right now, he's in a lot of pain. If Eli had asked me before he challenged Emma to race, I'd have told him Emma doesn't like to lose at anything." Hal laughed. Then she put her hand over her mouth. "I'm sorry, John. I shouldn't laugh. Eli could have been very badly hurt. As it is, he has to have a few days bed rest."

"That happened to him in a horse race with my daughter." John shook his head as he headed back inside to finish milking. He turned. "Hal, did Emma win the race?"

Hal puzzled a minute. "I think the race was a draw."

On the way to the Yutzy farm, Eli slumped in the seat and closed his eyes against the pain while they bounced along.

Emma turned Ben into the Yutzy driveway and said softly, "Eli, you awake? You are home."

"I have been thinking," he said in a strained voice.

"About what?"

"Since I won the horse race I still need to collect my kiss."

"Nah, you did not win," Emma scoffed. "The bet was the winner was the first one through the hayfield gate hole."

"Jah, and I was the first one through," Eli insisted.

"Nah. You flew over the gate hole not through it on your horse. You did not win. Now let me help you into the house," Emma insisted. "When you are feeling better we will discuss when I can watch you kiss your horse."

After a groan, Eli's replied, "Do you not want to know what it feels like to be kissed?"

"I already know what it feels like. I've been kissed twice," Emma said, looking away from him.

"Did you like it?"

"Jah, then I woke up," she whispered.

"You dreamed it! That's not the same thing as a real kiss. Want to try it while you are awake?" Eli asked eagerly, leaning toward her.

"I do not feel like I sinned when I dreamed about being kissed. I have no control over my dreams. It would be a much different thing to be awake and break with the teaching to abstain from physical contact." Emma opened the door. "If you want a kiss, you kiss the horse. Let me help you climb down so you can get in bed. I have to do as Hallie told me and explain to your parents what the doctor said."

Something inside Emma kept her from being honest with Eli about being kissed. His pushy personality was too much like the farm hand that took her for that horrible ride on Bender Creek Road. That man forced his kiss on her, and she was forced to run away into the timber. Thoughts of what might have happened to her if Levi Yoder hadn't come along and saved her still made her cringe. Now when she thought about a pleasant kiss as Eli suggested, that man's kiss didn't count so there wasn't any need to bring it up.

Chapter 4

One afternoon, Emma hitched up Ben to the enclosed buggy to pay a visit to the previous teacher, Ellen Yost. She had just thrown the lines up into the open windshield when the raccoon chattered nonstop. She wasn't eager to go into the barn to see if Barabbas was out of his cage, but with the hens wondering around the yard, she decided she should make sure they weren't in danger.

Emma rounded the corner as the door flew open. Out popped Daniel with Noah right behind him. Daniel had a rope around the raccoon's middle and was trying to lead the bulking animal. His efforts were more dragging than leading as the half grown raccoon braced all four paws, digging into the ground.

"What are you doing to that poor thing?" Emma asked.

Noah elbowed his brother in the ribs. "Listen to her, will you, Daniel? Now Barabbas is a poor thing."

"You are torturing him," Emma declared.

"Nah, we ain't. Just teaching Barabbas to get used to a lead rope so we can bring him outside to play," Daniel explained.

"He is not enjoying it," Emma retorted.

Daniel picked the raccoon up. "He will when he understands he has to walk when I do."

Barabbas crawled onto Daniel's shoulder and wrapped himself around the boy's neck. He stretched a front leg down, stuck his paw into the boy's shirt pocket and brought out a sugar cookie. Holding it in both paws, Barabbas relaxed on the boy's shoulders and munched, showering Daniel with crumbs.

Emma's nose flared. "You are feeding that animal my gute cookies now?"

28

"I did not mean to," Daniel defended. "That was my cookie for a snack later. He accidentally found it."

"Make sure he does not get away from you," Emma ordered. "I am going to visit Ellen Yost. I do not want to worry Barabbas will accidentally find my chickens while I am gone."

Hearing Emma scold, the raccoon put his front paws over his eyes, causing the boys to laugh. Emma scowled, refusing to find the animal funny.

"See how cute he is. He will be gute," Daniel promised.

The raccoon rose and stepped gingerly onto Noah's shoulders and put his front legs around the boy's neck. His head snuggled up by Noah's ear. "I like you, too," Noah said as he rubbed the raccoon's belly. With the swiftness of an experienced pickpocket, Barabbas reached down into Noah's shirt pocket and stole his cookie. Noah proclaimed, "Ach, nah!" He made a grab, but it was too late to save his cookie.

Daniel slapped his leg and laughed. Emma marched away, fearful they weren't going to heed her warning about her hens.

The warm breeze didn't do much to cool Emma off in what was the hottest part of the afternoon, but she relished the time alone. She needed the quiet time to think. She wanted to come up with questions to ask Ellen Yost that would help her do a good job as the teacher.

Once in a while, Emma caught a whiff of sweet fragrance as Ben trotted on the gravel road. Blooming wild honeysuckle, intertwined with foxtail and wild purple asters to vine along the sides of the ditches. Emma couldn't imagine a more pleasant smelling wild flower in Iowa than honeysuckle vines that bloomed several times each summer.

At the next patch of honeysuckle, Emma whoaed Ben and stepped down from the buggy. She walked to the edge of the ditch and yanked an armload of blooming sprigs from the vines. Now the buggy would smell sweet, and when she put the vines in the vase Hal gave her so would the kitchen. Normally, she'd use artificial flowers, but once in awhile, fresh flowers like honeysuckle brightened up a room.

If she was lucky, some of the sprigs might make roots. She could plant them below her bedroom window. In the cool of the evening, the scent was the strongest. She'd love to go to sleep, smelling honeysuckle.

Emma cradled the bouquet in her arm and took pleasure in sniffing the flowers. Suddenly, she remembered she had somewhere she needed to be. She settled into the buggy, laid the flowers in the seat and snapped the lines over Ben.

When she pulled up at the Yost house, she admired the farm. It was one of the neatest in the community. Emma visited often with Ellen's sister, Katie, and had stayed all night with her sometimes. Eliza Yost, a robust woman, and her daughters, Katie and Sallie, were hoeing in the garden. Eliza waved and called, "Go on in. Ellen is waiting for you."

Ellen welcomed Emma and led her to the kitchen. "We will sit at the table. I can get us tea to go with the chocolate chip cookies I baked." Ellen slid the plate closer to Emma. "Help yourself."

Emma reached for a cookie. "Sure is hot out, ain't so?"

"Jah. Reckon we will be glad to see fall come," Ellen agreed.

Emma bit into her cookie and chewed. It crossed her mind this may be the only cookies she'd get until she had time to bake if her brothers kept feeding her cookies to the raccoon. "The cookie is gute." She took a sip of tea from the frosted glass. "How are your wedding plans coming?"

"We are doing fine so far. After our schtecklimann, Andy Hershberger, talked to my family for Melvin about marrying me, he started his visits between Bishop Bontrager and us to come up with a wedding date in November. Melvin and I publish our announcement at the first worship service in October."

Emma giggled. "That announcement will be the worse kept secret of any wedding published for a gute long while. The minute you told the bishop a new teacher would be needed everyone in the community put two and two together."

"Jah, I expect that is so. Anyway, the last minute rush is a worry, trying to get the house and yard cleaned during fall harvest, and all the food prepared. That will be our endurance test," worried Ellen.

"You and Melvin have plenty of relatives so all should go well. You know my family will help. Just tell us what you need done when you know." Emma sighed and turned the conversation to the subject that interested her at the moment. "I just hope my teaching this year goes as smoothly as I know your wedding will."

"It will. Let me go get all the material I collected for you to use as teaching aides to help you have a successful year." Ellen came back, her arms loaded. She placed a stack of magazines on the table.

Emma eyed the stack, wondering when she'd find time to read through all those magazines in time to do her some good. "How many pupils do you expect this year?"

"Should be close to twenty-five," the former teacher guessed.

"Really. That many?"

"One teacher should be able to handle that many pupils and a few more. I did not have any trouble," Ellen said.

"But I am not experienced," Emma complained.

"I was not either three years ago. The parents are very helpful, and most of the pupils try hard which makes teaching easier," Ellen explained.

Emma looked doubtful. "I hope so."

Ellen picked up a ledger. "This is the record book from last year where I recorded names, grades, absentees and what grade the pupils will be in this year. Study it to get acquainted with the names and ages of the children and grade levels. The first day have the children stand up by age and say their names. That helps you put a name to the faces. I assigned seats to the children the last day of school so they already know where they are to sit the first day of this term. Boys in desks on the left side the aisle and girls on the right."

"That is helpful. Denki."

Ellen smiled. "You may not be so agreeable with the seating arrangement once school starts. Watch out for the pupils that are close friends. If too much whispering goes on, you need to part them. Sometimes, the children do not get along. They need to be separated so they are not disruptive to the rest of the class. The long table at the back is where I gathered each class when I worked with them." Ellen placed her hand on the stack of magazines. "This is a teacher's guide called *Blackboard Bulletin*. These have been a great help. You might find it a gute idea to subscribe to keep up with what is current."

"Denki. What about the board of directors?"

"I have always gotten along well with them. You will, too. They are Amos Coblentz, Deacon Enos Yutzy and your father."

"Next week is clean up day," Emma said.

"You should be there," Ellen informed her. "It will give you a chance to visit with all the parents. That day will be much different from talking to them at worship service. At clean up, they want to tell you about their children, and what they expect from you as a teacher."

"Really?" Emma asked in a squeaky voice.

"That is not necessarily a bad thing. It is helpful to know where the parents stand about their children's education so you know how to keep them on your gute side," Ellen encouraged.

∂

The morning of the school clean up, buggies and wagons parked along the edge of the yard. The women and children climbed down as the farmers tied up to lower tree limbs and the fence bordering the timber.

Bill Boxholder organized everyone for what needed done. Some men ran reel push mowers. Others raked dried leaves and fresh grass clippings. Some of the boys tossed the mounds into metal baskets and carried them to burning piles.

Three men carried ladders, paint pails and brushes over by the school while three more men painted the horse barn. Emma watched as one man's brush swiped over the black block letters above the schoolhouse door. The words Timberview School, disappeared. Later after the paint dried, one of the men would get on the ladder with a small can of black paint and redo the school name.

Girls carried filled mop pails from the pump inside to women and dumped out dirty water. Two women, on step ladders, washed windows on the outside, and others washed the panes on the inside. Some women swept down cobwebs on the ceiling and swept the floor. Two others followed behind the sweepers with pails and rag mops. Others washed the desks and blackboard and dunked the erasers in the wash pan.

Amos Coblentz, a handsome, muscular farmer and one of the board of directors, was raking in the corner of the yard on the ball diamond. The area was bare of grass from years of so many young feet running bases. In dry weather, leaves fell early and tumbled across the diamond, lodging in the fence row. The man had already piled leaves in several small piles in the middle of the diamond for the boys to pick up.

Emma wanted to get better acquainted with this director. She carried her rake over to where he worked. "Gute morning. Looks like you can use someone to rake in your corner." She hooked into leaves banked around a fence post.

Emma guessed Amos to be ten years older than her. She knew he was a widower with two young children. He gave her a cool, blue eyed, detached gaze that Emma imagined went along with his numb feelings of loss. She was familiar with that hang dog look. She saw it in her father's eyes and on his face after they lost her mother, Diane. Her father stayed that way until Hallie Lindstrom came along. Afterwards, John Lapp became a changed man and so did his children.

Amos nodded. "Gute morning, Emma Lapp." He shook loose a bunch of speared leaves from the rake teeth. "Not so much to do here once we get the fence row raked. The children keep the diamond bare so leaves do not stay put long."

"Are your children old enough to go to school this year?" Emma asked, looking for something to say.

"Jah. My son, Jake, is in third grade already, and my girl, Marianne, is just starting. School is gute for the children. I have to always leave them with someone while I work." His face grew gentle and his voice kind when he spoke about his children. With his next thought, his eyes took on a dark, sad

33

intensity. "They miss their mother. School will take their mind off her."

"How long has it been since you lost your wife?" Emma asked as she tugged her rake away from the dead grass rooted in the fence ridge.

"A bit over three years now," Amos said quietly.

Emma recalled when Gladys Coblentz died in child birth along with the baby. Everyone in the community felt so sad for the young family's loss. Emma leaned on her rake handle and eyed Amos sympathetically. "I know how your children feel. My brothers and I lost our mother awhile back."

He turned to eye her. "Jah, I remember that now. Diane Lapp died about the same time as my Gladys. I reckon it just takes time for us to get over the loss, ain't so?" He asked kindly and focused on raking.

"Jah, time and being fortunate enough to have someone new come into our lives. Hallie has made a world of difference in our home," Emma said to comfort the man.

Amos stopped raking again. Interest in her words registered on his face. "Denki for the comforting words. I understand you are going to be the teacher this year?"

"Jah, I am," Emma said.

"That is gute. My children will like having you as teacher," Amos said sincerely.

Not knowing how to take the compliment, Emma ducked her head and hooked the rake into a clump of leaves. "Denki. I will take gute care of your children."

Amos leaned on his rake handle, regarding Emma for a long moment. Finally, he said with gratification in his voice, "I know you will."

Near lunch time, the women headed for their buggies and carried food to a shade tree. A couple men set up saw horses with planks on them to lay the food on. The parents took turns welcoming Emma as Timberview School's newest teacher. As soon as the prayer had been given, everyone sat in a shady place, eating and visiting.

The mothers decided among themselves which ones would

bring the snacks for the different holidays. Every parent had a tidbit to share with the new teacher about their children. Emma listened and thanked them for their information.

It was chore time when the Lapp family pulled into their driveway. Emma and Hal headed for the kitchen with an infant seat in their arms. John and the boys went to the barn.

In just a few minutes, Noah came running to the house. He breathlessly rushed through his message. "Emma, we found new chicks in a pen in the barn. Looks like a pretty gute hatch. We need you to come help catch them so they do not scatter and get lost."

"Sounds like fun. The girls are asleep. I'll come, too," Hal offered enthusiastically.

When they walked into the barn, the generator hum was loud. The coon started his usual upset chatter at the sight of Emma and Hal. In the pen, the mother hen heard the coon. She clucked crossly to warn whatever she heard to stay away from her chicks. The first cows, John let in, tensed up, lifted their head and listened. John had his hands full calming the cows down.

Daniel was standing outside the pen, waiting for help. He had an empty five gallon bucket beside him. Several cats grew nervous at the increase in humans and skittered up the loft ladder. Just a couple of scared yellow kittens huddled together in the alley between the pens. They were too little to know what to do now that their mother deserted them.

Noah unbuttoned his shirt and took it off.

"What are you doing?" Hal asked.

"You will see," he said, grinning. "I go in first. The rest of you follow me. As soon as I catch the hen, start grabbing chicks and drop them into the bucket."

"Sounds like a plan," Hal said.

They edged into the pen with Noah in the lead. The hen made a creaky growl as she stood up, exposing the chicks. The yellow balls of fluff peeped loudly when cool daylight flooded their warm, dark hiding place. The hen saw the invasion of humans coming at her. She bristled up and squawked angrily.

35

Slowly, Noah eased toward the hen, holding the shirt out in front of him. With a screeching growl, the hen charged into the shirt. Noah wrapped the shirt around her and held onto the protesting bundle. Hal, Emma and Daniel rushed around Noah's feet, grabbing chicks.

One chick flashed by Hal's foot. She grabbed and missed. The chick ran out the open pen door. Hal took off after it. She couldn't believe how fast a tiny newborn chick could run. The cheeping chick ran past the two kittens. They sat up and took notice of a possible snack.

Hal hollered, "Scat, kitties." She flipped her apron wildly as she raced toward them.

The kittens saw Hal looming over them. The flapping apron signaled danger. They ran around the corner of the alley to near the coon cage and hunkered down. Hal rounded the corner and spotted the backend of the chick as it burrowed under a handful of hay bedding in front of Barabbas's cage.

The raccoon had his eye on a possible chicken dinner. He sat up on his backend, flattened his body against the cage wire and reached his paw through to get the chick.

"Nah, don't do that," Hal scolded as she came at him.

The raccoon saw Hal's quick movement as an attack. He growled, hoping to back her off. This meal was his. He continued to stretch his front leg toward the clump of hay.

At that moment, the kittens decided between an angry raccoon and a yelling woman their spot wasn't a safe place. With the intention to get out of the way, the two kittens took off. They ran in front of Hal, intending to make it past her, but they ended up under Hal's skirt. Her bare feet tangled up with the yowling kittens. She fell in front of the raccoon cage, giving the kittens their chance to escape up the loft ladder. She hit the hard floor, face down.

Back in the pen, Emma cried, "Ach! Hallie fell."

As she landed, Hal was in a panic. Her only thought was to save the chick from the raccoon. She lifted her head, stretched her arm out and slipped her hand under the clump. Just as she wrapped her fingers around the warm, fuzzy body she felt sharp pains in the top her head.

"Ouch!" Hal snapped as she rolled over and sat up, hugging the peeping chick to her chest.

Instantly, Emma was on her knees beside Hal, and John bent over her. John asked, "You all recht?"

"I think I am, but I just had the most awful pain in the top of my head. Felt like needles stabbing me," Hal replied as she handed the chick to Daniel to put in his bucket.

Daniel and Noah's distressed faces stared at Barabbas. The raccoon quit chattering.

Emma cried, "Hallie, that awful coon has your kapp."

"Ach, nah! He's eating it," Hal cried, putting her hand to her frizzy, copper red hair, straying wildly from the braid.

"You want me to make Barabbas give your kapp back?" Daniel asked innocently.

"Not now. Not in that shape," Hal said disgustedly as she rubbed her head. "Ouch! My head is sore."

Emma parted the curly hair. "Hallie, you have some open places on your scalp. The coon clawed you when he grabbed your kapp."

"Am I bleeding?" Hal asked in concern.

John leaned over and checked. "Not much."

"Not much," Hal squealed. "Quick, Emma, come with me. Now is the time to get some of that nursing practice you wanted. You can wash the open areas with alcohol to disinfect them. I don't want to get sick because of that animal."

Hal glared toward the cage. Now that all the excitement was over, Barabbas calmly licked himself like a cat. In front of him, all that was left of Hal's prayer cap were the strings, curled up on the cage bottom as if he'd saved them for a trophy of his latest catch.

Chapter 5

The next worship service was at the Beiler farm in mid August. During the common meal cleanup, Margaret Yoder handed Emma a plate to dry. "You all ready for school to start?"

Emma nodded half heartedly "Jah, Sister Margaret, as ready as I will get. I have noticed a leg on the teacher's desk is about to fall off. Wonder who we could ask to fix it?"

Lovina Keim folded her dish towel over the line behind the cookstove as she said, "Adam will be glad to fix the leg."

"That is voonderball gute, Sister Lovina. Tell him he can come when he has time. I will be careful with the desk until he gets to the school." Margaret dried her hands on the end of Emma's towel, and Emma draped the towel next to Lovina's. "Now that we are done, the other girls and I are going outside."

Emma's youth group walked over to a spot in the shade of the house and sat down on the wiry, brown grass. The teenage boys had gathered in the driveway until they saw the girls. They sauntered over and sat down among the girls with the exception of Eli Yutzy and Jason Fisher. They slouched against the house. Eli still had his braced arm in a sling. He laid his good hand protectively over his brace, rubbing along it as a sign the arm was painful.

Emma walked over by him. She wondered if Eli was trying to make a point of being wounded to get sympathy from the girls. Or, was the action just for her benefit to keep her feeling bad for his getting hurt?

Emma leaned a shoulder against the house and nodded a greeting at Jason. She said to Eli, "Are you up to going to the singing with me tonight?"

Eli said regretfully, "I am not going to be able to make the singing. Some of the soreness left my body, but I have not been going much by myself. Not up to it yet."

Jason had a smirky grin. "Poor Eli. Ain't so, Emma?"

Eli glared in Jason's direction to quiet him. Eli saw the disappointment on Emma's face and added, "My poor horse is not the same yet, either. He has been stove up ever since he hit that gate. I will not be using him for awhile."

Without comment, Emma folded her arms over her chest and turned to face the group on the ground. *Was Eli just making excuses to ease out of their date?*

Levi had been listening. He twisted around in the grass. "Eli, I have a young, broken gelding for sale if you are interested. Sell him to you for a gute price so you are not afoot."

"I am interested. I will be over to look at him real soon," Eli said, sitting down by Levi to talk about the horse.

When Eli first asked Emma to go to the youth singing in his courting buggy, she considered trying to find a way to get out of the date without hurting his feelings. She had an uneasy premonition she couldn't trust him. She'd had one bad experience with a boy. She didn't want to get herself trapped into a similar one.

The next moment, she grew excited at the thought of another date with Eli. After all, wasn't he the one all the girls wanted to date? She was the envy of her friends since they heard Eli had a riding date with her. Then the girls buzzed like bees when they found out Eli asked Emma to the singing. All except for Katie Yost, her best friend. The girl barely spoke to Emma these days since she found out Eli was dating Emma.

So for two weeks, Emma continued to switch hot and cold about the date with this young man who wore a T shirt, jeans and high topped, black tennis shoes. Now at the last minute, he tells her he isn't well enough to go on their date. In the next breath, he's sure well enough to go look at Levi Yoder's horse.

Emma glanced over at Levi and Eli. Levi heard Eli tell her he was breaking their date. Now Levi had the chance to ask her to go with him, but would he offer? Maybe he thought she should bring it up to him if she wanted to go with him, but she couldn't do that. Not now. Not after the way Levi acted so disappointed when she told him she already had a date with Eli. That would be rubbing it in that he was her second choice.

What bothered Emma even more was the gloating look on Katie Yost's face. She was pleased Eli turned Emma down, leaving Emma to come to the group singing without a date.

Tired of the uncomfortable way she felt with the group, Emma walked with her brothers to get the enclosed buggy. She might as well go home and drive back to the singing after supper. While she waited for Noah to untie Ben, Bobby and Adam Keim came after their buggy.

While Bobby backed the horse into the hitch, Adam tapped Emma on the shoulder with a question on his face.

"Jah?" Emma asked.

Adam took his notepad and pen out of his shirt pocket and wrote, "You need the desk leg fixed at school?"

She nodded. "I sure do. When I want to move the desk around for the Christmas play, the leg is going to fall off."

Adam wrote, "I fix."

"Denki. I know you are busy at your carpenter shop so come when you can. I do not plan to move the desk for a while." Emma grinned at Adam. "I will try not to lean on that corner too hard."

Adam's mouth opened in a silent chuckle.

Bobby threw the lines in the open windshield. "We can go now, Adam."

Adam nodded and stepped up into the buggy. Bobby smiled at Emma. "It has been a gute day of fellowship, ain't so?"

"Jah, it has," she replied.

"How is the coon doing, boys?" Bobby asked.

"Growing like a weed," Noah said.

Daniel bragged, "He is learning to walk with us on a lead rope. He is a smart coon."

Adam wrote on his notepad and leaned down in front of Daniel. "Coons are smarter than some people. Be careful he

40

does not hurt you."

"We will, but I am not worried he will hurt us. He likes Noah and me," Daniel defended.

Bobby rubbed the side of his face as he looked at his shoes. "Emma, are you coming for the singing?"

"I will be back later after I help Hallie cook supper."

"I would like to come get you for the singing. That is if you want?" Bobby suggested slowly.

Trying not to show too much pleasure at once again having a date, Emma replied, "I would like that very much."

"See you later," Bobby said as he climbed into his buggy.

Emma watched in wonderment as the Keim buggy pull up by the house yard so Lovina could get in. She was going on a date with Bobby. Going to singings with him wasn't a new thing. Plenty of times, she'd ridden along with Bobby when he dated Annie. So had Adam and Levi Yoder. Maybe she was making too much out of the invitation. After all, Adam probably would be along and maybe even Levi.

After supper, Bobby Keim pulled into the Lapp driveway in his open buggy to pick Emma up. He was alone. Emma wondered why at least his brother, Adam, wasn't with him, but she decided not to ask. She knew she'd have a good time at the singing. She always did, and she was comfortable being alone with Bobby. He was a good friend. She trusted him.

As soon as Bobby and Emma entered the large Beiler machine shed where the singing was held, Emma caught the surprise on Levi's face before he turned his back. He hadn't expected her to come with anyone.

It tickled Emma when she saw Katie Yost's disappointment that she'd found a date on short notice. Emma had to try very hard to keep her pleasure from showing. She knew for sure gloating over someone else's discomfort was not the Plain way. As long as she was secretly harboring feelings of pleasure, Emma would have liked for Eli to show up and see she had a date, but true to his word, Eli didn't appear.

After the singing, the buggy ride back to the Lapp farm was a leisurely one. Bobby let the horse amble down the road. On such a mild night, he wanted the ride to last awhile, and Emma didn't mind. She was willing for the pleasant evening to last as long as possible.

After a time of not talking, Emma broke the silence. "I had a gute time at the singing tonight. Denki for asking me."

"I had a gute time, too. Our youth group sure shook the rafters," Bobby said, smiling at her.

"That we did," Emma agreed cheerfully.

Bobby asked, "Are you eager for school to start?"

"I do not think eager is the right word. I am very nervous," Emma said honestly.

"You will do fine. You always do gute at whatever you try." Bobby examined the back of his hands on the lines as he asked, "Do you plan to teach school long?"

"If I do all recht after the first year, I have no idea how much longer I might teach."

"Ever think about getting married?" Bobby asked out of the blue.

What a switch? Emma was suddenly filled with a curious dread about this conversation. "Some day I expect to get married like every young woman in the community."

Bobby persisted with, "You are at an age when girls start thinking about a home of their own. If some man was to propose to you soon would you stop teaching school?"

Emma gave the side of his face a hard look. Was Bobby Keim thinking about proposing to her? She hoped that wasn't the case. "Bobby, why all the talk about marriage? If not for what happened to Annie, you would be married. Are you thinking about marriage again so soon?"

Bobby's voice sounded sadly strained. "Marriage was what I wanted with my Annie. It has been hard to accept she is gone." He glanced at Emma. "You remind me of my Annie. You were as close as sisters toward the last, ain't so?"

"Jah, we were, but Annie and I were not anything alike. Her life had been much harder than mine. I can not imagine my life will ever be that hard," Emma insisted. "And as for marriage, I am not ready to think about that just yet. I am almost seventeen, with a gute home and a new and different job in my future. I am content with the idea that I have enough in my life for now." She glanced at Bobby. His face was blank. The only sign that this conversation wasn't going the way he wanted was a slight clinching and unclinching of his jaws. "What is it you yearn for out of this life?" Emma asked.

After a moment's thought, he said sadly, "Right now that is human companionship and not any more human misery coming my way, God willing, for a long time to come."

One date and Bobby was rushing into a hint of marriage just because they were friends. Emma decided it was time to change the subject. She looked above them. Maybe Bobby would take her home a little faster if he thought he was going to get caught in a storm. "Where before the stars shone, the sky has clouded over. I think it might rain soon."

Bobby took a deep breath as he looked toward the heavens. "Smells like it."

Emma inhaled. "Jah, it does."

"It does," Bobby agreed.

Emma ended the conversation with an agreeable, "Mmm."

On a distance hill, a coyote yipped. A faint string of cries answered from the opposite direction. As Emma listened to the wild calls of coyotes on the run, she realized Bobby was right about people when they reached his age. Everyone needed human companionship. Even wild critters cried out for mates, but she hadn't reached that age of longing for a companion yet. Bobby Keim might as well hunt somewhere else for a wife if he was in such a big hurry to wed.

Emma stepped down from Bobby's buggy. A pale glow flickered in the living room window. Hallie must have left the lamp on for her. She slipped quietly through the front door and found Hal in John's rocker, mending a tear in the knee on Daniel's pants. She looked up from her work. "You're back."

"And you are still up," Emma said, surprised.

"Jah, I kind of like mending after everyone's in bed, and the babies are asleep. It's a peaceful time. Anymore, there is always

43

plenty of clothes to mend. The stack in the basket keeps getting higher, and I'm not getting any faster." Hal looked toward the stairs. "Your father went to bed awhile back. I should go, too. Five in the morning comes awfully quick." Hal laid the pants in the mending basket beside the rocker. She busily wound the thread around the spool and stuck the needle in it as she casually asked, "How did your evening go? It was sort of a surprise when Bobby Keim came for you instead of Eli."

Avoiding the hint about Eli, Emma said, "I had a gute time with Bobby, but he seems interested in continuing to date me." She looked worried as she flopped down on the couch.

"That isn't gute?" Hal asked.

"Dating any girl might not be gute for Bobby as long as he is mourning the loss of Annie. He still is grieving, and he is comparing me to Annie. He said as much and even mentioned he thinks about getting married soon," Emma related.

"Well, you're a very sensitive, smart young woman. As long as you're aware of how Bobby feels, you can act accordingly." Hal tried to stifle a yawn.

"Bedtime, Hallie." Emma urged, knowingly, "You do not have to wait up for me after each date."

"That really wasn't what I did," Hal said half heartedly.

"Jah, recht." Emma laughed. "You did not stay up this late when I went out with a group to the singings. You should not do it now that I am dating. You need your rest."

Hal climbed the stairs behind Emma. She entered the bedroom as John dropped one of his farmer shoes on the floor. As Hal walked around the bed, John twisted to look at her. "Emma got home all recht?"

"Jah." Hal pulled her cotton nightgown off the wall peg.

"I reckon I should not complain. Bobby is a better choice as a special friend, but what happened to Eli?" John wondered.

"Don't get your hopes up about Bobby. It sounds like he's looking for a replacement for Annie. I don't think Emma intends to play second fiddle to anyone," Hal said. She unpinned her dress, slipped out of it and pulled her nightgown over her head. She thought for a moment as she pulled the covers back. "As for Eli, I'm not sure what happened with him. She didn't want to talk about it tonight. Perhaps, I'll get that out of her soon."

"It is gute Emma talks to you. She needs you to help her make sense out her feelings now that she is dating," John said, blowing down the lamp's glass globe.

In the darkness, Hal replied. "I'm glad she wants to confide in me. I enjoy watching Emma sort through her thoughts about her special friends. Reminds me of my teenage years."

That night, Emma slept fitfully. She rarely dreamed, but her head was filled with a slide show. Through her dreams slid faces of men coming out of the darkness. First was vain Eli smirking his disinterest about dating her. Levi showed up with his pained look. Bobby Keim's grieving face hovered over her, looking for sympathy. All of them were fading away when out of the darkness, a pair of large calloused hands beckoned with curled up fingers for her to come near. Emma strained to see the man's face, but it was too dark to make out more than the outline of his head. The dream repeated itself several times while she tossed and turned. Finally exhausted, she fell into a deep sleep, safe from the accusing intrusions of special friends.

Chapter 6

Before daylight, the alarm clock in John and Hal's bedroom rattled, signaling 5 a.m. It was the first day of school. Doing his job, Abraham, the rooster, crowed to start the morning for the chickens and the animals.

Everyone dressed and went at their chores. John and the boys headed to the barn. Emma and Hal carried the babies downstairs and set them on the table.

Diapering the babies in the baby bed woke them. Now they fretted about being hungry while Hal heated bottles. As soon as the babies latched onto their bottle, Hal sorted the laundry into piles in the mud room and filled the gas motored washing machine with water. She propped the back door open a crack, tossed the exhaust hose outside and started the motor. She dumped a load of underwear and soap in the agitating water and went to help Emma.

The girl had breakfast well under way. While she mixed the biscuits, rolled and cut them, Hal filled the coffee pot and set it on the stove. Once Emma had the biscuits in the oven, she mixed up a skillet of tomato gravy.

Hal tread barefoot through the dewy grass to the clothes line with the first load of laundry. After she set the table, she carried out the second load. The sun was just peeking over the eastern horizon, waking up the birds. They flitted nervously from trees to roof tops and back. Not quite sure what to do with their day. As the morning brightened, short snappy chirps turned to bursts of song that filled the air with a joy that made Hal appreciate her life on the Lapp farm.

As she moved along the clothes lines, she felt the cold, dewy grass between her toes. She'd grown accustom to going barefoot, as much as possible, like the other women and children. It was good not to get her tennis shoes wet. They would dry stiff. Besides, she enjoyed the feel of the earth beneath her feet.

A jenny wren hovered on the end of a limb in the maple tree and chortled a tune as Hal put a clothes pin on the last sock. She loved to listen to the wrens. Their tunes were so cheerful. When Hal entered the living room, she heard the wren sing again. He sounded loud enough to be in the house. She turned around. The wren was perched on the back of the swing, peeking in the open window at her.

As Hal entered the kitchen, Emma's humming sounded as cheerful as the birds. It was good to see the girl so lighthearted. Emma must have come to terms with her new teaching job. "Emma, I'd swear one of the wrens has been following me around this morning so he can sing to me."

Emma broke eggs into a skillet to scramble. "I know the one you mean. He is not afraid of much, but you get near his nest and see how his tune changes. He scolds a cross tune just as loud as he sings a cheerful one."

By the time the eggs were done, John and the boys came in through the mud room. After breakfast and devotions, Noah and Daniel changed from chore clothes to school clothes. Noah hooked Mable, a small, rust colored horse, up to the open buggy and pulled up by the house.

Emma was eager to leave early. She wanted to check out the building one more time and get her assignments listed on the blackboard before the pupils arrived. She made a handout for each pupil. Written on it was First Day Of School in block letters to color and lines for names.

John thought this would be the last day of cutting corn to fill the silo. He met Jimmie Zook, sixteen, and Adin Mast, seventeen, in the driveway. He hired the boys to help him. They hopped on the flatbed wagon and rode down the lane. In the field, John drove the tractor pulling the binder while the boys stayed along side, stacking the bundles on the wagon. At noon, they would be back to empty the wagon and eat lunch.

After the family left, Hal filled all three clothes lines. When the last dress was pinned, she backed up and put her hands on her hips while she surveyed the clothes flapping in the gentle breeze. She was pleased so far with her morning efforts. Emma had shown her how to hang clothes in an orderly fashion from small sizes to large ones.

When Hal entered the front door, she felt the house's emptiness. Without the school children and Emma, the place was too quiet. She realized the stillness wouldn't last long. One of the babies would soon be awake and wake up the other one. The kitchen would be noisy again, but that wasn't the same.

Hal opened a kitchen window to let in fresh air and heard chattering in the barn. The raccoon must be missing Daniel already. Tom Turkey strutted fast across the driveway from the direction of the barn, headed to the hen house. His head was high in the air and on the alert as he looked around him, chirping crossly. He, too, was calling for Daniel, but what he wanted was help to protect his hens. The raccoon sounded dangerous to him.

The outside noises disturbed Redbird and Beth in their infant seats. They set up a whimper. Feeding time again. Hal warmed them a bottle. She hummed a few minutes as the girls nursed. When they dozed off, Hal picked the babies up, took them to the living room and placed them in the crib.

She wondered what to do next. She always depended on Emma to tell her what needed to be done. Homemaking didn't come natural to her like it did Emma or even her own mother, Nora Lindstrom. Nursing was so much easier.

Emma said she'd leave a list of chores, but she was so anxious about her first day at school she forgot. She did leave a menu for the day. It read fried potatoes and sausage cakes for dinner, but Hal decided she was hungry for sugar cookies since the last ones Emma baked didn't last very long. She really should come up with dishes to fix on her own to go along with the potatoes and sausages. Rice might be easy since it practically cooked itself. Just put it in the pan and let it boil.

48

That would go well with the other dishes on the menu.

She got Emma's recipe book out of the drawer. As she flipped through the pages, she found several recipes, but the very first recipe was Sugar Cookies from Mammi Naomi Lapp. John's mother had handed that recipe down to his first wife, Diane. Now it was Emma's. Hal couldn't recall Emma making the cookies since she moved in. It should please John when he and his helpers came in from the field if he found a plate of his mother's cookies on the table.

Hal flattened the book in front of the bowl and laid a knife across the top to keep the pages from closing. The recipe called for five cups of flour and plenty of butter to give the cookies that buttery flavor. She grew hungry for a warm cookie just reading the recipe. Hal mixed the ingredients and read on. The dough had to chill so she put the bowl in the icebox.

Next Hal peeked at the babies. They were dozing. She had time to put on the rice. She stared at the cookstove. How did Emma build the fire? Hal reached for the stove lid handle from its place on the warming oven and picked up a front lid. She laid it aside and grabbed the poker propped in a corner of the wood box. Now, she mentally told herself, stoke up the coals and add a couple sticks. Watching the dry sticks catch fire, Hal breathed in wood smoke trickling up at her and sneezed. Quickly, she stepped back and covered the hole.

Soon the kitchen was warm from the heat off the cookstove. Hal pulled a gallon sized, stainless steel kettle from the stack in the cupboard. She filled it half full of water and set the kettle on the stove to boil while she hunted the rice.

Emma bought many items in bulk. Hal found the sack and discovered it was a large one. She debated how much rice to use. She got a cup measurer out of the cupboard, filled it twice and dumped in the simmering water. The small grains sank to the bottom of the kettle. That wasn't going to be enough for hungry men for dinner and the whole family for supper. Hal added two more cups. Still it didn't look like much underneath all that water. Maybe two more cups of rice would be enough.

She took a minute to count people she needed to feed again.

Three men for dinner, two hungry, growing boys, one daughter and a hard working husband to eat supper. She dumped the rest of the sack in. The grains mound up above the water. That wouldn't do. Hal poured enough water from the sizzling tea kettle over the rice until it was covered and put the lid on.

Just as Hal tossed the empty sack in the waste can the babies woke up. They needed changed. After that was done, Hal decided maybe she could rock them for a few minutes. After all it was just mid morning. It was too early to prepare dinner, and cookies didn't take long to bake.

With a baby in each arm, Hal sat down in the rocker in the living room. She hummed softly. The babies responded with smiles and coos. Finally, their eyes grew heavy, and they dropped back to sleep.

Hal rocked gently until she heard sizzles and splatters. Awkwardly, she eased herself out of the rocker with a baby in each arm and headed to the kitchen. Her mouth popped open when she saw rice flowing over the sides of the kettle and burning black under wispy smoke rising from the stove.

She laid the babies in their infant seats. The sudden movement was enough to wake them. They added their wails to the sizzling splats. Hal grabbed a potholder, pushed the kettle over to a cool spot on the end of the cookstove and jerked the lid off. The rice simmered down to just below the rim of the kettle, but the grains were still hard.

Hal got another kettle from the cupboard. She added water to that kettle and ladled out about half the rice into it. She slid both kettles back to the heat. Now she was satisfied she'd taken care of that problem. She'd have to wait for the stove to cool before she washed the boiled over mess off. Maybe by that time, some of the rice would burn away.

She turned her attention to the infants, sniffling that they weren't happy. By rocking their infant seats back and forth as she talked soothingly and hummed, the girls settled down. Once Mama was attentive again, Redbird and Beth dozed off.

While she watched the rice, Hal thought she'd cut out the sugar cookies. It should only take a few minutes to roll out a portion of the dough and cut out two cookie sheets full.

Hal brought the dough to the table. She floured a spot and hunted up the rolling pin and a tablespoon. She jabbed at the dough with the spoon, thinking to dump a chunk of dough on the flour. The spoon bounced off the hard dough.

"I've got to use more force. For some reason, this dough set up like cement," Hal muttered to herself.

She leaned over the top of the bowl and thrust the spoon harder into the dough. She sank the spoon up to the handle. She pried back on the handle, and watched it bend into a U shape.

"This isn't gute," Hal grumbled, inspecting the bent handle. She jerked the spoon out and chipped away at the outer surface of the mound. With her hands, she formed a ball out of the crumbles and floured the cold dough and the rolling pin. She set the rolling pin on the dough and pressed down with a grunt.

Hal put all the effort she could muster into smashing the rock hard dough, but it refused to roll out smoothly. She mumbled and grunted as she pushed the rolling pin, trying to squash thicker areas without any luck. For the most part, she rolled right over the cold dough. She grew more discouraged by the moment. At this rate, she'd never succeed at getting the roller coaster dough into a flat surface.

Finally, Hal gave up on perfection and cut the uneven dough into round circles with a glass. She filled a cookie sheet and opened the oven door. Before she thought about it, she stuck her hand in to test the temperature like she'd seen Emma do. She chastised herself. "Big expert I am. I don't have the slightest idea if the temperature is recht." The oven felt hot, and the gage registered 400. That must be hot enough to bake cookies.

"No offense Grandma Naomi, but I wish I'd picked out an easier sugar cookie recipe than yours," Hal said to the ceiling.

By the time she'd filled another cookie sheet, her arm muscles pulled, and her midriff was tense. She felt as if she'd tried to fight a rock into submission instead of cookie dough. "If I wanted to do a cardiovascular workout I would pick an easier exercise to start with than this one," she groused.

She stared at the rest of the dough in the bowl, dreading another try at filling a baking sheet. One glance at the wall clock told her, she had a reprieve. It was time to peel potatoes if she was going to have the meal ready on time. Besides, she didn't have enough energy left to fight the rest of that dough at the moment. She could finish baking the cookies after dinner. Hal took the bowl back to the icebox and went to the basement for potatoes and a jar of canned sausage patties.

When she came back upstairs, she found the rice bubbling out around the lids of both kettles. "Oh fudge! Another mess."

At the same time, she smelled the cookies. She opened the oven door and took out both cookie sheets as she listened to the mess smolder on the stove. Then she rushed to the cupboard and got another kettle. She ladled out half the rice from the two kettles on the stove into the empty kettle, and the brew settled down. She pushed all three kettles to the back of the stove so she could use the front and hoped she could get the black puddles off the stove before Emma saw them.

When John and the hired hands came in the back door, John smelled potatoes and sausage frying. He told the boys, "Something sure smells gute in ----." His voice trailed off as he spotted three, bubbling kettles, with a cloud of steam escaping from under the lids, lined up on the back of the stove. "Hal, what is in the kettles?"

"Hal turned her back to him as she placed plates on the table. She said quietly, "Rice."

John asked innocently, "What is in the other two kettles?"

Hal spoke with an edge to her voice, "Rice."

"I see. That is a lot of rice," he commented as if he needed to point that fact out.

The boys looked at each other and grinned. Hal's head went up as she slowly turned to face all three of them with narrowed eyes. The boys turned serious. John knew better than to stay on the subject. "Boys, we better get washed up." As he washed his hands, he said, "I have been ready for dinner for an hour. We will eat and get back to the field. A few more hours and we can stop the binder and bring the last load in."

"The food's ready. Sit down and rest while I put it on the table." Hal dished up the potatoes and sausages and filled a bowl with rice to which she added milk, cinnamon and brown sugar. "For dessert, I made sugar cookies."

John eyed the thick and thin cookies stacked on the plate and decided to be more diplomatic. "So you did. They look gute."

"I used your mother's recipe," Hal offered, hoping for a more favorable reply than she got about the rice.

Jimmie leaned over to Adin and whispered loudly, "I remember eating Naomi Lapp's sugar cookies. They did not look like that."

Hal's eyes narrowed at Jimmie as John said, "These are going to be just as gute a cookies as my mother's. I can see that." He winked, and Hal relaxed.

When Hal had the kitchen to herself again, she finished kitchen cleanup and reluctantly brought the bowl of cookie dough back to the table.

"Now if I could just beat this dough into submission I'd have this job done." Hal suddenly felt sheepish for talking to herself. "I shouldn't get in the habit of talking out loud in case someone in the family walks in. They would think that's just another sign I'm losing it."

At the sound of Hal's voice, Redbird let out a happy squeal and Beth a coo. Hal giggled. "Denki, girls. I don't know why I worried. I forgot I have two mother's helpers to talk to." She turned the infant seats so the babies could see her and waved the bent spoon in front of them. "All recht, I want you two to look at this poor spoon so you're smart enough not to try your Grandmother Lapp's sugar cookie recipe ever."

Chapter 7

Emma prepared her first day of teaching in her mind for days. Ellen Yost laid out the daily plan, and Emma went over it again and again.

Get to school early enough to write the day and date on the blackboard. Below that list the subjects and assignment pages for each grade.

At 8:30, ring the bell on the schoolhouse roof. The pupils file in and go to their seats. Tap the bell on the desk for silence. "Good morning, boys and girls," she will say. The children greet her with, "Good morning, Emma."

Emma scans over the room to see if anyone is absent and records them in the record book. Before she reads devotions, she reminds the pupils to sit very still with their hands on their desks. After the reading, the pupils stand by their desks with bowed heads and hands clasped to say the Lord's Prayer.

Next sing three hymns in front of the blackboard to get the pupils used to facing the back of the room for programs. Have the eighth graders go up first. That way the tallest children were in the back. Watch out for boys that don't want to share a song book with girls, or those that want to talk while everyone else sings. That meant Emma had to rearrange the group.

Emma had the song books Ellen gave her. The rest were at school. Some books were German songs to be sung two times a week. The other three mornings, the pupils sang from an English song book *Favorite Songs*. She was to let the pupils take turns picking the songs.

The night before school started, Emma couldn't eat much of her supper. When she went to bed, she tossed and turned all night, dreaming the same ominous dreams repeatedly about Levi, Bobby and Eli. She had rarely dream until now. That morning after she woke, the dreams she remembered so vividly filled Emma with a dreaded premonition that something terrible might happen that day but not necessarily at school.

After she entered the school without mishap, her nervousness stayed with her. She tried to calm herself with the thought that she had this ominous feeling because she was so worried about teaching. She hoped that was all it was.

While Noah opened the windows to let fresh air into the stuffy room, Daniel filled the water bucket at the well, dropped the dipper in the pail and set it on the washstand. Emma brought the broom and dust pan from the utility room and swept the floor, dusted the desks, and chalked a welcome sign on the blackboard.

She had just finished copying and passing out the posters when one by one, bright eyed, excited pupils rushed through the door, full of high spirits and eager for school to start.

After the pupils sat down, Emma asked them to stand to say their name and grade, starting with smaller grades. This way the children became used to speaking in front of others. For the first few days, pupils were always bashful from spending much of their summer with their family.

She felt her heart lift at the sight of the children's fresh, happy faces. Soon a lively dialog between teacher and pupils had been established. The pupils liked that Emma was their new teacher. She could tell.

There were two girls in first grade. Sweet, little Marianne Coblentz, Amos's daughter, ducked her head and spoke with a lisp. The other was Rebecca Jacobus first child of Joe and Beth. She smiled sweetly and spoke softly.

In second grade, Andy Stoll, son of Dan and Kaziah Stoll, stuck his hands in his pants pockets and spoke boldly. There were two girls. Nonnie Zook, with bright red hair and blue green eyes, made Emma think of Hallie. She must have looked like this child at that age. Nonnie's parents were Ella and Andy. Sarah Muhlenberg, a dark haired child, was the daughter of

Abe and Linda.

In third grade, Amos Coblentz's son, Jake, was a quiet child that spoke to his desk. The very opposite, David Mullet, a cheerful, loud voiced boy, was the son of Hank and Mary, and Rose Yoder was the youngest child of Luke and Linda.

There were two fourth graders, Marvin Bender and Ella Miller. Marvin was the son of Adin and Anna. Ella was the daughter of Roseanna Miller Nisely and stepdaughter of Samuel Nisely. Ella wasn't shy about speaking up. Her family had been friends with the Lapps for years.

The fifth graders were Malinda Bender, sister of Marvin, and John Mast, son of Butcher Ben and Edna Mast.

In sixth grade was Daniel Lapp, and Rueban Rogies, son of Cooner Jonah and Ellen. Freda Manwiller, daughter of Lizzy and Skinny Samuel Manwiller, and Mark Yoder, son of Luke and Linda and Levi's younger brother.

The seventh graders were Jimmy Miller, Roseanna's son, Edna Stolfus, daughter of Chicken Plucker Jonah and Freda and Matthew Stoll, the older brother of Andy.

In eighth grade, beginning their last year of school, were Sallie Yost, Hamish and Eliza's daughter and her friend Katie Yost's sister, Mark Bender, the older brother of Marvin, and Jennie Boxholder, the oldest daughter of Bill and Linda. Also, she'd be teaching her brother, Noah, his last year.

In all, Emma counted twenty-one pupils. She tossed review questions at them to see how much information they retained over the summer. The pupils were prompt to answer. Emma was impressed. Most of the answers were correct.

An eighth grader, Mark Bender, was knowledgeable about history. Emma smiled a challenge at him and tossed out another history question at random so the other pupils had a chance. Mark waited. After a pause indicated no one else knew how to respond, he answered.

Next, Emma pointed at the posters on their desks and ask the pupils to color and sign them. When they finished, the children taped the posters above the blackboard. While the older pupils put their name posters up for display, Emma helped the two first graders spell their names so they could sign their posters.

Once the posters were displayed, Emma called all the pupils to the front of the room. The older boys seemed lazy about singing, but Emma motioned for them to speak up, and they finally did.

At 10 a.m., she tapped the bell on her desk for recess. She reminded the children to go to the outhouse, get a drink of water and sharpen pencils so they wouldn't have to do these things during class. Then they could play. Fifteen minutes later, Emma pulled the bell cord. The loud clangs alerted the children to come inside.

After that, she gave assignments in history and geography and let the pupils study. The rest of the morning past quickly.

At 11:30, Emma dismissed the children by rows to wash their hands, get their lunch coolers off the shelf in the utility room then return to their desks. When they were seated, Emma said, "It is time to eat. I'll set the timer for ten minutes." Ellen had warned her to use the timer. Some of the children gulped their food down so they had more playing time.

Her mind was racing about what she should do before she ate lunch to give herself a good start in the afternoon. She looked up and noticed all eyes were on her.

Emma repeated, "It is time to eat."

Jimmy Miller waved his hand.

"Yes, Jimmy?" Emma asked.

"Teacher, we can not eat. We have to pray first."

"Thank you for reminding me. I am sorry I forgot," Emma said sheepishly. "Bow our heads."

The pupils recited a prayer in unison and then opened their coolers. Before they went outside, the children took turns wiping off the desks and sweeping up crumbs. After that, they had until 12:30 to play.

After lunch is story time for 15 minutes. Emma set the timer so she didn't go over the allotted time. Geography, history and health were the afternoon lessons. After the last recess at 2 p.m. for fifteen minutes, the pupils worked on English lessons. That happened were two days a week and spelling lessons the other three.

At 3:30, the children ended the day by going by grades to get their coolers then they returned to their seats. When everyone was ready, Emma tapped the desk bell, and the pupils filed out by rows.

≈

Later that afternoon when Noah and Daniel burst into the kitchen, Daniel counted five plates stacked high with cookies. "Oh boy! Cookies!"

Hal glanced up from Emma's recipe book. "Help yourselves, but remember these took hard work and a lot of sweat. You aren't going to feed them to that raccoon," she warned. "There's tea and milk in the icebox to go with the cookies."

Emma came in behind the boys and eyed the plates of irregular shaped cookies. "You have been busy today. You baked ---- a lot."

Hal emitted a tired sigh. "I didn't know I was going to make a bushel basket full. I just used the first recipe in your cookbook." She waved her hand over the table. "This is what I got. Let me tell you it was not an easy job."

"You should have turned the page. The other sugar cookie recipes make smaller batches." Emma picked the U shape spoon up from the counter. "What happened to the spoon?"

"I mixed the cookie dough with it," Hal said blandly.

"Next time use oleo. The dough will be softer," Emma suggested, trying not to smile.

"I'll remember that. Boy, will I remember. I'm sorry about the spoon. Do you think it can be straightened?" Hal worried.

"Daed can put it in the vise, but it will probably break," Emma said, her eyes on the three kettles lined up on the stove, spitting steam. "You have been busy cooking. What are we having for supper?"

"Rice."

When Hal paused, Emma looked at her. "And?"

"That's it so far. Rice." Hal stared at Emma's hand written recipe book as the words burst out of her. "Oh, Emma, I have a big problem. How can such a small grain swell up so big? I'm

58

looking through recipes for all the ways to fix rice."

Emma's eyes widened. "How much did you use?"

"All of the sack," Hal admitted tentatively.

Emma couldn't believe what she heard. "That was a brand new six pound sack!"

"I don't know how much it weighed. I didn't think that mattered when cooking rice," Hal protested.

Emma heard Hal's flustered tone. "That is all right. We can come up with some use for supper. Then we will work on what to do with the rest after supper."

"Thank goodness, you're home. You're always my lifesaver." As an after thought, she asked, "You know how my day went. Tell me how did your first day as teacher go?"

Emma shrugged. "Fine, I think. I will get used to the routine soon I hope. At lunch time, I had my mind on what I needed to do in the afternoon and forgot we should pray before we ate. The children had to tell me."

"It has been awhile since you were in school. You will get back into the routine soon enough," Hal encouraged.

That night, Emma dreaded going to sleep. She didn't mind pleasant dreams if she could have them. She wished for a subject, any subject, in her dreams other than special friends giving her an awkward time.

For some reason, she had a sudden longing to talk to her mother about what was bothering her. That surprised her. Emma missed her mother the most right after Diane died even though they hadn't been close toward the last. Diane closed herself off from the family until she killed herself.

When Hallie came into their lives, Emma knew she could always turn to her stepmother when she needed comfort. She could tell Hallie anything, but she wasn't comfortable talking about boys. With the problems her mother had in the last few years of her life, Emma knew she was fooling herself. Diane wouldn't have been one to go to for advice. Anyway, it wasn't something Plain daughters did with their mothers. Still she couldn't help feeling cheated that her mother wasn't there to go through this portion of her life with her.

Why couldn't she have the kind of hopeful dreams all Plain girls had in their teen years? Her dreams should be happy ones about a husband, a home and babies.

Late that night, the full moon beamed into Emma's room and woke her. The room was so light she thought for a moment she'd overslept. She focused on a white light illuminating the wall at the foot of her bed and gasped as she reared up on her elbows. Not sure she should trust her sight, she rubbed her eyes and blinked. The light was still there, and it wasn't moon light.

She must be dreaming for sure. That was the only explanation unless this was a vision from God. Her mother, Diane, was sitting on the blanket chest against the wall. Arms crossed over her chest, she calmly watched Emma's shocked expression. "Hello, my daughter," she said softly.

"Mama, you – you are dead," Emma stuttered.

Diane smiled. "That is right."

"Why do I see you?" Emma implored.

Diane looked puzzled. "Because you asked for me to come. Why do you need to see me?"

"Earlier I wished I had you to talk to sometimes, but that was if you were still alive. You are dead. I can not talk to you. I should not talk to you. You are a figment of my imagination," Emma reasoned.

Diane agreed in a hushed voice, "I know."

Emma was befuddled. "Then why are you here?"

Diane chuckled. "How should I know if you do not. Like you said I am just a figment of your imagination. If you do not want to talk to me I will take my leave. Gute bye."

Her mother faded in an instant from transparent white to a filmy spot. Darkness enveloped the blanket chest. In a cold sweat, Emma slipped down in the bed and pulled the covers up to her chin. *What is happening to me? Am I losing my mind?* She shut her eyes tight to keep from seeing anything else. Her last thought before she dozed off was, *I better be really careful what I wish for from now on.*

Chapter 8

It was a fairly cool morning on September 15th. Hallie put the wash on the line, bathed the babies, fed them and put them in their infant seats to nap.

She had the whole day ahead of her. John was helping harvest corn at Samuel Nisely's farm. On the to-do list Emma left her that morning was pick the last of the tomatoes to make ketchup on Saturday while Emma was home to help. Before Hal did that she had one other task that was not on Emma's list. She was determined to make a cake for Emma's seventeenth birthday. She couldn't buy cakes from the Weber sisters forever. It was time to work on her cooking skills and hope she did better with the cake than she did with the sugar cookie flop. Hal looked through Emma's recipe book and found a yellow cake. To be on the safe side, she went through the whole book just to make sure there wasn't a better cake recipe.

The first one seemed the easiest, and she had all the ingredients. No need to try a fancy cake. Emma wouldn't expect one of those from her.

Hal placed a large mixing bowl and wooden spoon on the table. She dumped flour in the bowl and added sugar, eggs, lard, vanilla and milk. She made a fast scrape around the stainless steel bowl. Flour belched over the top of the bowl into her face and dusted her apron, the table and the floor.

"Fudge! What a mess," Hal mumbled. She grabbed the dish cloth from behind the stove and soaked it in water. In no time, she had the powered spot on the table cleaned, rinsed out the cloth and folded it over the wire. She filled the mop bucket at the pump in the back yard and dunked in the rag mop head, squeezed it dry and mopped the floured spot on the floor. She threw the water out the back door and leaned the mop against the house.

Hal stretched across the table and moved the bowl toward her so she could stand in a dry spot. "You girls just saw what kind of mess I made. I'm going to go at the mixing step a little slower this time," she said softly to the sleeping babies. Hal ran the spoon around and under the liquid ingredients and mixed that into the flour. She'd just gotten the hang of mixing when a loud racket outside startled her. "What on earth was that?"

The noises came from the barn. A combination of hissing, growling, screeching and a metallic rattle that was hard to describe. Hal went to the window. In front of the barn, chickens cackled and scattered, running for safety. Cats appeared on top the half door, leaped to the ground and skittered behind the barn. Back of the barn, the horses whinnied nervously. In his pen beside the barn, the bull braced his feet, cocked his tail and snorted as he stared at the barn.

Hal wheeled around to race outside. Her hand hung up on the long handled wooden spoon in the bowl. She kept going as the bowl toppled over the edge of the table. She stopped at the barn door, out of breath and panting. The various noises had escalated with slapping sounds. She peeked hesitantly over the half door, worried Daniel's raccoon might be loose and after Emma's chickens.

Barabbas wasn't loose, but he really wanted to be to get the best of Tom Turkey. Tom instigated the battle by flying into the barn to tease the raccoon. At the moment, the brown bird was doing his usual high pitched chirping challenge from a few feet away. Tom lowered his head, and stretched out his neck. His wings extended and flapped as he attacked the cage.

Barabbas didn't give an inch. He growled and snarled as he stuck a paw though the cage and batted the turkey. His claws connected on the side of Tom's neck and brought blood. Tom backed off and ruffled his feathers in anger with the intention of charging again.

The last thing Hal wanted was to place herself in the middle of this battle. She knew first hand what kind of reach Barabbas had. Tom was really mad. He wouldn't give up without some friendly persuasion. She didn't want Daniel to come home and find Tom Turkey dead. He'd not like hearing she knew about the battle and didn't try to stop it.

"Tom, stop that!" Hal yelled.

Tom and Barabbas turned toward her voice.

Tom chirped at her.

Hal unhooked the door, opened it and stood to the side. "Come out of there this minute," she demanded to Tom.

Barabbas growled at Hal's tone. He sounded like he was ready to join ranks with Tom and take her on.

The turkey took a few steps in Hal's direction and paused.

"I mean it, Tom. Shoo!" She waved her apron tail at him then stopped. That might be like waving a red hanky at the bull. Tom wasn't used to her scolding him. He might think she was ready to take Barabbas's place in the fight. "Come outside, Tom," she said calmly from behind the half door.

Now that her voice sounded friendly, Tom gave a squeaky chirp and stepped out the door. Hal quickly went inside and closed the door. She didn't trust the turkey to be over his mad fit. He tilted his head to the side, studied Hal a moment, fluffed his feathers again and walked away.

"Gute, that's over," Hal said in relief.

The coon growled.

"I suppose you're mad at me for breaking up your fun. Not much I can do about that, but you should be grateful I saved you from that turkey," she scolded, shaking her finger at him.

This is not how I want to spend my morning, she thought as she hurried back to the kitchen. For a second, she stared at the upside down bowl on the floor. Flour and batter leaked out from under the rim and puddled around it. "Ach nah, did I make that mess? Now I have to start all over."

She scooped up the batter and threw it in the chicken yard. Chickens ate just about anything. Emma's hens would clean the batter up before anyone saw it. After she mopped the sticky spot on the floor and got rid of the bucket and mop, she washed the cake bowl and started over. "I have to be more careful this time. If I keep this up I can add mopping the whole floor to my to-do list for today," Hal grumbled.

She mixed a new batch of batter and poured it in two round cake pans. "Girls, keep in mind this cake should have been easier to make than the sugar cookies," she said to the cooing babies as she placed the pans in the oven. "Just don't let your sons bring home raccoons and pet turkeys that get into fights which you have to break up while you're mixing the cake."

While the cakes baked, Hal went through the icing recipes searching for Emma's seven minute icing, but it wasn't in the book. She was disappointed. She'd have to let Emma make the icing before supper for her own birthday cake.

Hal put the babies in the living room crib, and they cooed as they kicked their feet to catch their toes. She'd pick tomatoes for a few minutes then stop to check on the cakes. She took four five gallon buckets to the garden, filled all of them and carried two of the buckets to the house. The minute she walked into the kitchen a scorched smell hit her nose.

"My cakes! I forgot them," she cried as she grabbed two potholders. She opened the oven door and got a face full of smoke. "Oh my, the cakes are black." She pulled the pans out of the oven and placed them on the table. "I have to make two more cakes. At this rate, I won't get the tomatoes chopped before Emma gets home." Hal wiped sweat from her brow with her apron. She suddenly felt harried by the tasks that needed to be done before evening. She'd always considered herself a multitasker, but she sure didn't feel like one now.

The babies cried, woke up by all the noise. Hal brought them back to the infant seats on the table. She looked at the black cakes. "Let's see. I need the pans for the next cakes. Where am I going to dump them so no one finds them? I don't think chickens will eat them. I know, girls. I'll feed them to the hogs. If they don't eat the cakes, they will nose them under the mud wallow and get rid of the evidence. Don't tell anyone. This is our little secret. Be gute. I'll be right back."

Hal washed up the cake pans and mixed the batter. She put the pans in the oven and added a couple sticks of wood to the fire. Then she hurried out to the garden to bring in the other two buckets of tomatoes. She was in the garden when Margaret Yoder drove in and climbed down from her buggy. "Wilcom, Margaret. It's gute to see you. What brings you over?"

Margaret shaded her eyes from the sun's glare as she came, taking in Hal's flour covered face and apron. "I wondered how you were getting along without Emma around so I thought I would come find out. Does it suit for me to visit awhile or are you too busy?"

"A visit from you suits me just fine. The house seems too lonely these days when it's just the babies and me in it," said Hal, honestly. "As for getting along without Emma, I do just fine as long as the girl remembers to leave me a to-do list except for all the mishaps this morning. I'm not going to be done with my list when Emma comes home. I just hope she understands when I tell her what happened. Come in and have a cup of coffee with me while I fill you in about my morning. Before I know it the babies will want fed, and I really should fix a bite to eat." Hal started to pick up both buckets.

"I can carry one." Margaret took the handle from Hal. "What are you going to do with these?"

"Peel and chop them up, salt them down and leave them for five days so we can make ketchup." Hal said it just like Emma told her as they walked into the house. "Doesn't five days seem like a long time to let tomatoes set?"

"Not if the recipe calls for it." Margaret set the bucket by the counter. She tapped the chest of each baby to see them smile. "Get me a knife and bowl. I can help you while we talk."

"You shouldn't have to work when you visit," Hal protested.

"You need help, and I don't mind. Actually, that was the reason for my visit. To see if you needed help." Margaret frowned, sniffing the air as she looked around the kitchen. "Smells like something burning. What are you baking?"

"Ach fudge, the cakes! I forgot them again." Hal's shrill voice sounded like two tree branches rubbing together in a stiff wind. That scared the babies. Margaret tried to comfort the howling babies as Hal jerked open the oven door. She relaxed when she saw the golden brown cakes. "Des gute. Today is Emma's birthday. I baked the cakes for her." She placed the cakes on the counter to cool then hunted knives and bowls. By that time, thanks to Margaret, the babies were cooing like pigeons.

After she sat down, Hal asked, "Do you know how to make seven minute icing?"

"Jah."

"Could you make a batch for my cake? That's what I wanted on it, but I couldn't find a recipe. I just don't know where that girl keeps everything yet," Hal said, stymied.

"Sure, I can make the icing. Get me the ingredients, rotary beater and bowl," Margaret said.

As they worked, Hal said glumly, "Doesn't look like it will be much of a birthday party. John's helping Samuel Nisely, and they won't stop picking corn until dark."

"Same at our house with the men in the field," Margaret said. "After Linda helps the school kids milk, we could come over for awhile to have cake if that would help."

Hal cheered up. "Ach, that would be super, but you're busy."

"Not too busy to be curious about what your first cake tastes like," Margaret teased. "Now what happened around here this morning. You look ferhoodled. Why did the cakes burn?"

By the time Hal finished describing her morning, she thought Margaret was going to get too tickled to finish the icing. "That's about it."

"That's enough for one morning. I knew you really threw yourself into your work. You have flour all over you," Margaret chuckled.

"I do?" Hal grabbed her apron tail and scrubbed her face.

Margaret laughed. "You always make my day, my friend. Only moments like these happen to you. I never get stories from any of the other women like yours."

"That's because they are too smart to tell you what goes wrong. Anyway, I'm glad you're having a gute time." Hal

66

looked at the clock. "My goodness! It's time to start dinner. Where did this morning go?"

"As soon as I icing the cake, I'll help. All we need is a sandwich. We can work up the tomatoes this afternoon. Stop worrying. We will be done before Emma gets home," Margaret chided.

That afternoon while the women peeled and chopped, Margaret said, "Emma must be really busy now with teaching."

"She is."

Margaret gave Hal a considering look. "We haven't seen her for some time. Is she too busy to go to the singings with Levi?"

"Nah, Emma goes." Hal paused to chop up a tomato. "She just isn't going with Levi."

"Have they had a falling out?" Margaret asked in concern.

"Nah, other boys ask Emma so she dates them."

"I'm sorry to hear that." Margaret sounded disappointed. "I had high hopes for Emma and Levi getting together."

Hal sighed. "John and I did, too, but at this point, I don't see the match striking between Emma and Levi."

"To be honest with you, I heard something about Emma having several special friends," Margaret said.

"Who was talking about Emma?" Hal asked.

"Stella Strutt is on her high horse again," Margaret admitted.

"What is her problem now?" Hal asked, annoyed that Stella was trying to cause trouble for Emma.

"You know Stella. She is like a dinkel vesgocket when she lays an egg," Margaret said in a vexed voice.

"Most of the time that cackling hen's eggs are rotten from the very start. So what is her rotten egg now?" Hal asked dryly.

"She is worried about the younger generation's rumspringa tales she has heard," Margaret explained.

"What has that to do with Emma?" Hal declared.

"Since Emma has been seen with more than one special friend, Stella thinks she is promiscuous," Margaret said.

"That's ridiculous. She should know Emma better by now," Hal snapped.

Margaret nodded in agreement. "But you know Stella. She

does not think when she is on a tangent. She talked to Bishop Bontrager about the young people and their sins."

"She shouldn't be meddling in something that is none of her business. What does she think he can do about the situation?" Hal implored.

"She says the bishop, as our leader, should make sure the Ordnung is obeyed, especially by the youth. Stella had a whole list of examples. Special friends should be using two separate chairs when they date. Sitting on a couch or porch swing together only leads to temptations. She feels it is a disgrace that the youth are wearing English clothes and the worst of English garments at that. They were raised in Plain clothes, and they should still be wearing them according to her. In fact, she felt it would not hurt if all of the younger married women went back to wearing black dresses and white aprons. We need to set a better example for the young girls she says."

"That's terrible. I don't look gute in black," Hal exclaimed.

"Exactly what I thought about the other young women. We waited so long to be able to wear pretty dresses. It is different at my age to wear black since I am a widow. Why should the younger sisters want to revert back to black now?"

Hal wrinkled up her nose. "How did you find out all this?"

"Jane Bontrager told me."

"I get it that the bishop's place is to keep his flock on the straight and narrow. He might be able to force the People to stick to the old ways and Ordnung, but when their children are in rumspringa that seems to be a difficult matter. Did Jane say what the bishop told Stella?" Hal asked.

"He reminded her he puts messages in his sermons all the time to warn the teenagers to be obedient to our ways and their parents. He told her he would have better luck preaching to take better care of our souls than he would our dress code or our youth group's rumspringa mischief. What the Plain youth did in their teen years, and how they dress was a problem for their parents to work on. Parents had to decide how far they let their children go during rumspringa."

"Gute for Elton," Hal cheered.

While Noah built a fire to warm up the school, Emma wrote Tuesday, September 15th on the blackboard. Soon the pupils arrived to a comfortable room. They put their jackets on the pegs in the utility room and stored their coolers. By the time they left for home, the day would be warm enough they would leave with their jacket thrown over their shoulders.

Third grader, David Mullet tromped up to Emma's desk. His heavy farmer shoes always sounded like a load for his feet to carry around. He boomed, "It frosted a little last night, Emma."

Emma finished writing the date on the blackboard and sat down at her desk. "It did? I hadn't noticed. September seems a little early for frost, ain't so?"

"Jah," David answered quickly and retreated to his seat.

By that time, the rest of the children had taken their seats, talking, laughing and fidgeting. Emma tapped the desk bell for quiet. She opened her bible to the book marker.

Suddenly, she heard a shrill whistle. Her head came up fast. She looked sharply around the room, getting ready to blame whoever looked guilty for the rude interruption. Clunking sounds on the floor drew her attention. Tin cans, with the labels off, were rolling and bumping into each other on their way down the two aisles toward her. Puzzled, Emma stood up and watched the cans roll. "What is this all about?"

The children grinned as they said in unison, "Happy Birthday, Teacher."

Emma put her hands on her blushing cheeks. "Ach! Who said it was my birthday?"

Many fingers pointed at Daniel and Noah.

"I might have known," Emma laughed, shaking her finger at her brothers. She looked at the cans in a log jam against her desk. "I am to get a surprise with each can I open, ain't so?"

Ella Bender said, "We all bought fruit. We thought you would like what is in the cans that way. David kept you talking so we could stick the cans in our desk until we were all ready to roll them down the aisle at the same time."

"So it didn't really frost last night, did it, David?" Emma

smiled at him as he shook his head no. She clapped her hands. "I am so proud of you for coming up with this surprise for me. I have an idea if you think it will be all right."

"The children wait expectantly.

"I will bring a can opener to school. Put a small bowl and spoon in your cooler so we can all share the fruit for our lunches. How does that sound?"

She was rewarded with yes and smiles. "Now help me pick the cans up. We can stack them under the wash stand."

After devotions, the pupils came forward for the songs. Emma asked Ella Miller to suggest a song. She said, "I pick *Happy Birthday* for the teacher."

Emma thanked her for the thought, clasped her hands together and listened as the children sang to her.

A couple hours later, pupils were busy working at their desks when Matthew Stoll stretched his neck to see out the window. "Someone is coming, Emma."

Chapter 9

A light breeze tugged at the curtains as Emma walked over to the open window. The fall smells mixed with the scent of new books and crayons. "That is Adam Keim. He is going to fix a leg on my desk before it falls off. It should not take him long." It was 9:30. Emma went to her desk and tapped the bell. "It is about half an hour early, but Adam will make a lot of noise. Take recess now."

The children filed out of the school past Adam. He smiled and nodded a greeting at them as he carried his tool box and a couple small pieces of wood inside.

"Wilcom, Adam. Reckon you are here to fix my desk leg?"

Adam nodded. He searched from one desk leg to the other.

"This is the leg." Emma pointed to the right front leg.

With a smile, Adam wiggled his hand back and forth.

"That is right. It wobbles. I fear any minute the desk might fall on my lap," Emma said seriously.

Adam knelt down to inspect. He chose a board and his saw to take out of the building. Emma heard Noah's voice. "Do you need help, Adam?" There was a pause before Noah asked, "Think laying the board across the top of a fence post will do?"

Emma heard the brief grate of the saw on wood then Adam was back. While Adam hammered, she sat at the table in back while she used a hectograph pen to draw pictures on paper. The first graders should like doing this activity sheet. Speaking English in school was a must, and that was hard for first graders when all they knew was Pennsylvania Dutch they spoke at home. On this sheet, they had to name each item in English, color the items and draw a line from the clothespin in

71

the middle of the page to correct items that would be found on a clothes line.

Once Emma finished the copy she took it over to the hectograph duplicator. She pulled the gray paper pad cover off the surface and laid the copy down on the gelatin to imprint it. Once she peeled the copy off, she laid a blank sheet of paper on the gelatin and peeled it off to dry. She only needed two copies for the first grade, but she decided to make three more for the second graders so she could see how advanced they were in English. Sometimes, it was one thing to speak English and another to read the words. Emma wrinkled her nose by the time she'd made the last copy. The purple ink had a strong peculiar smell that kept getting stronger with each copy she made.

Emma dipped a sponge in the wash pan and washed all the ink off the gelatin very carefully so she didn't tear the surface. Once the gelatin dried, she could replace the cover. Her fingertips turned purple from the ink. After she scrubbed her hands with soap and washed them, she threw the purple water out a window along side the foundation where the pupils wouldn't step in it.

Adam's hammer and saw clanked against the metal tool box when he put them away.

Emma asked, "All done?"

Adam nodded and waved for her to come as he pointed.

Emma inspected under the desk. "Here is the true test." She tried to wiggled the heavy desk. "I am so glad you fixed it. It does not wobble now."

Adam gave her a big grin as he patted his chest. He took out his notepad and pen and wrote, "Anything else need fixing?"

Emma thought a minute and pointed to the wall under the windows. "Nah, but sometime could you build some book shelves. We really need space to hold all the library books instead of leaving them stacked up on that table in back where I help the pupils with their lessons."

Adam nodded yes.

"You can come whenever you have time. If it will take awhile, you could come on a Saturday when school is not in session," Emma suggested, hoping he'd take the hint.

Adam wrote, "I will have to buy lumber, nails and paint."

"That is fine. Give me the bill for what you buy so I can present it to the board of directors."

Adam waved good bye.

"Have a gute day, Adam," Emma replied.

She picked up the dried copies she made and placed them on her desk. The clock read 10:15. She reached for the bell pull as Noah raced through the door and collided with her. "Noah, you know better than to run in the school. What is your hurry?"

Noah stammered, "You – you must come quick! Hurry! Adam Keim is holding Matthew Stoll up in the air by the back of his shirt."

"Oh nah," Emma said disbelievingly.

"He is shaking Matthew like a dog shakes a rat," Noah insisted, pointing a trembling finger.

The children were standing huddled together, wide eyed. Emma sprinted across the yard with Noah right behind her.

When she came up behind Adam, he was shaking a warning finger in the twelve years old boy's face and looking stern.

As he struggled, Matthew snapped angrily, "Put me down."

Emma scolded, "Adam, put Matthew down right now. You should not treat a child like this." She pointed at the other pupils. "You are scaring the children. You need to leave."

Adam looked hurt by the sting of Emma's words. His eyes bored into hers as he set Matthew on the ground. His back stiffened as he walked to his buggy. He gave an extra loud snap of the lines over his horse and sent the horse out of the driveway at a fast pace.

Emma look at the children, wondering what happened. They crowded together, studying their feet. Emma couldn't imagine what came over gentle Adam to cause him to attack a pupil. From the look on the children's faces, they were just as surprised as she was.

Third grader, Jake Coblentz, had smudges on his face where he'd wiped away tears with dirty hands. Though the other children looked scared, Jake was the only one really upset. He must have been involved somehow with Adam's tirade, but Emma was mystified as to how.

She took the seventh grader, Matthew Stoll, by the shoulders and leaned down to him. "Are you hurt?"

Matthew swallowed hard before he answered, "No."

"We all know how easy going Adam is. What upset him so much to cause him to treat you that way?" Emma implored.

The boy scuffed the dust with his shoe toe and shrugged.

Emma couldn't let this go with a shrug. Now was the time to figure out what happened. "Very well, Matthew, I want you to come inside with me. Jake, I can see you are upset so I want to talk to you, too. The rest of you can take a little longer recess. I will call you when I want you inside."

She marched to the building with the two boys lagging behind her. The boys stood in the aisle while she brought her chair from behind the desk and sit down at the edge of the riser. "Sit while we talk."

The boys went to their desks which were as far apart from each other as they could get. Emma shook her head no. "Matthew, come up to the front and take a seat in front of me."

He came forward and plopped down.

Emma demanded, "Now I want you to tell me what happened, Matthew?"

"I did not know Adam Keim was behind me until he picked me up," Matthew evaded.

Emma asked, "What were you doing just before Adam picked you up?"

She heard sniffles from Jake. He was crying again.

Matthew looked over at him. "I had Jake by his suspenders, and he was trying to get away from me."

"Why did you do that to Jake?" Emma asked sharply.

"I was just teasing him," Matthew excused softly.

Emma narrowed her eyes. "How was that teasing him? When you let go of his suspenders you knew that would hurt."

Matthew shrugged his shoulders.

Emma held a hand out and said quietly, "Jake, come to me."

The little boy sniffled and wiped his nose on his shirt sleeve as he approached her.

Emma put an arm around his shaking shoulders and wiped a tear off his cheek. "Stop crying so you can talk to me. You are not in trouble. I just want you to tell me what happened," Emma urged gently.

Jake pulled on his ear as he looked her in the eyes. "Matthew caught me by my suspenders. He said I had to say I was a dummkopf horse's tail, or he would snap my suspenders."

"I see." Emma clasped her trembling hands tightly together in her lap as she turned her attention on Matthew. This was one of those difficult moments she didn't foresee happening. "I repeat, to turn loose of this little boy's suspenders would hurt Jake. You know that. Tell me again why you would do that to him? He is much smaller than you."

"I was just teasing him," Matthew said half heartedly.

"Does Matthew do this to you often?" Emma asked Jake.

Jake darted a quick glance at the older boy. Matthew's eyes narrowed in warning. Emma realized this was not the first time Matthew had bullied Jake and maybe others. "Look at me, Jake, while I talk to you. Don't be afraid. Nothing will happen to you. Does Matthew tease you often?"

The little boy directed his attention back to Emma as he wiped his runny nose on his shirt sleeve. "Jah, he does."

"It is not fun at school, knowing Matthew is going to tease you while you are here. Can I make it better for you by giving you my word I will not let this happen at school again? You will want to come to learn and have fun from this day forward. I promise you."

Jake smiled slightly.

"You boys go back to your seats now." Emma carried her chair behind the desk, walked down the aisle and pulled the bell rope.

When the children were seated, Emma folded her hands on her desk top. She took a deep breath, praying she'd say the right words. "We need to talk about a serious matter. Jake and Matthew told me what happened between them at recess. I am willing to believe Matthew when he says he thought he was

75

just teasing. That he did not realize he was hurting Jake's feelings and scaring him. In his own way, Adam Keim was trying to defend Jake. Adam can not talk so he showed his disapproval the only way he could by stopping Matthew.

Plain people are taught to forgive those who do something against us. Jake, do you want to forgive Matthew for the bad way he treated you? I know you are upset. If you would rather wait and think about it I understand."

Jake paused for a moment as if to summon up courage. He stood up, took a deep breath and turned to face Matthew.

Matthew bowed his head and glanced briefly at Jake as the boy said, "I forgive you."

"Now while we are at it, is there anyone else that wants to tell someone you forgive them?" Emma asked.

She wasn't one bit surprised when most of the smaller children stood and offered their forgiveness to Matthew. As bad as she hated knowing, she suspected the pattern of behavior Matthew developed as a bully included more pupils than Jake. It didn't give her any satisfaction that Matthew looked uncomfortable, but this was his doing. She just hoped her talk to the children would be his undoing.

"Now listen to me. Six, seven and eighth graders, helping the younger children should not be different from helping your younger brothers and sisters at home. We should all remember to be kind to them as they enter this new strange world at school that is so different from home.

I gave Jake my word he will want to come to school from now on, because things will be different. I tell all of you in the lower grades that goes for you, too. I mean to keep my word on that, but all of you older pupils will have to help me. From now on, I will be watching to make sure that happens," Emma declared with meaning as she eyed Matthew. "There is a verse I think you have probably heard before, but this is the right time to repeat it. She wrote the proverb on the blackboard as she said it. *I must be a Christian child. Gentle, patient, meek and mild. Must be honest, simple and true in my words and actions, too. I must remember, God can view all I think and all I do.*

76

"Now back to our lessons. Six, seven and eighth graders, I have a school proverb I want you to practice writing until you remember it." She got up and walked between the windows and the desks. Matthew Stoll had a pencil clamped in his mouth with his head slanted toward the ceiling. He might look like he was concentrating on what she was about to say, but then again, he might be daydreaming. As she past him, she took the pencil from his mouth, laid it on the desk and pushed the back of his head upright.

"No one is useless in this world who lightens the burden of it for someone else." Emma walked down the middle aisle and back to the front of the room and wrote that proverb on the blackboard. "Once you have given this proverb some thought I want you to write an explanation about what it means on your paper. By the end of the day I want you to hand it in. Remember to write neatly. That counts for penmanship, and do not forget the end of the week your first book reports are due."

First and second graders, I have an assignment for you that I copied off." She handed out the sheets.

When lunch time arrived, Emma said, "It is too nice outside to sit in here. We are going to eat in the sunshine."

The children sat around in the grass, talking while they ate. As Emma promised, while the children played she watched.

Matthew was among the older boys and girls playing softball. The five first and second graders gathered fresh mowed grass and made nests. They played they were birds as they flapped their arms like they were flying and landing in the nests. Emma asked Marianne, "What kind of bird are you?"

Marianne smiled and lisped, "I am a robin."

"Why?"

"I like robins. They are the birds that tell us spring is here," the little girl said, wrinkling her turned up nose.

"I am a wren," Rebecca Jacobus said cheerfully. "They are a happy bird and sing all the time."

Emma thought, *Just like you.*

Nonni Zook offered, "I am a cardinal. They are bright red."

"Just like your hair," Marianne pointed out.

"I am a bluebird," Sarah Muhlenberg said. "They are a pretty blue."

"Like your eyes, Sarah. That leaves you, Andy Stoll. What kind of bird are you?" Emma asked.

"A crow," Andy replied.

Emma gasped, "Why?"

"We pay attention when crows are around," Andy boasted.

Sarah put her hands on her hips. "Because they are noisy."

"They are loud. That is for sure and certain," Emma agreed. She couldn't help but wonder if Andy would be a handful in a couple of years just like his brother, Matthew.

"Emma, I made you a birthday cake, but I couldn't find the recipe for the seven minute icing," Hal said as she sipped tea later that afternoon.

"Sorry about that. I make that icing from memory. The recipe was handed down from my mother's mother to her, and Mama told it to me. I can write it down for you to use next time. You watch while I make it, and that will help you remember how."

"No need to make the icing. Margaret came to visit, and she made it," Hal said. "After supper, the Yoders are coming to have cake with you to celebrate your birthday."

"Des gute," Emma said as she washed her hands. "Are all the Yoders coming?"

"Nah, just Margaret, Linda and the smaller children. Levi is helping Luke in the field, and Mark might, too."

"I see," Emma said flatly. She was disappointed Levi wasn't coming. This would have been the reason for them to be together that he'd been looking for.

Hal noticed how drained Emma seemed. "How has your birthday gone so far?"

"All recht," Emma said much too quietly.

Hal leveled her gaze on the girl. "What happened today?"

Emma plopped down across from Hal and put her head in her hands. "It was one of those unexpected, awful moments I dreaded happening except I did not know what it would be. I sure found out this day. I hope I handled it recht."

"Tell me about it. You have a habit of taking everything to heart. Maybe it wasn't as bad as you think," offered Hal.

"Ach, jah. It was bad. Adam Keim came to work on my desk leg this morning. After Adam left the building, Noah came to get me. Adam was out in the yard swinging one of the older pupils around by the back of his shirt, shaking him, as Noah put it, like a dog does a rat."

"That doesn't sound like Adam," Hal said, mystified. "Have you ever known gentle Adam to explode in anger and attack someone? Especially a child."

"Ach, nah, I would not have believed it was possible," Emma avowed emphatically.

"There has to be a reason," Hal defended.

"Jah, in Adam's mind but not one that would be satisfactory to Matthew Stoll's parents when they find out about this. The blame will fall on me for not watching the pupils close enough since I am the teacher," Emma said, rubbing her forehead.

"Knowing Matthew as I do, I imagine his parents are pretty understanding when something like this is explained to them. I don't think their son's behavior will come as a surprise. Just tell them honestly what happened, and what you did about it," Hal explained.

"I would like to defend Adam so they do not blame him, but he should not have picked Matthew up and shook him. Adam scared all of the children. You know how sharp my tongue can be. I was so angry I scolded him gute. He put Matthew down and left in a huff.

I took Matthew and Jake Coblentz, who was crying, inside and talked to them. It was not like Jake to cry, because Adam was hurting Matthew. What happened did bring out the fact an older child is bullying younger children on a continued basis. I think I settled that problem. Reckon I would not have found out about it if not for Adam," Emma said ruefully.

"So you did fix the problem. That sort of thing happens all the time in schools. Always some tough kid trying to bully younger ones," Hal said.

Emma eyes filled with tears. "Maybe, but I wish the student getting bullied had been anyone besides the son of a director."

That night, Emma went to bed full of worries. What could she have done differently? She chastised herself. She should have been watchful at recesses for something to go wrong instead of trusting the pupils to behave themselves. Finally, she came to a decision to make the situation better, before the directors came down on her.

With the problem on her mind settled, she thought sleep would come, but it didn't. She peeked over the covers toward the far wall at the dark image of her blanket chest. Like a child, she found herself lying awake, waiting for the ghost of her mother to appear without warning in another vision. The next thing Emma knew the rooster crowed and woke her up. It was time to rise.

Chapter 10

That morning, Emma draped her towel over the wire next to Hal's dish cloth. "I have been thinking about yesterday. I will send a note with Matthew and Jake to their parents, telling them I want to talk to them. That way I can explain what happened and tell them I talked to the children. As for a solution from now on, I will be outside at every recess, watching the children so teasing will never happen again."

"I think that is the right thing to do. That should make the parents feel better," Hal agreed. "Would you have time to make me a grocery list? I'm going to take the girls into Wickenburg to Doctor Burns for their checkup, and I can get groceries while I'm in town."

"I can make one right quick. For some reason, we seem to be about out of flour already," Emma said.

Hal thought of the big batch of cookie dough and the cake she ruined. "It takes a lot to make bread," she hedged.

Emma handed her a paper. "I wrote down the ingredients needed to make laundry soap. We are about out. Make sure you get the washing soda and not baking soda. Better get another sack of rice. I know we are not hungry for it right now, but one of these days we might be."

Hal knew homemade gifts were what went over the best for Christmas in a Plain family. She wanted to go shopping by herself. One of the stops was at the cloth shop where she bought material to make Emma a fer-gute dress. She could use a new dress for her dates with special friends.

With Emma away all day, it was going to be easy to work on

the dress, but Hal was eager to start on the sewing project. She feared she wouldn't be done with the dress in time with all her other household duties. After she put away the groceries and had the babies settled in the crib for a nap, she got out Emma's pattern box. She hunted the paper pattern for Emma's dress and unfolded the material on the kitchen table. She laid the pattern pieces on. Carefully, Hal cut into the cloth. As the scissors snipped along the edge of the pattern, Hal realized that was the only noise breaking the heavy silence in the house. She found herself wishing for the afternoon to pass faster. She missed Daniel banging doors, Noah looking for something to eat and sorely missed Emma to talk with and work along side.

࿐

Late that afternoon, Emma was at the kitchen window when she heard the slow clip clop of a horse drawn buggy, pulling into the driveway. Bobby Keim stepped down and met John by the barn. Adam wasn't with him. It didn't look like she'd be seeing that man any time soon. He intended to avoid her like a bad wind storm. She'd never forget the hurt look on his face when she scolded him. Adam thought she was unfair. She wished he'd give her a chance to explain. She wanted to tell him she was sorry she talked to him the way she did.

She should talk to Bobby about Adam. Now would be easier than at worship service with other people within ear shot. The sooner the better so Adam and she could get past this.

She threw her shawl around her shoulders and walked across the driveway. Her father said to Bobby, "Sounds like a gute idea to buy feeders to put on the cornstalk ground, but if I was you I would buy the calves and dry lot them until you have the corn picked. If you wait until harvest is over, other farmers have the same idea. The price of calves go up."

"Jah, I think you are right. I know you are busy. Would you have time to go with me to help pick out the calves? My judgment on ones that gain fast is not gute," Bobby said.

"I will be done soon. Twelve acres a day goes pretty fast. Maybe it will rain sale day so I will not be able to go to the field, but if it does not, we can go anyway," John said. "Let me

82

know when you are ready."

"Denki. Gute afternoon, Emma. How are you today?" Bobby greeted quietly.

"I am fine. Could I talk to you a few minutes?" Emma asked. Bobby looked surprised. "Jah."

"I have to check the sows," John said, sensing he should go.

"Walk with me down the lane," Emma invited.

It was a pleasant afternoon though overcast. The sun had been stuck behind a cloud haze for a couple hours, a pale orb resembling a white dinner plate. Mourning doves chortled to each other. Somewhere in the hayfield, a rooster pheasant clucked for his hens to gather around before dark.

Emma looked at Bobby, and he smiled at her. She wondered if this walk had been a good idea. She didn't mean to give him the wrong impression. She'd better get this over with quickly. "Bobby, what I want to talk about is Adam."

Bobby looked forlorn. "I think I know about what. I am sorry for what happened at school. Adam told me what he did to Matthew Stoll. He was so upset, because he made you angry at him. He thinks a lot of you. You treat him like anyone that can talk."

"I think a lot of Adam. The fact remains he might have hurt the child if I had not stopped him. He looked so angry while he was shaking that boy. To make matters worse, the other children were frightened. It was an awful moment I am sure none of them will forget. I can not imagine Adam doing such a thing. Why did he act that way?" Emma implored.

Bobby cleared his throat. "Adam was teased in school, because he could not talk. When he saw Matthew grab Jake's suspenders, he was trying to protect the little boy."

Emma persisted, "I thought that was it, but there was a better way to handle the problem. Adam could have come after me. Or, he could have stopped Matthew a little more gently."

"He could have, but Adam did not think. He was angry. He knew what being teased felt like, and Jake was crying. Adam just reacted," Bobby defended.

Emma let out a long sigh. "I will have to talk to Adam the

first chance I get and straighten this out. He did bring out a problem that would have grown worse before I realized it. I am grateful to him for that. Now that I am aware of Matthew's bullying I intend to keep it from happening again by keeping an eye on the children at recesses.

What goes wrong at school reflects on my job as a teacher. I am glad I found out about the bullying before it went on any longer. Now we best go back. I need to help Hallie with supper."

They didn't talk on the walk back to the buggy. When they neared the house, Emma said, "Tell Adam I want to talk to him, and, Bobby, denki for explaining about Adam's behavior. It will help me when I explain what happened to the parents."

In the night, a yellow light gleamed through the window across the bedroom, sweeping over Hal's face and John's back. Hal rubbed her eyes and turned her head to see where the light came from. She rose up on both elbows and watched the light complete a circle several times from the wall to the baby crib and up to the ceiling. Her heart pounded, and her voice vibrated as she shook John's shoulder. "There's a car driving around in our back yard."

"There is?" He rose up on his elbow, watched the yellow circling motion and listened for a car motor. "Hal, that is not car lights. Just one of Emma's boyfriends with a flashlight."

"This time of night? Why would he wake us up this way?" Hal said, astonished.

John grinned at her. "He did not mean to wake us up. He is looking for Emma. It is permitted when a girl is dating for a boy to shine a flashlight into the girl's bedroom window to wake her up so she will go downstairs and talk to him."

"He doesn't seem to want to give up and go home. We need to tell him he has the wrong window before he wakes the babies." Hal threw back the covers and pattered to the window. She looked below. With the flashlight's glare wavering in her eyes, she could make out a man's dark form behind the light but not who he was. She raised the window and called testily, "Who's down there?"

"It is Eli Yutzy," came the timid reply.

Hal snapped, "This is the wrong window. You woke up Emma's father and me. Emma's room is the third window."

"I am sorry," the boy called as she closed the window.

In a few minutes, John and Hal heard soft, quick steps moving in the hall and on the stairs.

John whispered in a disbelieving tone, "That was Eli Yutzy? What happened to Bobby Keim?"

"I'm as disappointed as you are that Eli is still around, but don't expect Bobby to come back soon," Hal said knowingly.

John sounded surprised. "But Emma just went for a walk with Bobby this afternoon."

"She talked to him about what Adam did at school. Remember Emma said Bobby's looking for a replacement for Annie. Trust me she isn't interested in him." Hal yawned.

Emma slipped out the porch door and leaned against the wall as she stared at Eli.

He pushed his Cardinals baseball cap back. "What?"

"It is really late. I need my sleep so I can go to work tomorrow with a clear head," she replied curtly.

"I have not said anything yet, and you are already mad at me." Eli sounded bewildered.

"I heard you were not as bad off as you led me to believe when you backed out on our date at the last minute. Now you are afoot? Have you wreck your nice courting buggy tonight on the way home from somewhere?" Emma asked peevishly.

"Nah, it is parked at home," Eli said evenly.

Emma asked testily "Why did you bother to walk over here this time of night when it is so chilly?"

"I needed the walk to clear my head, and I wanted to see you. To tell you I am sorry for the other night. I wish I had not upset you. I know it was wrong to give you such short notice."

The words hit her hard. He sounded so sincere she felt a lump in her throat. "I am glad to hear you say that. I knew you were not in bad shape so why did you do it?"

"I got cold feet. You do not approve of rumspringa. I was afraid you would not like a date with me. The more I think about it the sorrier I am I upset you," Eli said honestly.

"I am sorry, too. Now it is late, and I have to get up early. So do you," Emma said curtly.

"I made a mess of that night. Can you forgive me?" Eli implored.

His hang dog expression was so remorseful Emma felt like forgiving him. She wondered if her being friendly to Eli would help him understand the rumspringa path he was on was a bad one. She felt herself relenting the anger she harbored toward him. Hadn't she just told her pupils they should forgive the people who upset them? "I'll think about forgiving you some day, but for tonight, I just want to get some rest." Emma put her hand on the screen door handle then turned back. "If it helps any, I will rest better the rest of this night, knowing you apologized for standing me up."

"It helps to know that. It helps a lot. I will see you soon," Eli called hopefully as Emma backed through the door and shut it.

At the next Sunday service the end of September, Lovina Keim and Bobby came but not Adam. Emma sat down next to Lovina after the common meal and came right to the point. "Sister Lovina, Adam has not been to the last two services. Is he not well?"

"Nah, he is fine." Lovina bit her lower lip a moment then blurted out," "Ach, Emma, he is avoiding you, because he knows you are mad at him."

Emma groaned. "I hoped Adam felt differently after I talked to Bobby. I want to tell him myself I am sorry for scolding him. I did not understand what had taken place on the play ground at school until after Adam left. I am glad I found out when I did so I could stop the teasing."

"I am sure Adam will like to hear that. He is so bashful he does not have many friends. He considers you one of the few. I just wish he would get out more with people his own age,"

Lovina said wistfully.

"You tell Adam I said he is to be at the next worship service. All is forgiven," Emma said.

Lovina gave her a grateful hug. "You are a blessing to Adam. I will tell him."

✿

Two weeks went by. At the first October worship service, Adam came. He slid onto a bench with Bobby, shoulders slumped and head down until the service ended.

After the common meal was served, Emma honed in on Adam in a corner, listening to the men talk. He saw her coming. His eyes held a frightened deer look. He wanted to sprint away, but she had him cornered.

"I am glad you came to service, Adam. I wanted to talk to you as you well know by now. Take a walk with me," Emma insisted. She took him by the elbow to show she meant for him to come with her and led him to the door.

As they left the porch, Emma raised her head and breathed deep. "What a pleasant day. Trees are such pretty colors, ain't so? I hate to see the leaves fall. Bare limbs always look cold."

Adam nodded he agreed as he shuffled along beside her. He stuffed his hands in his pants pockets and watched the ground in front of his feet. It struck Emma hands in pockets was what her father did when he was upset.

"We can walk in the orchard." Emma headed Adam that direction. She wanted to be far enough away from the rest of the congregation to keep anyone from overhearing her. By the time they walked half way down the grassy area between the apple trees, Adam still hadn't looked at her. Emma clasped her hands behind her back and stopped walking as she studied him. No use letting the poor fellow suffer any longer. She might as well get to the point. "Please look at me while I talk to you so I know you are really listening."

Adam blushed as he looked up.

"That is better. I know you are upset with me. Avoiding me will not get my new bookcase built at school. So I want to discuss what happened the day you fixed the desk leg. You

87

need to know I understand why you shook Matthew. Bobby told me how you were teased when you were a child.

What Matthew did was wrong. Because you brought his teasing the children to my attention I put a stop to it.

I am not used to what can go wrong for a teacher yet, but I am learning. I want you to know I am sorry. I should not have been so sharp with you before I talked to you and the children to find out what was going on."

Adam nodded he agreed as the tension eased from his face.

"Do not think this lets you off the hook. That does not excuse you for what you did to Matthew. You could have hurt him by dangling him in the air," Emma scolded gently.

Adam ducked his head again.

Emma crossed her arms over her chest. "Adam, I am the teacher, ain't so?"

Adam nodded.

"Look at me," Emma demanded.

Adam glanced up at her with his head still bowed.

"Disciplining the children is my job as teacher. Do you agree you should have told me what was happening so I could take care of the problem myself?" Emma insisted.

Adam nodded and shrugged his shoulders without showing any expression, leaving Emma to wonder what he was thinking. "No telling how long Matthew would have tormented the other children if I had not been made aware of the problem by you. Maybe I should say denki for that," Emma replied offhandedly.

Adam's left eyebrow went up.

Emma laughed. "All recht, as much as I hate to admit it you win. No maybes. Denki, Adam Keim, for helping me discover a problem with my pupils. I would have been in trouble with the directors if the problem had gone on for a long time. You are forgiven for what you did."

Adam took out his notepad and wrote, "I did not do anything to be forgiven for. A big boy should not tease small children."

Emma read the pad. "I agree Matthew should be stopped. It was the way you stopped him I object to. Let's consider this matter over and done with. Now will you stop hiding from me? At this rate, it will be the next teacher enjoying that new book shelf you promised to make me."

Adam wrote, "I will only say I am sorry for scaring the children."

Emma giggled. "Ach, Adam, you mean to make this difficult for me I see. I know you are sorry for that. All recht, will you at least accept that I forgive you for scaring the children."

Adam grinned as he nodded yes.

"I had a talk with the pupils right after you left about being kind to each other. They have forgotten all about what happened, and I keep an eye on them at recess now. Rest easy. There is not a chance Matthew will cause a problem again if he was to revert to his old ways. Now if I remember right you like to fish, ain't so?"

Adam nodded.

"I would like to go again while this Indian summer holds. How about taking me fishing next Saturday afternoon?"

Adam's eyes lit up as he clapped his hands.

That evening as the youth group broke up, Levi came over to Emma. "Want to go for a ride with me next Saturday?"

"I am sorry, Levi, but I can not. I am going fishing with Adam Keim." Again she watched him try to hide his disappointment under a weak smile. Levi had never asked her to go for a ride before for no reason other than to enjoy the ride together. Though she felt bad about refusing him, Emma reasoned, how was she supposed to know when Levi wanted to date her. She wasn't a mind reader, and he shouldn't be taking her for granted.

Chapter 11

On Saturday afternoon, Emma climbed in Adam's open buggy and leaned her pole along side his. She set her can of worms next to Adam's worm can. "Looks like we have high expectations with all these worms."

Adam nodded as he made a U turn with the buggy. Once they were on the road, he lifted a hand palm up and looked at Emma questioningly.

"Why not take the Bender Creek Road? I like fishing in a deep hole in the creek I know about," Emma suggested.

Once they turned onto the dirt road that wound along side Bender Creek, Emma watched for a path and pointed out a beaten down area in the underbrush. "Stop. There is the path my brothers and I take to the creek."

They had their hands full with poles, Adam's tackle box and the worm cans. Emma took the lead. She had to be careful to keep her pole pointed straight ahead so it didn't tangle up in brush or trees. Finally, she paused and held up her hand for Adam to stop. She said in a hushed voice, "Listen!"

An intense concentration crossed Adam's face before he looked doubtful.

"It is running water, Silly. We are just about to the creek. The two sounds I like best are a crackling bonfire and the whisper of a flowing stream. What do you like, Adam?" Emma asked.

He laid his fishing gear on the ground, pointed up to the trees and waved his hands up and down like flapping wings.

"The birds singing?" Emma guessed.

He shook his head yes.

"Listen again," Emma said. "See that hickory tree full of

noisy blackbirds. They are getting ready to leave before winter comes." She pointed at another tree. "Hear how joyful the sparrows are chirping. They are happy the blackbirds are leaving." Adam grinned. She pointed ahead of them. "Listen! A squirrel is chattering crossly. We are invading his territory. Hear that blue jay squawk. I think bossy jays just talk loud so they know they are heard."

Adam wrote on his pad, "Like some people I know."

He held the pad in front of Emma's face. "You have any certain person in mind?" She asked, squinting at him.

Adam wrote, "Jah." As she read the word, he grinned at her.

"I am not going to ask who, because I am afraid I will not like the answer," Emma retorted and took off.

They walked a short way through the trees until they came to Bender Creek. They stepped out of the dimly lit timber and squinted in the bright sunlight.

Emma waded through a patch of tall foxtail and stirred up a bunch of monarch butterflies. The sight of so many butterflies floating up and down in synchronized flight was magical.

"Ach, my," Emma whispered as she took hold of Adam's arm. "What a sight to behold."

Adam barely nodded that he agreed, but his eyes sparkled.

When the butterflies flew away, Emma said, "To watch so many monarchs on their migration was voonderball gute. Now we can fish." She took a few steps forward and twisted back. Adam hadn't moved. "Come on. I know where I am going. It is a favorite fishing spot my brothers and I do not usually share with anyone else. Consider yourself lucky I am showing you where it is." She came back, grabbed his hand and tugged.

Grinning, Adam submitted to being led along the bank.

When a large cottonwood tree loomed up in front of them, Emma said, "This is the spot. We can sit in the tree's shade and fish as long as we want."

Adam touched her arm. When Emma turned to him, he pointed at his watch and grinned at her.

Emma smiled back. "All recht, Smarty. We will fish as long as we can within reason. If we stay too long a search party will be looking for us to make sure we did not drown."

In between bites, stick bugs skittered over the water surface and dragonflies fluttered into their lines. They took turns reeling in fast biting bullheads and bluegills. Adam unhooked Emma's catches and put the fish on a stringer he'd secured at the bottom of the bank.

The happy look on Adam's face told Emma he was enjoying himself. Inviting him to go fishing had been a good idea. Once her eyes met his as he unhooked a fish for her. She smiled. "After the way things have been lately, I needed a time with you just for fun. How about you? You having a gute time?"

Adam smiled his yes then the smile faded. He took out his pad and wrote, "Anything besides me bothering you?"

Emma read the note. She sighed as she ran her fingertips along the edge of her rod. "Adam, I think I am having growing up pains. When I was younger I could not wait to grow up. Now that I am old enough to date, I find it a troublesome time."

Holding up his notepad, Adam poked her on the upper arm with, "Why?"

Emma opened her mouth to answer then changed her mind. "Nah, I should not sound like a complainer. I am sure everything will work out all recht."

Adam nodded his head no. He turned his hand over toward her for her to tell him.

"You would be sorry if you let me continue. I am sure of that," Emma warned.

Again, Adam turned his hand over toward her.

"All recht. Do you think that dating is supposed to be fun?"

Adam gave his answer serious thought and shrugged.

"Ach! We are two of a kind. You don't know, and so far for me, dating is not fun. Eli Yutzy invited me to go with him to a youth group singing then backed out at the last minute. I was very upset. Levi Yoder has been more like a brother than a friend while we were children. Now he takes it for granted he can invite me out on short notice, and I will say jah. I tell him I have other plans, and he looks so disappointed I wind up

92

feeling bad for hurting his feelings. About as bad as I feel for Bobby." Emma stopped talking when Adam stiffened. He motioned for her to go on. "Nah, I said too much already."

Adam wrote on his pad, "I want to know about my brother."

"All recht. Bobby asked me to go to the singing after Eli backed out. I was glad he did. I like Bobby. It is just he would like to date me again, but Bobby is missing Annie. He is thinking he should get married soon and settle down like he would have if Annie had not died. He thinks he sees Annie when he is with me. It makes me uncomfortable so I refuse to go on a date with him again. It would only hurt him more to encourage him. I can never be Annie. Do you understand?"

Adam nodded yes. He wrote, "Bobby will be all recht. He has to get over Annie. It is a wise thing you are doing."

"Denki, I am glad you understand. Ach, I caught another fish," Emma cried excitedly and reeled in her line.

After a couple hours, the fish stopped biting. A turtle's head bobbed up in various spots. A few times, they felt tugs and reeled in to find their hooks empty.

Emma became bored. "The fish are not biting anymore, but that turtle sure is. All we are doing is feeding him our worms. Want to skip some rocks for awhile?"

Adam nodded and pointed at Emma to throw first.

Emma picked up a stone and skipped it as she counted the bounces. "Five times. Your turn."

Adam picked up a pebble and gave it a strong toss.

Emma counted. "That was six. I want to try again."

She hunted as if she was trying to find just the right stone to produce more skips. She picked up a stone and gave it a toss. She counted to seven. "Gute. I won."

Adam grabbed her arm. He shook his head no and wagged a finger at her.

"I did so win."

Adam wrote on his pad. "Do you always have to win? I should get one more throw."

He was questioning her with such an intense look Emma didn't know how to take him. Adam didn't look like he was teasing. "Is winning a bad thing?"

Adam shook his head no as he pointed at himself.

"So next time you can win if it matters that much to you," Emma said pensively.

Adam shrugged his shoulders, seeming to give in, but he didn't look very satisfied with Emma's answer as he turned away. She took hold of his arm so he'd look at her. "Adam, it is not just about winning with me. I have this need to do the best I can at whatever I do whether it be teaching or fishing."

Adam wrote, "You could do that quietly without turning your success into a contest. That seems to matter to you."

Emma moved her eyes heavenward, feeling guilty. Of all people, she hadn't expected Adam to lecture her on her faults. "I am sorry you are upset with me. I do agree with you. I will try to work on being a better person," she said submissively.

Adam wrote, "You are the best person I know." He gave her a smile and pulled her to him for a quick, forgiving hug. Then he pointed at his wrist watch.

Emma looked overhead at the western sun filtering through cracks in the dark clouds. The rays bounced off the current, turning the water a brilliant red. "I suppose we should go. It will be dark soon, and it will take time to clean all our fish."

She slid down the bank to pull the fish stringer out of the water. As she leaned over the creek, the clay bank caved away under her feet, staining the water a rusty murk. Emma yelled and flapped her arms like a bird trying to take flight as she plunged into the creek, producing a loud splash.

Adam laughed silently and smacked his knee. Emma glared at him. She slapped the water with both hands. "This was not funny. Help me out of here, Adam Keim," she ordered as she stretched an arm up to him.

Grinning from ear to ear, Adam carefully stepped down to the edge of the water and reached for her. Emma got a good grip on his hand and jerked hard. Adam dove into the creek.

He gave her a narrow eyed stare.

"Since you thought it was so funny I wanted to see how you like getting wet." Emma bobbed around him, laughing until he

94

smiled back. "Now help me out of here."

On the way home, Emma asked, "You staying for supper?"

Adam pinched his wet shirt, held it out away from his chest and wrinkled his nose.

"Ach nah, you are not going to use that excuse to get out of cleaning fish. You can wear a shirt and pants of Daed's until your clothes dry," Emma insisted.

They left the string of flopping fish in a five gallon bucket of water by the pump in the back yard. In the mud room, Emma and Adam took turns dunking their dirty feet in a pail of water. They dried with a towel taken from the stack by the pail and entered the kitchen.

The first thing Hal said was, "You two are all wet."

"I know. We need to put on dry clothes before we clean the fish for supper. Can Adam borrow a shirt and pants of Daed's?"

Hal nodded as she followed them into the living room. "Sure he can. What happened?"

"We fell into the creek," Emma said, starting up the stairs.

"I can see that much," Hal retorted to her back.

Adam wiggled his finger back and forth to say that wasn't exactly what happened.

"Ach, really," Hal said with interest and folded her arms over her chest. "Go on, Adam."

Emma turned around.

Adam pointed at Emma, reached over and took his left wrist with his right hand. He yanked, did a rolling motion with his hands and pinched his shirt, giving Hal a dolorous look.

"Not our Emma!" Hal said, pretending to be shocked.

Adam slowly shook his head.

"She really did that to you?" Hal asked in mock disbelief.

Adam shook his head again. As Emma eyed them innocently, Hal and Adam stared up at her accusingly. Seeing she was out numbered, she put her hands on her hips and hissed at Adam, "Squealer!"

"Come upstairs with me, Adam. I'll find you some dry clothes," Hal said sympathetically. "If I were to give you a word of advice about Emma, it would be not to go near the edge of the creek when she's fishing with you from now on. What did you do? Catch more fish than her?"

Adam slapped his leg and grinned from ear to ear.

When Emma came downstairs, John and the boys were at the kitchen table with Adam and Hal. John was laughing heartedly as he told about how he talked to Deacon Yutzy on the road. Seems Levi Yoder sold the deacon's son, Eli, an ornery horse. Every time Eli turned his back on the horse, it butted him and flattened him. Levi named the horse Popcorn. Deacon Yutzy said he could see why.

Hal laughed with John and her brothers, and Adam smiled as if he enjoyed the story. Emma didn't find the story one bit funny. Normally, Levi wouldn't have sold an ornery horse to anyone without first explaining the horse's faults. Levi must be trying to give Eli a hard time for paying attention to her. This was a new side to Levi she didn't know. One she didn't like.

Hal and John's bedroom lit up in the night. This time Hal knew what the yellow circles floating around the room meant. She grabbed John's shoulder. "There's another boy outside."

"How do you know it is a different one?" John grumped, rubbing his eyes.

"Eli knows better than to wake us up again. He knows which window to shine the light in so this has to be a different boy," she reasoned

"I will correct this one," growled John as he got out of bed. He pattered to the window and raised it. "You have the wrong room. Emma's room is the third window. Best get directions straight from Emma before you make a late night visit after this and wake me up."

Instantly, the bedroom went dark. Levi Yoder called apologetically, "I am so sorry, John Lapp. Go back to sleep."

The loud voices woke up Abraham. He crowed, thinking it was morning and set all the hens to cackling that it was time to start their day.

John groaned as he slid the window shut.

"Guess you said that plain enough," Hal said dryly.

John combed his fingers through his hair. "That was not a gute thing to do to Levi, ain't so?"

"I would say nah," Hal agreed.

"You said Emma was not interested in Levi. How did I know it would be him?" John moaned. "I do not want to scare away Levi. I like Levi."

Hal stifled a yawn. "Don't worry, dear. I don't think there is anything we can do that would scare the boys away from this house. They seemed to be drawn here like flies to the horses."

෴

"Gute evening," Levi greeted, turning his black felt hat brim in his hands. "As dark as it is, I can still make out the frown on your face is deep. Was ist letz?"

"Come away from the house so I can tell you what is the matter." Emma took off with a stiff legged gait, folded her arms over her chest and leaned against the maple tree. She inhaled a deep breath and scolded softly, "You knew when you sold that horse to Eli he butts. How could you do that?"

"Eli will learn to handle the horse. It is his horse now." Levi tried to sound casual. He leaned down, and before Emma realized what was going to happen, he gently kissed her.

Pink, warm splotches colored her cheeks. Levi had never tried to kiss her before. Since she just scolded him, she knew she hadn't given him cause to kiss her this time, but she liked the kiss. Because she liked his kiss, she knew later she'd feel guilty for not abstaining. Why did he put her in this miserable position?

Levi studied the displeasure on Emma's face. "I am sorry if I surprised you."

"You should be sorry. You know it is wrong to kiss me. Why did you do that?" She implored.

"It is just I feel like you are slipping away from me. I want to spend time with you, but you never have time for me anymore," Levi complained.

Emma looked into his face, a face she knew as well as her own. At least she thought she knew Levi well enough to know his likes and dislikes. This young man had been a childhood playmate, practically part of the family and a dear friend.

He had just made his intentions clear to her. He wanted to be more than her friend, a *special* friend. Except somehow she couldn't picture this boy she thought of as a brother as her husband and head of her household. She managed to say lamely, "I see."

Levi said bluntly, "Since I have to get in line for a date with you, I want to ask you to go for a ride with me one evening next week before anyone else does. Will you go with me?"

Emma didn't have a reason to turn him down. After all, Levi had taken her to the singings for sometime. Even if she wanted to turn his offer down to take her riding, she knew she'd get another one of those hurt looks from him. She couldn't bare to see that again. She smiled at him. "Jah, I would like that."

The tension drained from Levi. In the moonlight, his serious expression turn into one of his rare smiles she found endearing.

Emma turned serious. "I will go with you if you promise to leave off the kissing. I do not like breaking the rule about no personal contact."

"If that is what you want, I will do it," Levi said eagerly.

Once Levi felt his mission succeeded, he told her he had to go home. He had to rest so he could get up early to pick corn.

After Emma went back to bed, she couldn't stop thinking about Levi's kiss. She crawled out of bed and went to her knees. "Lord, I am sorry I sinned. Please forgive me for the kiss between Levi and me. I promise I will be more watchful of Levi from now on and not let that happen again. Amen."

Emma was so very tired. When she closed her eyes, she dozed off right away, but Levi's kiss was stuck in her mind and her subconscious.

The two of them were standing knee deep in a fog like haze. Levi's head lowered toward her. He kissed her.

She asked, "What just happened here?"

Levi grinned at her. "You kissed me."

Indignant, Emma retorted, "I did not. You kissed me."

Levi took her by the shoulders, pulled her to him and kissed her again. "Now we are even." Suddenly before she could chastise him, he faded away into the mist.

Emma woke with a start. She looked around her dark room and realized she was still in bed. She touched her tingling lips. How could that dream kiss seem so real?

Two evenings later, Levi pulled in and waited. Emma peeked out the kitchen window when she heard the buggy. She tore half a loaf of fresh bread out of a pan and rushed through the living room. She turned around at the front door and said to Hal and her father, "See you later."

Emma climbed into the courting buggy and waited until Levi flicked the lines. She tore off half the chunk of bread and handed it to him.

Levi took a bite. "This is gute. Fresh and still warm from the oven. Reminds me of the gute way you smell sometimes."

"The way I smell?" Emma puzzled.

"Jah, like fresh bread baking," Levi told her.

Emma didn't make a reply to the bread comment. It wasn't much of a compliment. Practical just like Levi. She still felt awkward around Levi. She knew that was silly, but every time she glanced at him, she thought about their kiss.

Finally, Levi asked, "Any place special you want to ride?"

"Nah, just anywhere will do. It is such a pleasant night for a ride, ain't so?" Emma replied breathlessly.

"Jah, that it is." Levi smiled wide as he flicked the lines so the horse would trot. "Come on, Broomtail."

When Levi smiled, his dimples deepened. Emma realized she hadn't seen those dimples in a very long time. These days the grown up Levi was usually too serious.

Levi asked, "So how is the school teacher job going?"

"I find I really enjoy the job," Emma said enthusiastically as dusk descended around them.

"Gute. At first, I know you were nervous," Levi said.

"I was. Now I realize I can handle teaching. That makes the difference," Emma said with confidence.

"I knew you would be all right," Levi contended, smiling.

"What made you so sure?"

"You can do anything," Levi declared.

Emma glowed inwardly at his assessment of her abilities, but she hated to make too much out of this compliment and seem prideful. Though it was better than his remark about her smelling like baked bread. Now that the stars were out, she focused on them. "Denki for the confidence in me. I do not always have that same confidence in myself."

"You should have," Levi insisted.

Emma grabbed his arm. "Look, Levi. A shooting star!"

"I see it." Levi halted the buggy. "Whoa, Broomtail." When he looked up again where Emma pointed, the sky was just twinkling lights.

"Like a flash, it is gone," he said as he laid his arm behind her across the top of the seat.

"Hallie says if we see a shooting star we should make a wish, and our dreams will come true." Emma closed her eyes for a second and wished that her life was simpler than it had been lately. "There. I did it."

"Everyone has dreams when they are our age. What are your dreams, Emma?" Levi asked.

Emma paused to think. She had the same dreams as other girls her age, but she wanted them to come true in the future when she didn't want to teach anymore. She wondered what made her unable to look away from Levi when she finally met his gaze. This wasn't a conversation she imagined she'd ever have with this man she'd thought of as a brother. Suddenly, she realized she didn't know the grownup Levi at all. "I am not going to tell you what I wished for just now, but a Plain girl's fate is always the same, ain't so? She ends up in a home with a gute husband and children if she is lucky. That should be in my future. It is something I dream about happening to me like it does other Plain girls." Levi's gaze was anything but brotherly as Emma continued, determined to make him understand how she felt. "I have to take things as they come and live in the moment. Right now that means teaching school for another year and helping Hallie at home while she still needs me."

Levi took his arm off the seat and fixed his eyes on the road as he flicked the lines, causing the horse to take off. He didn't look happy. She expected that, but she had to speak the truth. She did believe a family of her own would happen some day. She didn't know when, and she wasn't in a hurry. She had to know for sure she'd found the right *special* friend first, then the rest of the dream would come true.

☙

That night Emma knelt to pray. She was too keyed up to sleep. Her insides were still in a churning motion as if she was still in Levi's buggy, watching him not take her answer about her dreams well.

She rose, pulled the chair over by the window and opened it. While she stared into the darkness, she took out her braid and brushed her waist length hair.

Moonlight gave everything in the yard a silvery glow. A light breeze ruffled the drying red maple leaves on the tree at the end of the house and gently cooled her face. Buttercat slinked along the yard fence and disappeared behind the outhouse, looking for a field mouse. The windmill blades turned slowly, creaking softly. A loud string of chatters came from the barn. Daniel's raccoon was trying to call in a friend to rescue him. Just another peaceful night in the country.

She thought back to her conversation with Levi. True to his word, he hadn't made an attempt to kiss her again. He probably didn't even want to after she said she wasn't ready to get married. Although if he'd admit it, they had fun on the ride.

She thought a lot of Levi and in a way loved him. So what was wrong with her? Why wasn't the feeling she had for Levi strong enough to commit to him right now? That was what he wanted. She knew a marriage with Levi would be a good one. He'd make a good husband and father.

Emma fought back the urge to cry. She lost the battle as tears coursed down her cheeks. Once her energy was spent and the tears dried, Emma shut the window, crawled under the sheet and closed her eyes. If only she could shut out her troubles as easy as she did that window.

101

Chapter 12

Emma glanced to the back of the room when she heard the school door open and close. She laid the chalk in the trough on the blackboard and said quietly, "Welcome, Amos Coblentz."

Jake and Marianne twisted around in their seats and waved at their father. Amos nodded at them and sat down on the bench at the back of the room reserved for parents. "Go on with school. I just came to visit."

Suddenly, Emma had jitters deep in the pit of her stomach. Amos was on the school board. The former teacher cautioned her the three directors took turns dropping in unexpectedly. As for all the other parents, Ellen Yost remarked it wasn't unusual for them to visit school unannounced. The pupils liked their parents to come. Emma was sure they did. She remembered when she was in school parents dropped in, but her parents didn't. Her mother was too sick, and her father was too busy taking care of the farm and her mother.

For which reason did Amos come, as a parent or a director? Amos should be upset about his son getting teased. Emma was upset that it happened, and she wasn't the boy's mother. Yet why didn't Amos meet with her right after she gave Jake the note. She asked Amos to come as soon as possible.

Amos crossed his legs at the ankles and folded his hands in his lap. He had a couple hours to watch until school let out, and he seemed to be patiently doing just that. What could he see? Lemon dusting spray hung in the room from the going over the third grade girls gave the desks that morning. It was the same smell so familiar in almost every Plain house. Fourth grade girls had sweeping duty this week so the floors were clean.

Besides that, there were neat rows of desks, colorful art

works displayed over the blackboard, and pupils working on their lessons. Emma had just put math problems on the blackboard for the upper classes. Once she put them through the math drill, the pupils went back to studying.

Near the end of the day, Emma asked Sallie Yost to pick up the monthly book reports and bring them to her desk. All the pupils scrambled to dig their reports out of their other papers except for Matthew Stoll. He looked out the window.

When Sallie handed the papers to Emma, she thanked her and rifled through the reports looking for Matthew's name on one. She didn't find it.

When it was almost time to dismiss the children for the day, Emma always took a stroll down the aisles to see how much the pupils had done. If anyone hadn't completed an assignment that day, they needed to take homework with them to bring back in the morning. Before she walked around, Emma wrote a note. "Please stay after school. I want to talk to you." She laid the folded note on Matthew's desk and kept walking.

When she reached the back of the room, Amos Coblentz said in a low voice, "I would like to talk to you before I leave."

"I thought you might," Emma replied softly. "I have to talk to one of the pupils first then I will be free." She walked back to the front of the room and sat down at her desk. "Gute job for the day, pupils. Put your books away and go get your things." She waited for all the pupils to get back to their desks then tapped her desk bell. "School is dismissed. Noah, take out the stove ashes, and Daniel, fill the wood box."

The pupils filed out. Matthew walked slowly to the teacher's desk with his head down, looking uncomfortable.

Jake and Marianne stopped beside their father. He told them, "You go out and play while I talk to the teacher."

Now Emma was really nervous. She hoped Amos thought she handled the bullying problem the right way. Not that he should have too much to complain about when he took his sweet time showing up to discuss the matter with her.

Suddenly, she was feeling less nervous and more irritated by the second. She had to force herself to concentrate on Matthew when he stopped by the desk. "Jah, Emma?"

Emma kept her voice low. "Say Yes not jah. You did not turn in a book report for September. Why?"

Matthew shrugged his shoulders.

"That is no answer. Explain to me," Emma demanded.

"Reading is boring," Matthew said blandly.

"Did you even take a book home to read?" She asked.

He shook his head no.

"That tells me you do not plan to ever take a book home or do a book report. Am I right?" Emma asked.

"Jah, I mean yes I reckon," Matthew said, shuffling his feet.

"All right. I do not want to fail you for not trying, and you should not want that, either. You have no way of knowing a book is boring if you do not attempt to read it. Come with me." Emma went to the books on the table at the back of the room. She picked up *Black Beauty* and handed it to Matthew.

He looked at her questioningly.

"Since you need help to make a decision, I picked this book for you. This one is about a horse which should not be boring since I know you like horses. I expect you to take the book home and have it read in time to hand in the next book report the end of October," she stated firmly as she stuck the book in Matthew's hand. "You can go now."

Matthew scurried past Amos and out the door. The director's eyes were on Emma as she came to him. Amos smiled as he stood up which helped ease Emma's fears to some degree. He couldn't be too upset with her if he smiled. Could he? "Gute to have you visit. Jake and Marianne were glad to see you here," she greeted.

Amos twisted his black felt hat in his hands. "I was thinking it was about time I came to see how they were doing once."

"Your children are very bright. They pick up their school work quickly." Emma sat down on the bench. "Please sit down." Amos sat beside her. Emma licked her lips nervously, before she had the nerve to continue, "I have waited for some time for you to come for this talk."

Amos looked puzzled as he laid his hat in his lap.

104

Emma wondered why as she continued, "Jake and Marianne must have told you what happened when one of the older boys picked on Jake. After that, I found out he picked on the other younger children, too."

"Jake mentioned it," Amos said offhandedly, folding his arms over his chest and crossing his legs at the ankles.

Emma narrowed her eyes as she scrutinized him. "I hoped he would. You should know I handled the problem to the children's satisfaction. I had a talk with them about bullying. From that day on, I keep a close watch on recesses to stop any more teasing."

"Jake told me. He is happy about coming to school now," Amos affirmed.

"Jah, this is true. However, I have been anxious to touch base with you about this so I could explain what happened, and what I did to correct this matter so you would not be worried about your children." Emma looked bothered.

Uncomfortable with the tone of Emma's terse voice, Amos rubbed his chin. He said with deliberation, "I was not worried. I knew from what my children told me you handled the matter to everyone's satisfaction. Jake and Marianne can not wait to get to school now, and they like it that you are their teacher. That is a gute thing for me to know. So do not worry. I was not going to bring it up."

Emma's face felt hot as she stammered heatedly, "You ---- you took the word of your children so you did not think it necessary to come talk to the teacher. When you finally show up you are not going to bring something this serious up. I thought after I sent the note you might be concerned enough about your son and the other pupils that you would want to hear what happened from me right away. If not as a concerned parent then as a board of director member."

For a moment, Amos considered how upset Emma was. Then it was as if a lamp lit in his brain. He raised a questioning eyebrow and said tentatively, "What note?"

"The note I sent home with Jake, asking you to come talk with me as soon as possible. I sent one to Matthew Stoll's parents at the same time, and they were here the next day," Emma said tersely.

Amos looked confused. "I did not get any such note. I am sorry there has been a misunderstanding. I will bring up the missing note to Jake to see what happened to it and make sure something like this does not happen again. All recht?"

"Jah, that would be a gute idea," Emma replied, still tense.

Perplexed that the teacher thought he was making excuses, Amos rubbed the back of his neck. "This might not be a gute time to discuss why I came today. I had another reason."

"Ach, what else is the matter?" Emma asked. Her shoulders slumped as she grew concerned again.

Amos spoke hurriedly, "Nothing. Nothing bad that is. The children just wanted me to invite you to go for a ride with us on Sunday afternoon since it is the in between Sunday."

The invitation threw Emma off guard. Her voice squeaked, "Go for a ride? With your family?"

Instantly, Jake and Marianne's heads appeared in an open window. Clearly, they had been listening.

Jake said, "Please, come along with us."

Marianne begged, "The ride will be a lot more fun if you are with us, Emma."

Emma paused. How was she going to handle this problem? She didn't want to disappoint the children. They seemed to be looking forward to spending the afternoon with her.

Amos looked at her in an expectant manner. Would he take affront if she turned him down? She didn't want to give him another reason to be upset with her on top of her just accusing him of not being a very concerned parent. She focused on the two small heads just above the window sill. "All recht, I would love to go with you on the ride."

"That is gute," Jake exclaimed.

Marianne giggled as she clapped her hands together.

"I want you to come in. We need to talk," Amos said sternly.

The children's feet made crackling whispers as they raced through the dry grass to the door. Marianne darted into utility room and slowed to a walk like the pupils were told to do. Jake

106

came in slower yet with his head down. Emma suspected from his hearing the conversation between her and his father, Jake knew he was in trouble.

Amos held his hand out and beckoned to the children. "Jake, you have some explaining to do. Emma tells me she sent a note home with you to give me. She wanted to meet with me. I did not get that note, and now I am in trouble with the teacher."

Jake's eyes welled up with tears.

Wide eyed, Emma exclaimed to Amos, "Ach, nah. I am sorry I gave you that impression."

Amos insisted earnestly, "You did!" He turned to Jake. "Explain to Teacher and me what happened to the note."

Jake wiped his eyes with his shirt sleeve. "I did not want to get Emma in trouble with you so I did not give you the note."

"Ach, Jake," Emma pulled the boy to her for a hug. "Denki for protecting me. It was Matthew who was in trouble. I just wanted your father to know what happened."

Amos explained, "Jake, your heart was in the right place, but you should have given me the note. When the teacher wants to see me, it is important I get her notes. I am not only a parent, but as Emma was quick to remind me, I am on the board of directors." He darted a twinkling look at Emma to watch her blush. "That goes for you, too, Marianne. Do you both understand from now on I need to see notes from Emma? The note might be a matter concerning school business or about how you are doing at school."

The children nodded solemnly.

"Gute. Now you know I have done nothing wrong does this mean I am not in trouble anymore, Teacher Emma?" Amos said with twinkling eyes.

Emma wanted to shrink to two inches tall and hide under a desk. Amos was teasing, but she felt miserably embarrassed. How did she manage to get herself in this mess, with a board of director member no less? As Jake and Marianne watched her, concern for their father was written all over their faces. When the teacher was mad at anyone it was not a good thing. Emma swallowed hard. She said remorsefully, "Jah, Amos, now that I understand what happened to my note you are not in trouble. I am sorry about the disagreeable way I talked to you."

"Do not think anything of it. You were just being the gute, caring teacher you are," Amos said sincerely.

"So since you are not mad at our father you are for sure and certain going for a ride with us?" Marianne asked hopefully.

Emma focused on Amos and his twinkling eyes. "Jah, Marianne and Jake, how could I turn you down now? I am for sure and certain going on the ride."

෨

Sunday afternoon rolled around faster than Emma would have liked. She still wasn't used to the idea of a ride with Amos and his children when the enclosed buggy arrived.

John glanced up from his bible as Emma went out the front door. "Where is Emma going?"

Hal put down the *Family Life Magazine.* "Amos Coblentz asked her to go for a ride with him and his children."

"Amos? Amos Coblentz?" John sputtered.

Hal nodded. "That's the one."

"I do not understand. Why would Amos ask Emma to go riding with him?" John asked, baffled.

"Keep in mind Emma's changing. She doesn't think like a little girl anymore, and she doesn't look like one. Though sometimes I think the newness of her change into a young woman has taken her by surprise," Hal said contemplatively. "As for Amos, I imagine he's thinking about his kids. They need a woman around, and they like Emma. Though I'm not sure Emma has figured out what Amos is up to yet." Hal was thoughtful a moment. "When she does figure out Amos's intentions, this may be a one time ride. Emma is trying to please two of her pupils and a board member. Besides, she feels guilty so she's making up for something she said when Amos came to school this week."

Hal had John's full attention now. "What did Emma say?"

"Emma chastised Amos for not coming sooner to discuss the teasing his son experienced from Matthew Stoll. She sent a note with Jake to ask Amos to meet with her, and he didn't

108

show up. She was upset."

"Ach! She did not give a hard time to a gute father like Amos?" John asked in disbelief.

Hal smiled weakly. "Jah, she did but giving him a hard time worried her more than it did him, because he's on the board of directors." John lifted an eyebrow. Hal grinned. "Don't worry. The misunderstanding has been ironed out. Jake threw the note away, thinking he'd get Emma in trouble. Emma told Amos she's truly sorry she spoke in haste."

John groaned. "With my own eyes, I see Emma act like she got up on the wrong side of the bed and speak sharp tongued. I worry she might turn out like her mother. I must admit I do not understand all that is going on with her."

Hal laughed. "You are the father. You may not be supposed to understand. Don't worry. Emma's not sick like Diane was. She's just a teenager, suffering from growing pains. Keep in mind, you have to go through this daughter dating game at least twice more in about sixteen years with the babies."

"Maybe I will have this dating business all figured out by then," John said uncertainly.

"I doubt it, but you probably won't have too much worry with our two little girls," Hal said. "I don't think from what I've seen of Plain dating the girls have many choices in boys."

John questioned, "Why does Emma have so many choices?"

"She's a good catch. Emma has been running a household for several years. She is a calm, quiet, kind, gute person. Her experience and personality make her gute wife material."

John said proudly, "Jah, she will make a gute wife."

Hal giggled. "Jah, so get used to all the competition, Daed."

Jake and Marianne opened the flap on the back window so they could watch the scenery go by. On an afternoon warmer than normal, Emma found the soft breeze refreshing as it filtered passed the kids to the front seat.

Amos looked straight ahead as he talked. "Jake and Marianne were looking forward to you being with us this day. Reckon you can tell my children have missed having a woman to lean on. They enjoy your company."

"You have two very nice children. They are polite and smart. You can be very proud of how you are raising them," Emma replied, watching the fall scenery glide by her window.

"This is true, but still, my children could use a woman to mother them," Amos remarked.

Emma darted a glance at Amos and met his warm, meaningful smile.

So much for the pleasant ride with a school board member and his family. Emma took note of the change in his manner and the softness of his voice. He'd rushed right to the reason he asked her on this ride, and she didn't know exactly how to respond. Her senses told her to be careful what she said. The man wanted her to know he was looking for a wife, and somehow she'd ended up on top of his short list. If she upset him now, she might wind up jobless.

Emma looked sincere. "That will happen for you someday."

"Jah, I am sure," Amos said shortly and watched the road.

Emma eyed a cluster of fiery red sumacs in the ditch. She stiffened. "Amos, turkeys!" The large birds scurried to the road and skittered across in front of the horse. The horse shied sideways. Amos pulled back on the lines. "Whoa, Joe!" The horse came to a quivering stop. After the turkeys slinked into the tall grass in the opposite ditch, Amos clicked to Joe.

Emma let out a gust of air. "The horse was surprised."

Amos chuckled. "Not any more than I was."

When they were close to the Coblentz farm, the children said in unison, "Turn in, Daed. Show Emma where we live."

"Emma has seen our farm many times when we have worship service at our house," Amos said reluctantly. "I am sure she knows we have a nice house."

"She has not seen my pet kitty," Marianne said, pouting.

"I wanted to show Emma our new colt." Jake said petulantly.

Emma whispered, "You will spoil their whole afternoon if you drive by."

Amos grinned at her. "Maybe you are right."

He turned into the leaf strewn driveway. They stepped out

of the buggy. Marianne grabbed Emma's hand and tugged. "Come with me. My kitty is in the barn."

Trailing along behind, Jake said, "The colt is in the lot behind the barn with the mare. You can look at her next."

As they entered the barn, Emma looked back for Amos, but he'd disappeared. When they came out, Amos was in the shade of the barn with a stack of glasses and a sweating pitcher of lemonade. "How about a cool drink before we leave?"

He handed each of them a glass and filled Emma's first. She met his kind blue eyes as he poured. She took a sip and said bashfully, "You make gute lemonade." Emma found herself thinking life would be pleasant if she lived with Amos's family.

Emma's dreams mellowed some of late after Eli's visit. Certainly her guilt wasn't as pronounced when she thought about Levi's kiss. After all, she reasoned his kiss wasn't her fault. Levi took her by surprise. He certainly was happier now since she went on the buggy ride with him.

That night, Emma's dreams were busy and confusingly full of men, circling her. Along with a sincere Eli, a smiling Levi and a sad Bobby, a new face came into focus. That of Amos, with his kind blue eyes, watching her carefully for a reaction.

She studied the men's faces and felt confused about her own feelings for them. She was gravitating out of the dream when a work worn hand came from the darkness. With palm up, the hand beckoned her to stay. Emma grew calmly peaceful as she saw the calloused hand, tempting her.

She was the first to admit she had more than enough special friends, but she was curious about this mystery man. When she moved closer to see the face connected to the hand, the man faded away.

Emma woke up with a start and looked around her. She half expected to find her bed surrounded by all the men, including the mystery man. With relief, Emma told herself she'd just had another disturbing dream. Not that realizing she'd been dreaming was any consolation. She felt as if she'd never have another uninterrupted, good night's rest.

Chapter 13

One mild day in October, Hal decided to spend the afternoon picking pumpkins while the babies napped. As she pulled the red wagon down the lane, she noted the day was one that all the animals seemed content to do nothing. The cows and sheep relaxed in the pasture. Some of the cows stretched out flat, letting the sun's rays warm them. Just so there wouldn't be any doubt that this was a farm, once in awhile, a cow bellowed. A ewe gave a sharp baa, and a horse added a neigh.

Hal stacked pumpkins in the wagon and unloaded them into a pile close to the roadside stand. She didn't plan to make much progress before the children came home since she stopped every trip to check on the babies. She was just helping Emma.

After a few trips, Hal was weary. She unloaded the wagon and went to the house. Redbird and Beth laid on a quilt on the living room floor. They snuggled up under a blanket, enjoying the comfort of being together. The babies were growing fast. Soon they would be crawling and need more watching.

Hal thought she could get one more trip in. By then, the babies should be fretting. She took a drink from the dipper in the water bucket and went out through the mud room.

The afternoon was cool enough to need a jacket but not really uncomfortable. The sun still had some heat to it as it lowered to the West. Walking certainly helped to warm her up, and she liked being in the fresh air more than in the house.

The jenny wren followed her from the patch to the road and back. He perched on a post and sang, encouraging Hal to keep trudging with her load. When she walked close, he flew away, perched and took up where he left off. How neat was that?

Hal pulled the wagon over by the acorn and butternut squash and various shaped gourds. They were smaller. She could load more of them into the wagon. She stacked the squash as high as she dared and plodded slowly down the lane, watching where she walked to keep the squash from tumbling off.

On the slow walk, Hal was deep in thought about a cold glass of tea and the chance to sit down. Suddenly, she sensed something was wrong. It was too quiet. The wren wasn't singing. She looked at the fence posts ahead of her. He wasn't there. The sheep bunched by the pasture fence and stared through the woven wire.

Hal looked where the sheep fixated. The worse of her fears had come true. Barabbas was rambling toward her. To make matters worse, Tom Turkey raced to catch up to the raccoon, chirping a war challenge.

Hal considered escape. It was too far back to the gate hole. She couldn't get out of the way, and she couldn't go around the raccoon and turkey. Barabbas must have gotten a whiff of her. He stopped, stood up straight and sniffed the air. That gave Tom time to close in on his predator. He pecked the raccoon in the behind. Barabbas whirled around, growled and batted Tom. The turkey backed away, bristled up and fluffed his feathered coat out to twice its size. Immediately, Tom went on the defensive. He raced at the raccoon. His feet came off the ground with all ten toenails aimed at the raccoon's face. Barabbas ducked and flattened. Tom sailed over the top of him and turned around, fanning his tail feathers out to the limit. He stomped a foot in warning. He wasn't done with Barabbas yet.

Hal watched helplessly. If only the raccoon would run away. That would solve the problem of persuading Daniel to let Barabbas go, but that wasn't going to happen. Barabbas accepted Tom's challenge. Hal had to figure out a way to stop the fight before Tom or Barabbas got hurt or killed. But how? Tom wouldn't be any friendlier to her than the raccoon if she interfered. Hal gazed around, frantically trying to come up with an idea as Barabbas and Tom connected in combat.

Her eyes lit on her wagon load. She picked up a sharply

pointed acorn squash, screamed like a banshee and hurled the squash. It connected with Barabbas's back and broke into chunks around him. He turned loose of Tom and attacked the offending squash pieces, scattering them at the turkey. Hal had halted the fight, but she didn't want the battle to start up again. She hurled one squash after another as fast as she could lob them, screeching loudly.

Tom backed out of the line of fire. Barabbas hunched down and waited for the assault to stop. Squash raining down on the warriors took the fun out of their battle. Tom was just far enough away to give the raccoon the chance to skitter through the fence. He took off across the pasture and headed for the protection of the picnic grove. Watching him scramble away, Hal hoped, for Barabbas's freedom, the raccoon kept going. She didn't want to run into the coon when they went picnicking and have Daniel bring him home again.

Tom's beak touched the wire fence as he watched the raccoon leave. He stretched his neck high up and chirped a challenge. "I took care of you. Come back, and I'll give you more of the same." With more pressing matters on his mind, Tom trotted away. Hal patted her chest with a shaky hand. She hadn't known which critter to fear more Barabbas or Tom.

Strewn on the battlefield were yellow and green chucks mixed with a pulp and seeds mess from her squash ammunition. Now she worried what would be the more difficult thing to do; clean up the nasty mess, tell Daniel his pet raccoon escaped or explain to Emma how she went about destroying the girl's roadside stand inventory.

Hal unloaded the remaining squash, cleaned up the broken squash and gave the load to the hogs. She parked the wagon and pumped water into the bucket at the well. As Hal washed her hands to rid them of dust and sticky squash goo, she noticed feathers scattered in the grass and heard Tom Turkey. He made mourning chirps as he circled around two half eaten hens. No wonder he was so angry at the raccoon. Barabbas killed two members of the turkey's family.

～

The youth singing group's annual picnic was set for October on a Thursday night. Emma packed a picnic lunch to take to the pasture at the back of Bishop Elton Bontrager's farm. With her coat over her arm, she set out for the picnic. The sun had been warm all day, but a chill would set in at dusk.

Emma walked toward the blood red sunset stretched across the horizon and high in the sky. She didn't remember the last time she'd seen such a striking sunset that made the sky on fire. Then again, she hadn't taken time to admire sunsets before.

Many of the teenagers were already at the picnic when Emma arrived. Since she didn't have a date she sat with the girls who came alone. When the evening was over, it was too dark for easy walking. Emma decided to cut across the pasture and head toward the road.

The peepers somehow seemed louder in the darkness. In the distance, the sound of a train whistling at a crossing, carried on the breeze. Emma was keenly aware of the different night sounds and was wishing she was home when she heard running footsteps behind her and stopped. She recognized Eli's voice before she could tell it was him. "Mind if I walk with you?"

Focusing on the big dipper, Emma shrugged her shoulders. "Reckon not."

"Is that all you got to say?" Eli asked.

Without a word, Emma picked up her pace again.

Eli tried once more, hustling to keep up with her. "Would you like it if I came and got you for the singing Sunday night?"

"Would I like it?" Emma mocked, looking straight ahead. "Do not do me any favors. Especially one you will not keep."

Eli felt the sting of Emma's words. He took hold of her arm and stopped her. "Sorry, I did not do a gute job of asking you. Let me try again. I would like to take you to the singing. Will you go with me?"

"Sure you mean to take me this time?" Emma asked uncertainly.

"Jah, I am sure," Eli insisted.

Emma debated just long enough to watch Eli squirm. "Jah, I

will go with you."

Sunday evening, John looked up from his bible as Emma rushed across the living room like the room was on fire and out the door. "She is hurrying. Which special friend is it tonight?"

"Eli Yutzy," Hal said flatly.

"I thought Emma was mad at him," John said, flustered.

Hal embroidered over Noah's initials in his coat lapel. "Something went wrong when Eli was supposed to date her. I don't know what, and she's not interested in talking about it."

"Eli is not a gute choice for Emma," John groaned. "I dislike him even more than finding a hair in my biscuit."

"I agree. Emma's so glum after she's been around Eli. I hoped what he did might be enough to keep her from dating him again, but guess I was wrong." Hal sighed.

Noah and Daniel came in from outside and flopped down on the couch beside Hal. "We wish we were old enough to go to the youth singing," Daniel grumped.

"You will get your turn soon enough," John told him.

"It is boring to be our age," grumbled Noah.

"Have you heard the saying that the grass is always greener on the other side of the fence?" John asked.

"Jah," Noah said.

"That is only true for cows that jump the fence. It is not so for people. All too soon, both of you will be old enough to work full time and go to group singings like Emma," John said.

Hal patted Noah's knee. "I know it's hard to believe, but a day might come when you boys will wish for the days when you were school children again."

"Daydreaming about how gute things might be on the other side of the fence just makes you more discontent," John told them. "Learn to take one day at a time and make the best of it."

The moment had arrived. Eli parked his courting buggy in the Lapp driveway. That buggy was the envy of most of the boys. It was shiny new with a bright red cushioned seat. A buggy that cost more than the other boys could afford.

As Emma walked across the yard, Eli smiled a slow smile designed to unravel her. "Hello, Emma."

Such an ordinary greeting yet the very earth seemed to shift beneath her feet at the deep sound of his voice. Suddenly, all caution flew to the wind. Eli showed up this time. Now she couldn't remember one reason why she shouldn't go on a ride with him to the youth singing, and plenty of reasons why being with him would be a fun experience if she was open to it.

That evening, Eli and Emma had a good time as a courting couple. Being the center of attention made Emma slightly uncomfortable. Others in the youth group kept watching them with looks of surprise, envy, curiosity and even a few puzzled looks from some of the boys.

During a break in the singing, Emma went to the refreshment table to get Eli and her a lemonade. She got in line behind Bobby Keim. He poured himself a drink from the pitcher and handed it to her. "Having a gute time?"

"Jah, I always do at singings," Emma said enthusiastically as she poured two glasses.

Bobby took a sip of his drink and looked over his glass at her. He lowered the glass and asked half heartedly, "Des gute. Want to go to the next singing with me?"

"That would be nice, but Eli is taking me." Bobby looked as surprised as Emma felt when she'd accepted Eli's latest date offer so quickly. She rambled on, "I have not talked to you since I talked to Adam. We had a gute time fishing, and he has forgiven me for scolding him."

"He told me," Bobby said shortly.

Emma picked up the glasses. "I better get back to my table."

Later while she put on her coat, Levi Yoder paused by her. "Emma, will you go with me to the next singing?"

"Nah, Eli is taking me." Before she looked to see how Levi took her news, she suggested, "Katie Yost may not have a date. You should ask her."

A strange cloud passed over Levi's face. Her suggestion about Katie hadn't been well received. Before she could say more, Eli showed up and asked if she was ready to leave. When she turned back to Levi, he was staring at Eli like he was a buck in the sights of Levi's hunting rifle. She let the matter drop and walked away with Eli.

They rode along at a leisurely pace. Emma's senses took in everything about the evening. The night before a rainstorm came up late. Emma was glad to see this night an orange harvest moon, surrounded by stars as bright as she could ever remember. She relaxed and listened to the creaks of the buggy as the wheels made lumbering circles in the mud.

The breeze caressed a wisp of short hairs that escaped from under her prayer cap. Eli stuck the lines in his braced hand and reached over with his finger to smoothed the stray light brown hairs back under her cap. His touch was as light and gentle as the breeze. "A nice evening," Eli commented, glancing up.

"Jah," Emma agreed then she sat up straighter. "Ach, look! We are not the only ones on this road tonight." She pointed toward an enclosed buggy's dim lights, coming to meet them.

Eli slowed to a stop and so did the other buggy. Eli whispered, "Jason Fisher. Where he is you find Diana Kingman." He called, "Gute evening. Nice evening for a ride."

Jason stepped down from his buggy with a beer can in each hand. "How about a beer?"

Eli said, "Reckon one beer would go down gute."

"Gute evening, Emma," Jason greeted.

"Gute evening. Eli, we should head home." Emma wanted to get away from Jason. From what she'd seen and heard about him lately, he spelled trouble.

"We will go as soon as I finish my beer," Eli promised.

Emma waited through the first can then the second. She wondered if Jason had the back of the buggy filled with beer. He wasn't running out of a supply any time soon.

It was too dark for her to see more than the form of Diana in the buggy. As meek as that girl was, Emma didn't expect her to be any help breaking up the drinking. The girl wasn't popular with the boys. Now that she had Jason dating her, Diana wasn't about to do anything to upset her boyfriend. Emma sighed. *Too bad. Diana could do so much better than Jason.*

Emma interrupted between each fresh can of beer to say she should go home. Finally, the anger in Eli's voice was strong. "Jason, looks like I better take my date home before she has a real fit. See you soon." He jumped into the buggy and snapped the lines over the horse's back as he glared at Emma. "You are such a nagger. If you are in such a big hurry to get home I will take you as fast as I can."

Emma held on with a white knuckle grip to the side and the seat as the courting buggy hurled through the ruts and bounced in and out of the water filled potholes. "Slow down before you throw us out of the buggy," she shouted, trying to be heard above the rush of wind.

"You wanted to get home in a hurry. I am taking you there," Eli growled, using his good hand to flail the lines across the horse's back to keep going at break neck speed.

"I want to be alive when I get home," Emma screamed. They verved from one side the road to the other as they rounded a sharp curve. Emma gazed nervously ahead through the darkness, trying to see home. As the buggy swayed, she bumped against Eli and cried out in fright. As soon as she could, she struggled back to her side of the seat.

He shouted, "Stop your gagrish noises. You ain't going to get killed. I am a gute driver."

"Depends who you ask," Emma shouted shrilly.

In a few minutes, Eli careened into the driveway and yanked the horse to a stop. He cackled as if he enjoyed scaring her. "Now you are home."

"I was afraid I might not get here alive," Emma said bitingly, trying to stop shaking now she was safely home. "You should not have been drinking or driving that fast. Look at how hard your poor horse is breathing."

Eli belched and gave her a grim look. "My horse is my concern. How are you ever going to know what is right for your future if you do not experiment during rumspringa?"

"Your kind of experimenting is not for me. I told you that already," Emma replied wearily. "For your information, I know

119

what I want. If you do not know what is right for your life I can not fix it for you anymore than rumspringa will. You have to find the answers yourself. If I do not know how to fix my life when it is messed up I pray to God to help me."

Eli's words slurred as he mocked, "That is the Plain way."

"It works for me and most everyone I know. It will work for you too if you let it. You are making a mistake by living your life this way. Please repent, and you will be forgiven. If you continue to drink and dress English, that will cause you to make a big mistake. Then there will not be a place in the Plain faith for you. You will be asked to leave. Think about what you are doing long and hard before that happens.

I need to go in and get some rest. Morning will be here soon." Emma jumped out of the buggy. Her knees wobbled. It took her a few steps to feel as if her legs would hold her weight up as she walked to the house. She quietly let herself in and closed her eyes as she leaned against the door to catch her breath. She held her hand over her pounding heart and listened to the groan of wheels and fading hoof beats.

By the light of the lamp Hal left on for her, Emma realized what a mess she was as she shed her mud speckled coat. The lower half of her skirt was spotted. She touched her face and felt of her head. She could feel flecks of mud on her prayer cap and face. She went to the kitchen and washed. She'd have to wash her clothes on the sly. She didn't want Hallie and her father to know about this night. She didn't need to be told what a dangerous idea it had been to date Eli Yutzy. Without her father telling her, she was smart enough to know she shouldn't accept another date from Eli.

Emma was in a state of numbed weariness when she slipped into bed, but she spent a restless night anyway. Her body wanted to rest, but her mind refused to sleep. She dreamed she was in Eli's fast buggy, speeding down a dark road. She felt helpless and scared as she sailed along at break neck speed. She looked over at Eli to demand he stop the buggy and let her out. Terror filled her. She screamed. No one was in the seat next to her. Eli had vanished. Just as she was about to scream again, the buggy rolled to a stop. Out of the darkness, someone held up his strong hands and helped her down. She'd been trembling until his arms went around her. Suddenly, she felt safe. She started to thank him for saving her, but he was gone. She was alone beside the rocking buggy and snorting horse.

Emma woke with a start. Her body was wet with cold sweat. Had she screamed out loud? She listened for running footsteps in the hall. Nothing but silence. The scream had only been in her dream. She snuggled under the covers. It took a long time for her to go to sleep. She feared a repetition of that nightmare.

Though the nightmare was gone for the night, another dream came. Levi appeared, staring intently at Emma with the same sad troubled look he had at the singing. "Just once I wish you would look at me like you love me."

Emma throat tightened. She couldn't speak. When Levi floated away, Eli hovered over her, taunting her to break away from her Plain ways. She should live life on the edge like him. Amos stepped between them to plead his plight. His children needed her for their mother. She should consider becoming his wife. Emma turned to run away and fled right into another man's arms that wrapped around her. Strong arms of an unknown man that made her feel safe. She started to say thank you when the dream ended but not for long. It started again from the beginning and repeated itself the rest of the night.

Finally with the break of daylight on Monday morning, Emma woke up, feeling as if she hadn't gone to bed. She heard the clattering bang of stove lids being rearranged. Hal was in the kitchen. Emma scrambled out of bed, reached for a dress on a peg and eyed her dirty coat next to it. She wished she hadn't worn her coat last night. If the air hadn't been damp and cool she wouldn't have. Now she had to figure out how to get the coat cleaned without Hal seeing it. She needed the coat for the next worship meeting.

The first streaks of dawn burst through the living room windows and slid across the floor as Emma made her way downstairs. She smelled sausage cakes and eggs cooking. The whine of the generator told her the milking would soon be over.

"Gute morning," Hal greeted over her shoulder as she flipped the sausage cakes.

Emma gave her a wan smile. "Gute morning."

"That was a weak greeting. You look tired. Out late last night?" Hal inquired, surveying Emma closely.

"Jah, afraid we lost track of time," Emma excused.

"That happens when you're dating," Hal replied casually.

Emma glanced around to see what needed done. She grabbed the coffee pot and filled it with water. As she ladled out the dippers of water from the bucket, she could feel Hal's eyes on her back. She turned in time to see the look of concern on Hal's face. Taking a deep breath, Emma forced herself to sound cheerful. "Sorry I overslept. What have you left for me to do?"

With that, the women finished cooking the meal. While they waited for John and the boys to come in, Emma made three lunches for school while Hal set the table.

On Saturday after breakfast was over and the clean up was done, Hal asked, "Did you remember we're going to Margaret and Linda Yoder's to work on a quilt this morning?"

Emma had forgotten, but she didn't want to admit it so rather than lie she just nodded yes.

Hal planned, "We have all day. John and the boys are cutting wood. We can send their lunch with them. Potatoes to roast in a bonfire and deer burgers in a skillet."

Emma worked at smoothing out the dish towel she'd draped over the line, thinking up an answer. She wasn't sure she wanted to deal with Levi if he was home. She was about to turn Hal down when she thought of her dirty coat. This would be the perfect time to clean it. "Nah, you go on. I have sewing to do. Noah and Daniel need new shirts."

"All recht. I'm going to take the girls. That way you won't be interrupted. I don't expect to be back until mid afternoon."

That is gute, Emma thought. *I can wash the coat and hang it on the wire line at the end of the porch with the Sunday best clothes. It will look like I am airing the coat along with the other clothes just like we always do before Sunday meetings.*

That afternoon, Emma looked out the kitchen window when she heard the clip, clop of an enclosed buggy drive in. Hal took Beth's infant seat out of the buggy and set her on the porch then went back for Redbird. Emma dried her hands on her apron and went to pick up Beth. "Gute afternoon. Did you have a gute time at the Yoders?"

"Jah, I did. You get very far with the sewing?" Hal asked, watching her feet as she climbed the steps carefully with Redbird. Emma muttered jah just as the clothes, waving in the breeze, at the end of the porch caught Hal's eyes. "You have the meeting clothes airing. Even your coat."

"Jah, seemed like a gute day for it." Emma held tightly to Beth's seat and opened the screen door for Hal.

Hal made her way to the kitchen. She placed Redbird on the table, and Emma put Beth beside her. She looked puzzled. "Why didn't you hang the rest of the coats out?"

"Hmm?" Emma stalled as she turned to the dishpan. "I need to finish dishes before the water cools. I am cleaning up now that I have a cake in baking."

"I can smell it. Makes me hungry," Hal said. "You didn't answer me, Emma. Why is just your coat airing?"

"I did not take the time to get the other coats after I decided to bake the cake." That was the truth. Emma had only been thinking about washing her coat without getting caught.

Hal paused to think. "Last time I saw you wear your coat was for the youth singing with Eli last weekend. You've looked like something is bothering you ever since. What's wrong?"

Emma sighed. "Hallie, maybe some day I will tell you, but right now it would not do any gute to discuss it."

"As long as you know you can tell me anything and share your problems with me when you want," Hal insisted.

"Jah, I know," Emma said, feigning lightness as she dunked her cake bowl into the rinse water.

❧

Late that night, Emma's room lit up. The light wavered in a circle on the wall and spread over her face. She slipped out of bed, her heart racing as she tiptoed to the window. Emma made out a dark form behind the flashlight, standing near the martin houses. She opened the window and called softly, "Who is it?"

"It is Eli. I need to talk to you."

"Nah, not tonight." Emma reached to close the window.

"Just for a few minutes," Eli pleaded.

Emma relented. "All recht, come around to the front porch."

She slipped outside. Eli was already leaning against a porch post, waiting for her.

"What do you want?" She snapped.

"To tell you I am sorry I lost my temper," Eli said contritely.

"Sorry for scaring me out of my wits? Are you sorry for making me sit in your buggy while you drank away the night? Are you sorry for trying to kill me, yourself and your horse, racing on the road in the dark?" Emma asked angrily.

Eli looked toward the barn. "All of that. I do not think sometimes. I wish I had. Now I can not take back what I did."

The words hit her hard. He looked pitiful as he struggled with himself. She felt a lump grow in her throat and tried to blink tears away as she shivered in the stinging wind. "I am glad to hear you say that, but now I must go inside. I am cold."

"Want to go get your coat so we can talk longer?" Eli asked.

Emma grunted. "Nah, I do not. About my coat. It was so covered with mud the wheels splashed on it the coat may be ruined. I just washed it. I can not wear it again until it dries."

"It is sorry for that, too, I am. I made a real mess of our date, ain't so? Can you ever forgive me?" Eli said as if he meant it.

His hang dog expression was so remorseful Emma felt like forgiving him. She almost did until she pictured her coat, and how she had to slip around to deceive Hallie to wash the coat. She didn't like to be dishonest. It went against her teachings. If this was a sample of what Eli caused her to do he wasn't worth it. "Maybe, but for tonight I just want to get some rest to make up for the sleep I lost last night." Emma put her hand on the door handle then turned back. "If it helps any, I will rest better tonight knowing you apologized."

"It helps. It helps a lot. I'll see you soon," Eli said fervently as she shut the door on him.

Chapter 14

Daylight, now that it was fall, had grown much shorter. John lit the red lantern to take to the barn to see what they were doing at milk time. One late afternoon when the lantern light flooded over the raccoon cage, Daniel did a double take. Barabbas was curled up in his cage fast asleep as if he had always been there.

"Daed, Noah, look in the cage," Daniel said gleefully as he squatted at the open door.

"Barabbas came back," Noah said in wonderment, kneeling beside Daniel.

"Be careful. That coon is wilder now since he has been free for awhile," John warned. "You can not keep him anymore."

At the sound of John's gruff voice, Barabbas woke up. He stretched, sniffed the air and chirped a greeting to the boys. Daniel reached slowly into the cage to pick Barabbas up. The raccoon put his arms around Daniel's neck and laid his head on the boy's shoulder.

"See, Daed, he is all recht. He came home to us," Noah said.

"He missed us," Daniel added as he eyed the raccoon fondly.

"I see, but you will have to let him go again. That is my last word on this," John ordered sternly.

"Ach, nah. What if we fix the latch better on the cage so Barabbas can not escape?" Daniel pleaded.

"Coons are very smart animals. He would figure out how to get out. Coons are always wild. It is cruel to keep them caged." John saw the sadness on his sons' faces. "Remember who named the coon?" John asked.

"Emma did," Daniel said, tearing up.

"Emma had a reason for picking that name. Do you know the story of Barabbas in the bible?" John asked as he slipped the handle of the lantern onto a nail so it lit up the milk parlor.

"Nah," Noah said.

"That name fits this coon. Barabbas was a robber and a murderer just like your coon. He was caught and arrested. At Passover, he was the one pardoned. He was never going to change, but they let him go anyway. Just like this coon is never going to change, but we need to pardon him. I want you to let him go but not around here. He has a taste for Emma's hens and Tom now. Take him farther away so he will not be tempted to come back. You hear me?"

"Jah," Noah said.

Daniel hugged the raccoon as he nodded.

"Tonight during devotions, I want both of you to read John 18 to learn the story of Barabbas," John insisted.

The next morning, Emma stared into the buggy. "Daniel, why are you putting the coon cage in the buggy. That wild animal can not come to school with us," Emma maintained with fervency.

"He is safe in the cage," Daniel contended.

"That coon's safety is not what bothers me. It is how safe the children will be around him," Emma worried.

Barabbas rumbled a low growl like a dog at her fretful voice.

Emma glared at the animal. "I do not like you any better than you like me."

Barabbas put his paws over his eyes and ducked his head.

Daniel and Noah laughed.

"Very funny." Emma tried hard not to smile at the raccoon's antics.

"We are going to turn him loose so he can live in the timber by the school. Daed said Barabbas will get mean one of these days if we keep him in the cage. We will give him his freedom far enough away he will not come back to our house and get Tom Turkey," Daniel said sincerely.

"Tom proved he can take care of himself. It is the rest of my hens I worry about. That coon has already eaten two of them. Remember those hens are what lay your food for breakfast," Emma replied through narrowed eyes.

"We know, but after today you need not worry," Noah said.

"You are really going to let him go?" Emma asked.

"Jah, after we show him to the boys," Daniel confirmed.

"All recht, but you make sure to warn the pupils not to stick their fingers in the cage. When you turn the coon loose have the children stand back. I do not want him to attack and bite one of them as nasty tempered as he can be," Emma exclaimed as she climbed into the buggy.

"Barabbas will not do that. He only gets mad at you," Daniel scoffed.

"The pupils are strangers to that coon. If they move too fast to suit him, he might think they were going to harm him and attack them," Emma warned.

"All recht," Daniel agreed.

During the first recess while the children played, Emma sat on the steps, grading some assignments and prepared the afternoon lessons. She kept a nervous eye toward the boys grouped around the buggy. Barabbas chattered nervously, not liking all the attention. He didn't want to be an attraction for all those noisy humans.

Not only that, the horses, in the pen next to the small barn, pawed and snorted. They didn't like being close to the raccoon. Emma worried about how fidgety Mable acted. The last thing she wanted to do was have Mable get away from them and have to hunt a runaway horse before they could go home. She short changed the children a few minutes when she called recess was over, but she wanted the boys away from the raccoon. The poor animal needed time to settle down and so did the horses.

That afternoon, the class room was too warm with the heating stove going and the sun shining in. Emma opened a window close to her desk. She was relieved to hear silence. Mable, her head lowered, stood quietly with one back hoof lifted as if she was asleep. The other horses stare over the fence toward the buggies.

Emma picked up a book from her desk and walked in front of it. Before she had time to speak, Barabbas perched on the open window sill and chattered a greeting.

The pupils pointed and laughed.

Emma edged between the raccoon and the pupils. She hissed at him, "Get out of here."

The coon pounced from the window into the room and sat up on his backend, surveying the room as he sniffed.

"Coons have bad eyesight but good smell. Barabbas is looking for me and Noah," Daniel explained. "When he smells the air, he is trying to pick up our scent."

Matthew agreed, "That is so, Emma."

Some of the other boys added their knowledge of raccoons. The girls tittered nervously and eased out of their seats to gather as far away from the animal as they could get.

"Daniel, get him out of here now," Emma ordered harshly.

Barabbas's ears perked up. Footsteps thudded on the wooden floor mixed with Emma's angry voice, signaling danger. He wanted protection in this strange place full of human smells. His twitching nose told him someone close smelled familiar. He sprang toward Emma and wrapped himself around her legs.

Emma screamed, "Get him off me."

At the sound of her voice, the raccoon responded with a long, low growl and tightened his grip with all four legs. His needle sharp claws dug into the back of Emma's thighs.

The girls, not wanting to be in the fix Emma was in, ran screaming from the building. The boys backed up by their desks, watching helplessly.

Nearly in tears, Emma yelled, "Brothers, you have got to get this coon off me." She was afraid to touch the raccoon herself. When she tried to walk, she had to shuffle her feet and almost lost her balance. She perched on her desk top with her legs stiffly in front of her. "Get up here now!"

The coon chattered nervously as he looked above him where the loud voice came from.

Daniel intoned, "We are in trouble now."

Noah replied, "What do you mean we? The coon is yours."

"Emma is looking mean at both of us. You help me," Daniel insisted.

As they walked down the aisle, Emma closed her eyes and tried to stop the panic welling up in her. She said through clinched teeth, "Will you hurry up?"

"If we run at Barabbas, he will be afraid and hold on tighter," Daniel told her.

"I can not stand this smelly creature. He is digging his claws into my legs, and it hurts. I want him off me now," Emma plead softly as she took a tighter grip on the edge of the desk.

Daniel reached out and touched the raccoon's back. "Come to me, Barabbas. Come on."

The raccoon's chatter softened, glad to hear a friendly voice as he laid his head on Emma's lap.

Noah encouraged, "I think he likes you, Emma."

"I do not like him and never will. Get him away from me," she said shrilly.

"He thought Emma is me when he heard my voice," Daniel reasoned. "Noah, help me. We can pry him loose."

Noah and Daniel tried to pull the raccoon's front legs away from Emma, but Barabbas was too strong for the boys. They couldn't budge him. He was not giving up the warm place he considered safe.

At the back of the room, the boys broke out in laugher when Daniel and Noah couldn't persuade the raccoon to turn loose. Outside, the girls talked excitedly, all at the same time, like a bunch of magpies. Emma heard them, but she wasn't in any position to find out what their problem was. She had enough troubles of her own.

Suddenly, the girls grew quiet. The boys stopped laughing. Hurried footsteps sounded in the middle aisle. She looked through tear blurred eyes as Adam Keim rush toward her.

"Adam, help me," she begged.

Adam looked stern as he held his finger to his lips and touched her lips with the fingertip. He turned to the tittering boys and glared at them with his finger to his lips. Then he

129

pointed to the door and waved them outside. All the pupils left except for Matthew Stoll. He walked slowly up front.

"Emma has Barabbas scared up," Daniel blamed.

Adam nodded he agreed.

Emma spoke softly with vehemence as she glared at Daniel, "We will discuss blame for this coon's actions, and about who is upsetting whom after you have gotten rid of this animal."

Adam pointed to the raccoon's front legs and at himself and Matthew. He pointed to the back legs and at Daniel for the right side and Noah for the left side.

"Got it, Adam," Noah said. "We better move all together before Barabbas figures out what we are up to."

Daniel asked Matthew. "You want to help us, ain't so?"

Matthew nodded and got in position.

Noah counted to three. "Now!"

They grabbed the appointed limbs and yanked. The raccoon's claws were embedded in Emma's skirt. The swift jerks caused her skirt to rip, but she was free. Daniel took the raccoon to the window and dropped him outside then jumped onto the sill and leaped to the ground. "Boys, help me scare Barabbas so he goes into the timber."

The boys didn't need to be told twice. They came running.

Emma pointed a shaky finger. "Noah, shut that window quick before Barabbas changes his mind about leaving."

Noah watched out the closed window. "I do not think Barabbas will come back. He is racing under the fence with the boys after him."

Adam gave Emma a sympathetic look and handed her his handkerchief to wipe the tears as he patted her shoulder.

Emma put her fingers to her quivering lips, breathed deep to get hold of herself and went to the door. The pupils stood at the timber fence, looking at the trees. She pulled the bell rope. "The excitement is over." After the children were seated, she said, "I need some fresh air. I want all of you to do a creative art picture for me in the next thirty minutes. Choose anything you want to draw. Each of you will show the class and talk about your picture when I come back."

Adam walked out behind her and closed the door. He pointed to the swings, swaying in the breeze.

"Jah, I would like to sit down. I am weak kneed." Emma lowered herself into the swing.

Adam sat next to her.

"Denki for saving me." Emma wiped her eyes on the handkerchief again and handed it back.

Adam waved his hand.

"It was something to me. I was in a panic. Daniel and Noah could not make that coon turn loose. I do not know what I would have done if you had not come along to rescue me." Emma's voice rose as panic built up again when she thought about the predicament she'd been in.

Adam put his finger over Emma's lips to silence her. Amusement sparkled in his eyes and then a look of concern.

"Reckon you are right. I should think about something else if I am ever going to calm down. Why are you here?"

On his notepad, he wrote, "To build the book shelves."

"Des gute. Maybe with you around that coon will not come back and attack me again. If he dares to show up you can run him off," Emma said with a slight grin.

Adam beat his chest to show he was fearless.

"Just the same, keep an eye open for that critter. Daniel has him spoiled. Barabbas thinks he is human," grumbled Emma.

Adam wrote on his pad. "Want to go fishing tonight?"

"It might be too chilly."

Adam shrugged and wrote, "Dress warm. Hot chocolate."

"I will bring enough chocolate for both of us," Emma said and managed a smile.

While Adam constructed the bookshelves, Emma tried to hold the children's attention with their art work. She noted whispers from the older boys, directed at Daniel. When the children were looking at her, Emma said, "Now I am going to let each of you show me what you drew. When I call your name, stand up and show the class your paper. Daniel Lapp, you first."

Daniel didn't expect to be called first. He stood up slowly

and held his paper out. Emma saw a round hole torn in the middle. The rest of the paper was blank. "Daniel, you did not draw a picture?"

"Jah, I drew a rabbit," Daniel said. His twitching lips reminded Emma of a rabbit.

The boys around him snickered behind their hands as Emma said sternly, "That paper is blank."

Daniel studied the paper as if looking for the rabbit and asked nonchalantly, "Do you see the hole?"

"Yes," Emma acknowledged tersely.

"That is the rabbit's hole. He must have disappeared down that hole," Daniel offered, sounding mystified. He chuckled as the other children laughed.

Adam quit hammering. Emma glanced at him. The man grinned. She narrowed her eyes, and he went back to work. She turned her attention on Daniel and managed a smile. "All right, Daniel. I reckon we all needed some cheering up after the scare we had with the coon. Now you sit back down and get the rabbit out of the hole and on that paper by the time the other children have shown us their art work. If you do not draw fast, you will not go to another recess until that rabbit is drawn."

That wiped the smile off Daniel's face. He sat down and worked feverishly. Emma knew missing recesses would motivate her brother.

Emma said, "Marianne, you next." The first grader stood up and proudly showed the class her stick figure woman. "Good job. Is that someone we know?"

Marianne said cheerfully, "My daed says some day soon we are getting a new mother. This is the one."

Emma studied the picture of a brown haired woman with a dress on green as the one she was wearing. Adam stopped hammering again. He was looking Marianne's picture which was similar to the teacher. He cocked his head over one shoulder as he eyed Emma with a curious expression. She shook her head slowly at Adam, before she said, "Thank you, Marianne. Now, Matthew, you next."

Emma half expected him to show a blank paper like Daniel,

but she was wonderfully surprised. Matthew drew a leafless tree with a squirrel perched on one limb and a crow on another. In the background, the sky had small clouds sailing across it.

"Matthew, that is a good drawing. Where is that tree?"

Matthew pointed out the window. "Right out there."

Emma walked over by Adam and looked out. Adam stood up to see. He looked at Matthew's drawing and back out the window. He turned to Matthew and winked then smiled at Emma. She wasn't surprised Matthew knew the view outside the window so well. He spent plenty of time gazing in that direction. What did surprised her was how well he could draw.

"Matthew, you should do more art work. You are very good at it," Emma praised, thinking Matthew would appreciate the compliment. Instead, he shrugged and laid the picture back on his desk.

❧

The next holiday was Halloween. Not a favorite for Emma with some of the Plain boys so much like their fathers, tricksters and jokers. A couple weeks before, Emma let the pupils put up Halloween art work. Most of the pictures were a selection of ghosts and witches with weird, scary faces and not very many jack-o-lanterns. Those were made by the younger pupils, because she gave them a pattern to trace, color and cut.

Rebecca Jacobus had her usual dramatic moment during the Jack-o-lantern making. Emma looked around while she called out the answers for the seventh and eighth grade math exercise. Rebecca sat with her sad face in her hands, watching the other pupils work. "Rebecca, work on your jack-o-lantern so you get done, before your class works in the phonic books."

"I can not," Rebecca cried in a high pitched voice.

"Why not?"

"I have lost my pencil," the little girl wailed.

"Again. How does this happen so often?" Emma asked.

"I do not know," Rebecca said, wiping tears.

"Quit crying. You can get one from the pencil can on my desk. As soon as recess comes, you hunt your pencil and bring mine back," Emma said and turned back to her math class.

"Now we can check page two of the math problems."

The pupils shifted the math papers. Edna Stolfus leaned out in the aisle to peer at Matthew's paper. She waved her hand wildly. "Emma."

"What is it, Edna?"

"Matthew does not have his math problems done," Edna tattled smugly.

Matthew gave the girl a woebegone look.

Emma said, "Matthew, count one problem wrong for each unfinished row. Why are the problems not done?"

Matthew shrugged. "Just slow at math."

Matthew was a very bright boy. His problem was he was lazier than most. "Now I will give the answers for page two."

That day at first recess, Emma looked up from grading papers to see Matthew followed by the other older boys as they eased up on Jake Coblentz. Matthew dangled a plastic skeleton on a string. Emma was too late to stop Matthew from trying to scare Jake. He jumped at the little boy with the imitation skeleton jumping up and down as he yelled boo. The other laughing boys surrounded Jake.

Emma tensed, ready to stop the boys from having fun at Jake's expense. As she listened, she realized she didn't have to help Jake. He didn't bat an eyelash as he looked at the shaking bones in front of him.

"You afraid of spooks and skeletons, ain't so?" Matthew sounded disappointed.

Jake gave him a big smile as he batted the skeleton to make it dance faster. "No such thing as a ghost, and a skeleton is nothing but a stack of bones with the people scraped off."

Daniel laughed. "Makes sense to me."

That afternoon, Emma looked over the small audience that showed up for the Halloween party. It occurred to her that these very parents, as children, had been up front performing for their parents in the Christmas programs. This might be the first and only Halloween program they ever attended, but Emma felt the Christmas program would be more successful if the pupils put on another program ahead of time.

The parents had their eyes on the children on benches at the front of the building. Emma picked Sallie Yost for the spokesman. She gave the nod, and the girl stepped forward. "Welcome to our Halloween Program. We hope you enjoy our efforts this afternoon. First, we are going to sing a song. She turned to the pupils behind her. "You may stand now." She turned back to the audience. "You are welcome to sing along with us. The song is *In The Still Isolation* set to the tune of *Twinkle Twinkle Little Star.*"

Sallie started the song, and the pupils and parents joined in. "In the still isolation you find my praise is read. Greatest God answer me for my heart is seeking you."

After the children sang all the verses, Sallie announced, "We are going to do a program called *What Did God Make On Day Six*? We have eight riddles read by the pupils. When each pupil finishes with the riddle, the audience gives the answer. Then we will tell you if you are right. Noah Lapp, step forward."

He carried a sheet of paper hugged to his chest as he walked to the edge of the riser. He thought for a minute to make sure he remembered to say the riddle just right. "You rarely will find me when you go to the zoo, but I think you will guess me if I suddenly moo! What am I?"

Almost all of the parents said in unison, "Cow."

Noah turned the paper around. "You are right. It is a cow."

Staying off to the side, Sallie said, "That was good. Edna Stolfus's turn."

Edna's face was flushed as she edged her way to the front. She took a deep breath and began, "You might get hungry if it was not for me. I provide the eggs for your whole family! What am I?"

"Chickens," came the fast replies.

Edna turned her sheet around to show them the word chicken. "Yes," she said shyly.

"Daniel Lapp," Sallie called.

Daniel marched forward and said forcefully, "Usually I am scary because I can roar! If I chase you, you would run for the

135

door! What am I?"

"A tiger," some of the women shouted.

"A bull," some of the men decided.

"A lion," others cried."

"Good job, Daniel. Now show the answer," Sallie instructed.

Grinning from ear to ear, Daniel turned his sheet around. In big letters was the word lion.

Sallie waited for Daniel to be seated. "Mark Bender."

Mark shuffled forward with his head bent. He didn't dare look up at all the faces focused on him before he said his piece. "If my nose were long, too, I would be quite a wreck. God thought it better to give me a long neck. What am I?"

A whispered discussion ensued among the parents. Finally after some nodded agreements, one of the women said, "We think it is a giraffe."

Mark nodded as he turned the sheet around to show them that was the right answer.

"Matthew Stoll, your turn," Sallie said, beckoning him.

Matthew grinned at everyone as he said, "If I would start showing off like I usually do, you would all start laughing. Maybe I would, too. What am I?"

Matthew's father, Dan, said, "Sounds like Matthew already, but I can tell everyone he is not old enough to have been around during the first six days."

Everyone laughed.

"No, Daed, I am not the answer this time," Matthew said seriously.

Everyone laughed again.

John Lapp suggested, "Monkey."

Matthew turned the sheet around to show he had it right.

"Next is Freda Manwiller," Sallie said.

Freda spoke quickly as if she wanted to get her part over fast. "I think I am quite special. My nose stretches long. I carry logs with it. God made me so strong. What am I?"

The men put their heads together in back and mumbled about the long nose. Samuel Nicely said, "An elephant."

Freda turned her sheet around. "That is good."

Sallie said, "Now Jimmy Miller is next."

Jimmy stepped forward with a grin on his face. Emma could tell he really liked this riddle. "I am not a Holstein, and I do not smell like flowers. If you get in my way you will shower for hours. What am I?"

Amos Coblentz rubbed the side of his face. "I know first hand this is a skunk."

"Jah," agreed the crowd.

Jimmy turned his sheet toward them. "You are right."

"Rueban Rogies has the last riddle," Sallie announced.

Rueban said, "The last one has a soul which is different from the rest. After God made it, He called it the best! What am I?"

Bishop Bontrager said, "I know. Man is the answer."

Rueban nodded, "Yes."

"Gute job, pupils," Emma praised as the parents all clapped and nodded proudly. "We have picked three songs we want you parents to sing with us."

As soon as the singing ended, Emma said, "Now to go on to the next portion of the program. Everyone, line up at the refreshment table to get a treat."

The next day was the time to hand in the monthly book reports. Emma ask for them at the end of the day. She hoped Matthew Stoll did his assignment on *Black Beauty.*

Jennie picked up the reports. Emma thumbed through them. She was pleased to find Matthew's name on the top of the last paper. Her feeling of success didn't last long when she scanned the page. His version didn't describe the book at all. Matthew hadn't read the story. He just made up a report. Emma was disappointed, but as she read, she realized Matthew had quite an imagination. He worded his sentences well. The report could easily have been about a book. Just not *Black Beauty.*

How should she handle this problem? Matthew would expect her to say something. His book report was actually quite good. If she hadn't read the book she wouldn't know the difference. She glanced over at Matthew. He was watching her for a reaction. Emma didn't give him one. Instead, she dismissed school.

The next day she handed out the graded book reports. She announced, "For October, Matthew's report was the best written of all the reports."

Matthew's mouth dropped open. Emma smiled at him. "Matthew, do not forget to pick up another book to read."

After Emma dismissed school, the other pupils went to the new book shelves to put away the book they had for a month and picked out another one before they left. Matthew held onto the book *Black Beauty* and stayed at his desk.

Emma asked, "Yes, Matthew?"

"I was surprised at the grade you gave me for the book report," he said with a guilty expression as he came to her desk.

Emma replied, "I could see you were. Why?"

The boy lowered his head as he confessed, "I did not read the book all the way through. I thought you might notice."

"I did. I did not give you the grade for reading the book. I gave it to you for a well written report which took a fair bit of imagination," Emma said frankly.

Matthew looked puzzled.

She explained, "I love to read. I know *Black Beauty* by heart. I knew your report was not about that book. Next month you should read the book all the way through and write a report on it. You will like the story, and as well as you write, you will do a good job."

Matthew said solemnly, "All right, I will do that."

"Thank you for telling me you did not read the book. That was the right thing to do," Emma told him.

Matthew gave her a weak smile. "Bye, teacher."

"See you Monday," she replied.

Emma felt as if she'd succeeded a little with Matthew by picking his as the best book report. His guilt, because he cheated, made him confess. Now he'd read the book and do the proper book report for November. She was pretty sure her work with him wasn't over yet, but she was very hopeful. She had plenty of time to work on bringing him around.

Chapter 15

Branches swayed in the brisk, chilly wind as Adam drove along the winding creek road. The western sun shone through the tree branches, throwing patches of wavering light on the shaded road.

"The sun stripes the road cheerfully, but after dark we are going to get cold, Adam," Emma predicted.

Adam put his hand out and wavered it back and forth.

"Ach, I know we will. When the sun goes down, its heat goes with it for the night," Emma insisted.

Adam smiled as he parked.

They stepped down and grabbed all the fishing gear and Emma's thermos of chocolate.

Most of the tree leaves were under foot now and rustled noisily as Emma and Adam tromped on them. Emma dropped her armload under the cottonwood tree. She tugged her coat tighter around her and sat down.

Adam placed his load beside hers and picked up his pole.

The northerly breeze softly whispered through the tree tops. The creek quietly lapped at the bank. Waves, pushing other waves, were small and barely noticeable.

Emma leaned back against the tree and crossed her legs at the ankles. She let out a long sigh. "Adam, this is my favorite place no matter what season I am here. It is peaceful tonight"

Adam nodded and looked around. He grabbed Emma's arm and pointed across the creek. An antlered deer edged down the bank. The deer lifted its head to check for danger before he sipped. He lifted his head again and wiggled his ears back and forth, listening for strange noises. After he didn't hear anything, he leaped up the bank and crashed through the underbrush.

"How nice was that, ain't so?" Emma declared.

Adam smiled.

Emma sighed. "This is much better than playing pranks on people for Halloween, ain't so?"

Adam wrote on his pad, "We got pranked last night."

"Ach, nah! What happened?"

He wrote, "Four boys came to our place in the night."

"Who were they?" Emma asked eagerly.

Adam nodded no.

"Why not? Maybe I do not know them," she baited him.

Adam wrote, "You know them. I will not tell."

"Tell me at least what they did," Emma insisted.

Adam wrote longer that time. "They took our open buggy apart and reassembled it on the barn roof. Bobby heard a racket in the night. He peeked out a window and saw them.

It was almost daylight so he woke Mama and me. He told Mama to prepare a big breakfast. When the boys came off the roof, Bobby was at the foot of the ladder. He said he wanted to invite them in for breakfast since they worked so hard. The boys did not know how to say nah so they came in and had breakfast. We were nice to them. The boys felt so bad they went back out to the barn and disassembled the buggy and put it back together on the ground."

Christmas was an important occasion at school. The children looked forward to standing up in front of their parents to put on a program. Emma wanted to make the program a good one. She was thrilled when she found the program book in the stack of magazines Ellen Yost gave her. *Getting Ready for Christmas* was filled with Christmas plays, poems, and songs suited for Amish schools. She jotted down suggestions for a good program for her pupils.

Noah helped her move the teacher's desk over to the corner to make more room on the riser. As much as possible before the Christmas program, the children rehearsed. It was hard for some of them to memorize all they were supposed to say. She prompted most of the time.

Snow hadn't been more than a skiff so far in December. Emma worried the day of the program would be the big snowfall, but that afternoon was sunny with not much breeze. A perfect day to travel, and it showed. Parents, grandparents and neighbors crowded into the school as soon as they shrugged out of their coats, shawls, felt hats and black bonnets and piled them in the utility room. When the program was over they would sort through the garments, checking for their embroidered initials in the necks.

The audience took their seats at the desks and on the backless benches. They looked at the artwork, trying to guess which decoration had been made by their children.

That morning, the older boys set up the manger scene. They stretched a wire across the room and threw a sheet over it for a curtain. Matthew Stoll lead in a small calf and tied its halter to the desk leg. Ella Miller carried in a cage of hens and one rooster. Noah brought a few bales of hay, and Daniel helped him stack them behind the cardboard box they painted to look like a manger. David Mullet tied his pony to a twine on the top bale in the stack. Nonni Zook brought two lambs, donated by her grandfather, Rudy Briskey. They were in a make shift crate with spaces wide enough to stick their heads out.

Emma picked Sallie Yost to be the spokesman again. She seemed comfortable with the job. When the school was packed, Emma stepped forward to introduce Sallie as a Christmas angel who would guide the audience through the program.

Sallie, in a white robe with wings and a construction paper halo on her head, stepped forward. She clasped her hands together in front of her and looked at the audience. After a deep breath, she said, "I am glad to see all of you today, because if you had not come you would have missed a good time. So for all of us scholars, I want to greet you with Merry Christmas. Now here are some of the pupils with a message about Christmas."

Noah Lapp came forward. He held a poster with simple handmade gifts on it. "Sometimes the gifts you make bring more happiness than anything you can buy."

Matthew Stoll stepped up beside Noah. His poster was covered with a yellow smiley face. "Making gifts and giving them away to make others happy is the best part of Christmas."

Malinda Bender held up a poster with a large red heart on it. "However, we all know the best gift you can give is simply called love."

The rooster crowed a string of times, and Edna Stolfus shouted over him. "This Christmas season let us try to do some Golden deeds."

"To carry someone's burden to help someone in need," stated Jimmy Miller.

Behind the curtain came a crack and a splatting noise which scared the hens. They cackled excitedly.

Mark Yoder's eyes rolled toward the ceiling as he supplied, "There are always those who need our help as we journey on life's way." Behind his hand, he said in a loud whisper, "Like those old hens in the stable."

That brought titters from the audience.

"The friends we win by helping people make us richer every day," Freda Manwiller said.

Rueban Rogies pointed his finger at the audience. "So remember what we say if you see a sad face as Christmas time grows near."

The children all said together, "Do your best to lift the load of someone and spread a word of cheer."

The audience clapped as those children bunched in the corner.

The older girls came forward and stood in front of the desk. On the desk were a large mixing bowl and other items.

Sallie said, "We are going to make a Christmas cake so listen closely to the recipe." She read from a recipe card, "Girls, gather for the bowl a bit of cheerfulness and a pinch of laughter." The girls reached out to pinch the air above the audience and opened their fingers over the bowl as they laughed robustly.

Sallie picked up a glass measuring cup from the desk and

handed it to Malinda Bender. The girl held the cup over the bowl. "Next I will dump this cup of thoughtfulness and stir all through and through."

Loud scratchy sounds came from behind the curtain as Edna Stolfus said, "Now to this bowl add tranquility which is a verse of *Silent Night* so that however quiet we may be God will send his holy light." Munching sounds behind the curtain brought snickers from the audience, highlighting a not so tranquil time. Edna stirred with a wooden spoon as the girls sang a verse of *Silent Night.*

Next Freda Manwiller said, "Set aside a moment while you go for spices, herbs and pine, for music, fun and candle glow." She picked up a cardboard yellow star and put it in the bowl. "A star was the sign that Christ was born."

Edna handed the spoon to Malinda. As she stirred the bowl, she said, "Mix and fold again and add some mistletoe."

Holding the bowl in front of her, Ella Miller said, "Add a bit of faith and love and into the oven your cake must go." She spooned what was in the bowl into a cake pan.

Sallie added, "Where warmth and affection will combine to make this cake come true." She pointed around the room. "Icing with happiness so fine. Enough for me and you."

All together, the girls said, "Serve with a prayer of peace on earth and a heavenly kingdom near."

Sallie said, "Now we sing, *O Little Town Of Bethlehem.*

After the song was over, Angel Sallie stepped forward. "Now it is time for our Nativity play. The children scrambled to get into place behind the sheet. Noah and Matthew pulled the curtain along the wire to expose the stable. They stopped to hide where the actors stood behind the desk.

The hay bales had turned into a mishapped hay stack thanks to the pony. He was still munching on the bales. A hen had laid an egg. The earlier noise was when it rolled out of the cage and splattered on the floor. The lambs stuck their heads out of the crate and baaed. The calf perked up at the activity around him. He bawled at the crowd, braced his hooves and jerked on his halter, vibrating the desk as he tried to free himself.

"I told you, Matthew, you should have brought the cow along. That poor calf is hungry," Dan Stoll said in good humor.

His wife, Kaziah, reached across the aisle and patted his arm. She hissed, "Listen to the play."

Adin Bender agreed, "Dan's recht. He wants his mother."

Joseph played by Daniel Lapp and Mary played by Sara Muhlenberg came past the pony into the stable. The stable hosteler, Jake Coblentz, petted the pony. Joseph stopped by him and asked, "Who do we see about getting a room?"

Marvin Bender stepped away from the two other shepherds, David Mullet and Andy Stoll, each holding a staff. He pointed to Marianne Coblentz standing by the calf, trying to get it to calm down. "Talk to that woman, but the inn is full."

"We must have a room," Joseph said. "My wife is going to have a baby tonight, and she needs a warm bed."

"There are no empty beds in the inn," Shepherd Marvin said. "Just ask this woman."

Joseph (Daniel) walked by the chickens to Inn Keeper Marianne. He stepped on the smashed egg and slid into her. She pushed him away. He said, "My wife needs a bed. Do you have one for us?"

Marianne said, "Yes, come with me." She turned to leave.

"Oh no," Shepherd Marvin declared, grabbing Marianne by the arm. "The inn is full." He looked imploringly at Mary (Sara). She shrugged, not sure what to do.

Daniel slipped up behind Marianne and whispered, "Say there is not a room in the inn left. No room for these people."

"That is right," Marvin said, nodding at Marianne. "They have to sleep in the stable."

Marianne put her hands on her hips and said definitely, "There is a room in the inn where it is warm. Mary is going to have a baby so I made room for them."

As a titter went through the crowd, Marvin looked helplessly at Emma. This wasn't the way the play was supposed to go.

Marianne grabbed Mary by the arm and was trying to take her away. Mary stood her ground and tugged back. They were wrestling when Emma whispered in Angel Sallie's ear. The angel pulled Mary and the Inn Keeper apart and got caught in the middle of the shoving match. By the time Sallie managed to separate the two girls, her bend halo tilted to the side of her head, and one wing was broken. She placed her hand on Marianne's shoulder. The girl gave the angel a defiant look, determined to take Mary to a warm bed. The angel said, "What a different story the bible would have in it if the inn keeper had been as kind hearted as you are Inn Keeper, but since we know Jesus was born in a manger in the stable we have to let Mary have him there."

Noah and Matthew pulled the curtain back in front of the stable. The angel came from behind the curtain, escorting Marianne to a seat and at the same time trying to hold her drooped wing up. She got back on the riser. "Now it is Christmas in the stable."

Noah and Matthew opened the curtain again. Mary and Joseph were kneeling by the manger, looking in it. Shepherd Andy was behind them, peering over their shoulders. He turned and called to the other two shepherds, "Come, I have found the babe wrapped in wrinkled clothes."

Mary looked up at him. "The babe's clothes are not wrinkled. They are dirty and rotten."

Marianne sprinted on stage. She grabbed the babe from the manger. "He needs to be inside where it is warm."

Mary grabbed for the babe. "His bed is in the manger. When she jerked the Amish rag doll from Marianne's hand it flew off the stage and landed at the feet of the parents on the front row.

Emma was beside herself at how the play was going. She put her hand over her mouth, wondering what could possibly go wrong next. It didn't help her frame of mind that the audience giggled at the exchange between the actors.

Angel Sallie, now missing the wing, came to the rescue. She picked up the babe and laid him back in the manger. "This is where he belongs on Christmas day," she told Marianne firmly.

Titters grew loud as Marianne huffed to her seat.

The three wise men, John Mast, Rueban Rogies and Mark Yoder, came from behind the curtain. Each carried a gift wrapped in white paper. They went to the manager and knelt down by Joseph and Mary.

Wise man, John, said, "We are bringing gifts to the babe of gold, common sense and fur."

That melted the crowd into a fit of laughter. Everyone clapped robustly.

The angel said, "The play is over. We want the audience to sing with us, *We Wish You A Merry Christmas.*"

Bishop Bontrager singled Emma out when the program was over. He was still wiping tears from laughing so hard. "That was some Christmas program, Emma."

"I am very sorry about the play. I thought the pupils knew their lines better than that," Emma apologized.

"Do not be sorry. I have never enjoyed a Christmas program, in all the years I have attended, as much as I did this one. Very voonderball gute play."

The Christmas party grew boisterous in the crowded school as gifts were exchanged and plates were filled with snacks. Emma had fixed each child a small paper sack of Christmas candy and caramel popcorn with a pencil sticking out of it.

The children drew names the first of December so now they exchanged their gifts while the grown ups helped themselves at the refreshment table. Some of the pupils gave Emma a gift. One gift in particular pleased Emma very much. She opened the brown paper wrapping to find Matthew Stoll's art picture of the tree she had liked so much. It was in a plain brown wooden frame.

When the gift exchange was over, the pupils lined up to get their refreshments; rice krispie bars, chocolate pretzels, coconut bon bons and hot chocolate.

Adam Coblentz paused by Emma. "The program was gute. You saved the day when Marianne changed the ending."

"You have a special little girl. She is so kind hearted she could not follow the script," Emma said cheerfully.

"Denki for saying so." Adam gave her a gentle smile. Her compliment about his daughter meant a lot to him.

Making the special Christmas cookies and candies were certainly a part of Emma's holiday home to-do list. She wanted plenty for the Lapp family use and extra to give out as gifts.

Noah and Daniel brought in sprigs of cedar from the pasture to lay around the living room shelves and attach over the windows. Heat from the stove warmed the cedar and stirred up the pungent scent that added to the holiday cheer.

Hal set candles on the window sills. She sent Christmas cards with letters for friends and family. She offered the rest of the box to Emma, but the girl said she'd make her own. She had a box full of rubber stamps, ink and other card making supplies. She spread the box contents on the kitchen table and worked on cards for her pupils while she watched cookies bake.

In the evenings, Emma helped her brothers thread together popcorn strings to hang with the greenery above the windows.

Hal found it fun to go to the mailbox every day to see who they had a card and letter from. In the evenings, John looked over the mail with her.

Christmas Day was on Thursday so school was out until Monday. As soon as chores were out of the way that morning, they fasted by skipping breakfast while they mediated and took turns reading bible scriptures until dinner time. This was the day to celebrate the birth of Christ.

Emma butchered two chickens the day before so there was plenty of roast chicken if visitors came. The rest of the menu included mash potatoes, gravy, stuffing, canned green beans, and Christmas pudding. The pudding was a cream cheese salad layered between red and green Jello to represent Christmas colors and snow. For dessert, Emma and Hal baked a cake, two dried apple pies and sugar cookies.

After dinner, the family exchanged gifts. John and the boys gave Hal stationary with a purple aster border and envelopes to match. She said she'd use the pretty paper to write her mother and Aunt Tootie.

Emma's gift to Hal was special. She'd bought a spiral

147

notebook and in her neat, cursive handwriting copied a pamphlet on the art of homemaking titled *Beatitudes of a Homemaker.* Hal read the first beatitude. *Blessed is she whose daily tasks are a work of love; for her willing hands and happy heart transform duty into joyous service to others and to God.*

As she turned the pages, Hal found eight more. The last was *Blessed is she who preserves the sacredness of the Christian home; for hers is a divine trust that crowns her with dignity.*

It was the duty of a Christian wife and mother to be discreet, chaste, keepers at home, good, obedient to her own husband, that the word of God be not blasphemed, as it says in Titus 2:5.

"Emma, what a thoughtful gift," Hal exclaimed.

"You can use it as a guide to help you be a gute homemaker. The beatitudes will help you understand what is expected of a Plain wife," Emma explained.

Hal laid the booklet aside and watched as John opened his gift from the children which were six blue work handkerchiefs.

The gifts Hal enjoyed the most were the ones for the children. Redbird and Beth were too small to know about the holiday, but Emma had made each of them a faceless rag doll from the scraps that matched the babies new dresses. Hal told her in a few months when the girls could walk they would be dragging the dolls everywhere with them. Emma and Hal had taken turns sewing on fer-gute shirts for Noah and Daniel. The boys were growing up, but they liked games so Hal and John gave them a Monopoly game.

The surprise for Emma was the new fer-gute spring dress Hal made. Emma tried it on and twirled around in the pale green dress with short sleeves. Not that she intended to point the matter out, but Hal had purposely left material out of the skirt so that the dress draped over the girl's hips. She was afraid if she said anything John and Emma might worry the style change would add more names to her special friends list.

Chapter 16

The next day was the Second Christmas. It snowed four inches in the night. The Lapp family was excited. That meant they could use the sleigh when they visited.

They had been invited to the Yoder farm for dinner. So as soon as chores were done, everyone climbed into the two seated sleigh. John called to Ben to giddy up, steered the horse in a wide circle and pointed him down the driveway. There was just enough north wind to blow the light snow from the ditches across the road around Ben's hooves, but the road had been traveled enough already to pack it under the runners.

Margaret met the family at the door. "Come in. We could hardly wait for you to get here."

"Cold it is out," Linda said from the kitchen. "I have coffee and hot chocolate ready. Come and get it."

Luke and Levi greeted the Lapps as they headed to the kitchen to sit around the table. Hal handed Margaret and Linda a bundle from Emma and her. "Some sugar cookies."

Margaret's eyes sparkled. "Are these cookies made from Grandma Lapp's recipe?"

"No way. Emma was too smart to let me get in that mess again. She didn't have time to help me mop the floor," Hal said. She laughed with Margaret, Linda and Emma at the thought of that horrible cookie making day.

Levi sat down between Emma and Daniel. He said to Daniel, "Did you have a big Christmas meal yesterday?"

"We did. Emma fixed two baked chickens," Daniel told him.

"How about that. Two of them," Luke exclaimed.

Emma smiled. "I thought I might as well butcher both of

them before Daniel's coon came back and got them."

Everyone laughed and even Daniel giggled.

Levi said to Emma, "How is your Second Christmas Day going so far?"

"It is a voonderball gute day," she declared, filled with enthusiasm for the holidays.

"As soon as we drink our chocolate, we can go outside and make a snowman," Mark said.

He was greeted with smiling nods from the others.

"Hold off on that plan," his mother said. "You will get into a snowball fight and be covered with snow. Wait until after you eat dinner."

"Ach, Mom," Mark groaned.

Luke suggested, "You got a new game for Christmas. Why not play that for awhile now that you have plenty of players?"

Mark brightened up. "Gute idea. It is called Uno. Come with me. We can play on the living room floor."

After dinner, the children put on their winter garb and went outside to make the snowman, leaving the grownups to wonder at the quietness in the house now that they could hear each other talk without raising their voices.

Emma stood beside Levi, watching her brothers and Levi's brother, Mark, and sister, Jennie, roll the snow balls. Levi asked, "Would you like to go for a walk?"

"Jah, might as well. They do not need us," Emma said.

As they trudged along, Levi studied her face. "Have you other plans for today?"

Emma's boots and dress hem become coated with snow. "Nah. The boys got a Monopoly game for Christmas. They are eager to play it after supper so that will take up our evening until bedtime unless we get visitors."

Levi gave a soft sigh of relief. It was obvious he was fishing to find out if she had a date that evening. "Since it has snowed, how about we go for a sleigh ride tomorrow afternoon?"

"I would love it. I can bring along some hot chocolate," Emma planned.

"As long as I am thinking about it, do you want to go with me to the Christmas frolic Sunday night? We can get another sleigh ride in," Levi added as enticement to get her to agree.

"That would be gute," Emma exclaimed. "We need things to do at the frolic. I was thinking we should bring Rook decks so we can play cards."

"Sounds like a gute idea." Levi looked over his shoulder. "Looks like the snowman is together, and the snowball fight is under way. Want to join the battle?"

"I certainly do," Emma said as she headed that direction.

In the evening under the flickering glow of the kerosene lamp, Noah and Daniel dumped the Monopoly game pieces on the kitchen table and unfolded the board. John raised the lamp wick so they could see better. The whole family gathered around the table. Hal didn't know who was more excited about playing the game, John or the boys.

The rest of Emma's school vacation past by fast. Her only dates during that time were with Levi. He took her for the sleigh ride, and he picked her up for the singing group's Christmas frolic at Hamish Yost's farm. Then it was time for school to start again.

Emma found January started out as busy as December had been. Various folks, beside relatives and friends, were invited to visit at get-togethers in different houses in the neighborhood. Those ask to come were single women, teachers, and others of like interest so Emma had a fair share of invitations.

One afternoon while his children climbed into the buggy, Amos Coblentz stuck his head in the school door. "Emma, I have an invitation for you from the Weber sisters."

Emma stopped erasing the blackboard. "It has been forever since I saw those women. What do they want?"

"They are planning a special dinner for you to show their appreciation to you as our new teacher," Amos told her.

"That is nice, but they do not need to go to all that trouble."

"Jah, they do. Since I am a director, they asked me and my children to bring you to the meal." Amos declared, "If you say nah then my family will miss out on all that gute food. You will be forcing my children to eat more of my cooking."

Emma laughed. "I do not think your children are suffering from your cooking, but I will accept. When are the Weber sisters cooking the meal?"

"They said Friday evening if you do not have other plans. I am to find out and let them know," Amos said.

"I will be able to go that night," Emma consented.

"Des gute, I will let the sisters know," Amos said.

Emma watched at the window as he trudged through the snow to his buggy. What a striking man he was, tall with broad shoulders and a straight back. Before he stepped in, he turned to call a greeting to Noah and Daniel as they came out of the basement with their arms full of wood to fill the wood box. Then Amos spotted Emma at the window and waved.

It seemed a bit strange to Emma that the Weber sisters would fix her and Amos's family a free meal. She couldn't remember hearing they gave any of the other teachers a meal. They cooked meals for a living and served Englishers and Plain people with reservations only. They raised a garden and used the vegetables in their meals. Plus, they had chickens to supply chicken dinners and eggs for different dishes.

On Friday evening, Amos picked Emma up. She walked around the horse and stayed in the pale yellow glow of the buggy's headlights until she was at the door. After she climbed in, Amos handed her a folded blanket to put over her lap. He steered his black horse around and headed toward the road. "Gute evening. How are you?"

"Gute," she said, thinking she should be truthful and say she had been better. The buggy was too quiet. Emma glanced over her shoulder at the empty back seats. "Where are the children?"

"They are spending some time with my parents. Since the kids are both in school, they do not get to see much of their grandparents. I thought it would be a gute time for them to visit," Amos said casually. "Ready for a gute meal?"

"Jah," Emma managed with a shiver, pulling the blanket tighter around her. *Ach, What have I gotten trapped into? No children. This evening is looking more and more like a date with Amos Coblentz,"* Emma thought and made sure to hug her end of the front seat.

The horse's hooves clopped loudly on the pavement but made more of a muffled sound when Amos turned onto the gravel road. When they reached the frozen branch that crossed the road just before the Weber sisters driveway, the horse slowed down. The buggy headlights bounced off the ice, creating yellow glares. That worried the horse.

Amos flicked the lines over his back. "Get up, Joe!"

The horse put one hoof on the ice and then the other, testing his footing. Amos shook the lines again, and the horse walked gingerly across. Loud crunches sounded under the plodding horse hooves and the buggy wheels as the thin ice broke.

Up ahead, Emma saw the brightly lit house. A lantern swayed on the rod attached to the front porch post, lighting up the path from the yard gate to the porch steps. The kitchen windows glowed with a warm cheery brightness, beckoning winter visitors. Emma shivered. She'd be glad to warm up.

Amos pulled up in front of the large, white farm house where Esther and Eve Weber lived. The sisters had cared for their parents until they died, remained single and continued living on the family farm.

The wind kicked up and funneled across the porch. Emma shivered as Amos knocked. Delicious smells met them as the door opened. Eve greeted, "Come in out of the cold. We have been waiting for you, ain't so, Esther?

"Jah," replied the short, brown haired woman stirring a steaming kettle on the stove.

Thin, tall Eve's complexion was as fair as her sister's was dark. She waved her hand toward the table. "Sit down. The meal is almost ready, ain't so, Sister?"

Esther nodded.

"Is there anything I can do to help?" Emma asked. She'd rather be busy than sit awkwardly by Amos.

"Nah, you are our guests. Sit down and talk to us." Eve asked, "How is teaching going, Emma?"

"Fine. I enjoy it," Emma answered.

"We knew you would like the job," Eve said. "Right, Sister?"

"Right," Esther agreed without turning around.

"This kitchen sure smells delicious," Amos said.

"We hope the food tastes as gute as it smells," Eve said. The sisters dished up mashed potatoes, pork chops, gravy, green beans and a sweet potato casserole.

Once they had the table filled with bowls and platters, the sisters sat down across from Emma and Amos. Eve said, "Let's bow our head for prayer."

After a minute, the sisters stared the food around the table. As she filled her plate, Emma admitted to herself being nervous didn't keep her from having an appetite.

Amos asked, "How is business, Sisters?"

"This time of year is slow," Esther answered.

"We expect that," Eve added. "We will have plenty of visitors to feed in spring and summer. It is time to rest now."

"That is gute," Amos replied as he cut up his pork chop.

Emma stated, "From what I heard from my customers at our roadside stand in the fall, Englishers would love to come to the country for a voonderball gute meal like you serve. I have given some of them directions to get here."

"We hear that from Englishers, too," Esther said seriously.

Eve smiled. "Your help in guiding people to our door explains the new customers we have had lately. Danki, Emma."

"People are trying to eat healthy. They appreciate food that has been raised on your land. It makes a difference to them that they can see where the meal was grown. Maybe you need to do some advertising to draw in more customers all year around," Emma clarified.

"That is a gute idea," Eve agreed, giving what Emma said some thought. "But we may have all the business the two of us want. We are not spring chickens anymore."

Esther placed her folded hands under her chin and said in a

dreamy voice, "Emma, I will always remember when your father brought Nurse Hal here on *their* date. That was a special time for both of them, too." She winked at Emma and said coyly, "Ain't so, Sister?"

Instantly, Emma felt butterflies fluttering in her stomach, and she concentrated at her plate.

"It was a nice day for all of us. Of course, you must remember John and Hal were already married when they came to visit, Sister." Eve corrected.

Emma concentrated on pushing her food around as color crept up her neck and covered her face. She was suddenly burning up. Hopefully, her face wasn't so red that her discomfort showed. She continued to eat, hoping Amos hadn't noticed Esther's wink. She prayed, *Please let the Weber sisters change the subject.*

No such luck as Eve added, "They were such a special couple. They were meant to be married."

"Ach, jah! When you stop to think about it, Eve, we have fed more than our share of special friends at this table that went on to marry," Esther inferred, looking at Amos with a coy smile.

Emma twisted on her chair to glance hard at Amos.

The man caught Emma's stern look and seemed to lose his tan. He swallowed hard and choked. With his hand over his mouth, he coughed and coughed.

Esther and Eve watched him in concern for a long moment. Emma stared at him through narrow eyes, wondering what he told the Weber sisters about this evening's meal that made them so sure they were feeding special friends.

Finally, Esther ordered, "Emma, slap the poor man on the back and help him out of his misery."

With her temper rising, Emma stood up with the intention of putting Amos out of his misery all right for letting her think this meal was a gift and for whatever he told the sisters about them being a courting couple. Amos caught sight of Emma's raised fist and grabbed his water glass. He put his hand up to stop her and took a long drink. Finally, he stammered, "Nah, I – I will be fine. Denki anyway."

Emma sat down and concentrated on the food in her plate again. The Weber sisters carried most of the remaining conversation through the meal and while they served the coconut cream pie. Thank goodness, they chattered about harmless topics such as what was happening in the neighborhood and the weather.

As soon as the meal was over, Amos and Emma were back in the buggy, headed to the Lapp farm. Amos didn't pay for the meal in Emma's presence. That didn't mean much. He probably paid before they arrived. She was afraid to speak for fear he'd hear the anger in her voice. Logic told Emma, she didn't want to be disrespectful to a director even if she did consider him deceitful. That meant she better not say anything at all until she had time to decided exactly what she wanted to say to this man.

Amos parked in the driveway. "You are back home now. I hope you enjoyed the evening?"

"I always enjoy a visit with the Weber sisters," Emma replied quietly. "Denki for taking me for the gute supper." Before she left the buggy, she added, "Next time you talk to the sisters please tell them how much I enjoyed their gute cooking. Tell them I am grateful they wanted to show their appreciation to the teacher. That was very thoughtful of them."

It was too dark to see Amos's face, but Emma didn't have any trouble imagining how the silent man looked. She hoped she'd made sure he was cornered into sticking to the story he told her.

Chapter 17

It was a frigid, sunny mid January day. The kind that made Emma's breath catch in her chest from the moment Noah drove the buggy into the icy wind on the gravel road.

Noah grunted when he saw a wagon coming out of the blowing snow to meet them. "It seems the worse the weather the more buggies are about."

"Folks are tough," Daniel surmised.

"It is a sunny day which helps them think traveling will be all right," Emma said.

"We have been traveling on days when the visibility was so bad in the blowing snow I couldn't see the road, hoping we would make it to and from school. Dummkopfs do not have to be out were on the road with just a couple dim lanterns on the sides of their buggy no one can see on a gute day. Let along in a blizzard. It is below zero this morning, and someone comes in a wagon," Noah complained.

"The man must think he has a reason," Daniel quipped.

"Why has he an umbrella in front of him?" Emma asked.

"I do not know," Noah replied.

As they came even with the wagon and recognized the man behind the black umbrella, the boys said in unison, "Gute morning, Jacob Helmuth."

The man nodded. His long beard was covered with frost and his lips were blue. "Cold day, ain't so?"

"Jah," Noah agreed.

Jacob continued on down the road, holding the umbrella in front of him so he could peer through a peek hole cut in it. He was using the umbrella to shield himself from the blowing snow.

That morning at recess Mark Yoder found out how cold it was. Emma was watching the smaller girls skip rope when David Mullet grabbed her hand. He shouted excitedly, "You have to help Mark. His tongue is stuck."

As David tugged on Emma to drag her along with him, she repeated, "His tongue is stuck?"

"Yes, on the pump handle."

Emma parted the children around the pump. "Oh, no. What has happened?"

"Pless, Emmmma, get me list this pump," moaned Mark.

"Stand still and do not try to speak. You will hurt your tongue," Emma said. "I need to go after warm water."

She went inside, poured some water in a tin cup and set it on the heating stove to warm slightly.

Daniel darted to the door to see what she was doing. "Mark is having a fit. Are you coming back soon?"

"Yes, I am right now." Emma hurried to Mark's side and slowly poured the warm water on the side of the pump over the boy's tongue until his tongue came loose.

"Mark, what made you do this foolish thing?" Emma asked.

"The boys dared me. I thought if I licked the pump quick enough my tongue would not stick," Mark said.

"Reckon you found out differently." Emma said to the other boys, "Mark is going to have a sore tongue for a few days. Let that be a warning not to try this dare again."

That afternoon, Adam Keim brought a wagon load of wood and stacked it in the basement. Emma grabbed her coat and trudged through the snow beside the building. "Denki, Adam. That wood is much needed."

Adam smiled and wrote, "Want to go fishing later?"

"I am not much for ice fishing. Sitting on ice makes me too cold."

Adam's eyes twinkled as he wrote, "Want to ice skate."

"I have not been in a long time. I would be terrible," Emma said. "Are you a gute ice skater?"

158

Adam nodded yes.

"Promise to catch me if I trip over my skates?" Emma asked.

Adam nodded.

"Then I will go. Our pond would be a gute place to skate, ain't so?" Emma suggested.

Adam nodded.

Emma slipped back inside. The pupils were working hard on their assignments. The timer rang as she sat down. "Recess time."

The children walked to the coat pegs, put on their coats and slipped into boots and went outside. Some of the boys brought sleds. The children loved sliding down the ditch in front of the school house. She could hear them shouting and laughing as she put her coat on to go watch them. Marianne rushed in. "Why are you back?"

"It is something I need to tell you," Marianne said, bashfully.

Fearing what the little girl meant to share had something to do with her father looking for a wife, Emma asked abruptly, "What?"

"Some of the big boys passed a note," the girl whispered.

"How did I miss that?" Emma asked.

"They did it while you were outside," Marianne hissed.

"Who did it?"

"It was Noah, Daniel and Matthew," Marianne related.

"I see. You keep it our secret that you told me so you will not get in trouble with the boys. I will talk to them. Thank you for telling me." Emma gave the girl a hug. "Now go play." *What is going to happen next?*

As time to go home approached, Emma knew she couldn't put off talking to the boys any longer. She prayed she'd say the right things. "Children, I want to talk to you. Some of you have been passing notes. I want you to be honest so I am not going to say your names. As soon as school is out today, I want you to come up front and talk to me."

She tapped the desk bell. "School is dismissed. Get your coats and boots on. I will see you tomorrow."

As the other children shrugged into their coats and boots,

Noah, Daniel and Matthew came toward her desk. "Sit down so we may have a talk." Emma looked at the other children now at their desks. "You may leave now."

Noah and Daniel looked remorseful. Matthew looked indifferent. As usual, he'd be the one she had trouble reaching.

"I am disappointed in all of you. Can you tell me why you should not pass notes?"

Silence while the boys squirmed on their seats.

Finally, Daniel spoke up. "It is against the rules."

"Good," Emma said. "We need to obey the rules. Why?"

"When we pass notes it keeps us from working on our lessons," Noah said.

"That is right," Emma agreed. She directed her attention to Matthew. "You older boys are an example for the younger boys. You do not want to teach them to break rules, do you?"

"Nah," Matthew said.

"Speak in English. The answer is no," Emma said.

"No," Matthew repeated.

"For your punishment I want you to write a composition titled *Setting a Good Example.* I expect that composition to be handed in tomorrow. If it is not, you will be missing recesses until it is," Emma declared. "The one thing that makes me feel better about this is you were honest enough to come forward. Thank you for that."

Emma opened the door when Adam knocked. His ice skates dangled over his shoulder. "Come in out of the cold while I put my coat on."

John laid the *Budget* newspaper in his lap. "Wilcom."

Adam smiled and nodded.

"Cold out tonight," Hal said.

Adam patted his ice skates.

Hal laughed. " I know. Just recht for skating."

Emma put her skates over her shoulder. "I am ready."

As Adam shut the door behind them, John gave Hal a puzzled look.

"I know," Hal answered, reading his mind. "Seems like the

special friends are missing out on opportunities to date Emma while for some reason Adam has the inside track. Too bad the two of them are just friends, ain't so?"

꩜

Adam put his arm around Emma's shoulders as she slipped in the snow. "Denki. That was close." She giggled. "It is a gute thing the moon is big. The reflecting light on the snow helps us picked our way between the drifts."

The wind had gone down so the pasture was wonderfully quiet. Emma listened to the stillness, and her worries dissolved, leaving her with a sense of serenity.

The icy air stiffened her cheeks as they sat on the pond bank in the dry grass to put on their skates. Emma shivered.

Adam looked worried. He wrote, "Diese katle winder luft."

Emma held the notepad close to her face. "Of course, it is cold, but that is all recht. Look how pretty the moon streaks across the ice."

Adam stood up and gestured toward the pond.

"Ach, nah! You first so you can hold me up," Emma ordered.

Adam stepped carefully onto the ice and held out his strong hand. Emma gripped it tightly and stepped onto the slick surface. She waved her arm in an up and down motion, trying to balance. Her hand was as cold as Adam's was warm when they circled around the pond. Their skate blades cut into the ice, making the sound of glass shattering. Icy slivers sprayed their skates and the pond surface.

Emma tilted her head upward. "What fun! I am so glad you thought of this."

Adam squeezed her hand as a sign he was enjoying himself, too.

They turned to face the West. Emma squinted at the moon glare in front of her on the ice and accidentally dipped the front of her right skate into the ice. She made a windmill motion with her free hand as she leaned forward. Adam spread his feet wide, caught her around the waist and held on until she had her feet under her and was upright again.

"I almost did a nose dive. Gute thing you are so strong."

Adam gave her a bemused look.

The couple made several more circles. Finally, Emma said, "I am getting tired. Time to call it quits for tonight."

Adam pointed above them.

The sky had turned overcast while they skated. Lazy snowflakes caught on her bonnet and cape as they took their time walking across the pasture. As they passed by a cedar tree, Emma said, "Reminds me of a poem called *The Snowflakes Song*. How many songs do the snowflakes sing as they fall from the leaden sky? In a twilight world devoid of sound, they drift down with a silken sigh. And the barren earth soon sleeps, tucked under soft cider down. While the lonely cedar is transformed, a king with an ermine crown."

Adam brushed a flake off of Emma's slender nose then clapped. Emma shuddered. Adam folded his arms around himself and made a shivering movement.

Emma snuggled close to him. "Ach, we are both cold, but this has been the most fun. We should do it again soon. Maybe my brothers and Bobby would join us next time."

Adam nodded approvingly.

৵

That night Emma snuggled under the covers, trying to warm up. When she tried to get out of bed in the morning, she feared her chilled joints would be stiff ones from all the skating exertion. She relaxed and quickly dozed off.

Emma felt like she'd been asleep for a good long time when a strange bumping noise woke her. She blinked her eyes, rubbed them and stared at the ceiling, wondering what she'd heard. Rustling sounds came from beyond the foot of her bed. Reminded Emma of a mouse gnawing its way through a stack of newspapers. She lifted up and rested on her elbow, straining to see through the darkness.

A white aura surrounded the blanket chest. Emma blinked again. The lid was open, resting against the wall. Diane Lapp was on her knees, rifling through the contents.

Not again! "What are you doing?" Emma asked.

Diane twisted toward her. "After my last visit I was

162

concerned. I had to see if you had your blanket chest ready just in case you change your mind about getting married soon."

"Mama," Emma hissed. "I am not getting married soon."

"All recht, but tell me how is it you have such a full blanket chest if you are not getting married recht away," Diane demanded. "There are more things already in here than most girls have the first four years of their married life."

"Mama Hal, ----," Emma paused when her mother's head perked up. Why on earth had she called Hallie Mama Hal. She hadn't done that before. This was a bad time to start in front of her mother. "I mean Daed's wife gave me their wedding gifts."

Diane let out a gusting huff. "That is not the way it is done. Why did she do that?"

"My ---- I mean your kitchen was already filled with everything Hallie needs. She thought I should have these new things for when I wed. The way it looks now my getting married will not happen for a long time if ever."

"I noticed you are having trouble picking a special friend out of all those gute choices. Perhaps, you are too choosy. Your duties on this earth do not permit crying over the could have beens or the will never bes, my dear daughter. Remember to pray for an answer to this problem for it is the Lord's will be done not yours. He will see to it that your life goes his direction, and hopefully, that means a husband and plenty of children not staying a maidel."

Emma sighed. "I have prayed more than once, but waiting for an answer is hard."

"Jah, but God has a purpose for putting you through these trials and temptations. So never give up on him being there when you need him. He wants to see how strong you are," Diane said knowingly.

"I think He is finding out I am weak when it comes to picking a man. I am just an ordinary, confused mortal," Emma said woefully.

"Practice patience with your situation, love for everyone and forbearance. God will eventually give you more insight. As time goes by, you will gain the wisdom to make the recht

163

choices in life. Until then, my advice is it might be a gute idea to not be so choosy when you have so many special friends to pick from. Settle on one and get on with your life." With that said, her body gravitated over the blanket chest and floated through the ceiling.

An eerie silence filled the room. Emma buried her head in her hands. Was her future going to be in such bad shape that she needed the specter of her dead mother to appear as a vision to scold her?"

Emma wiped at her stinging gray green eyes to catch the tears before they rolled down her cheeks. As a child, the thought of facing life without her mother hadn't been easy, but she let go of her mother long before she died. Back then, Emma didn't have time to think about her loss. She had to take care of her two younger brothers, her father and the house. Her mother deserted Emma when she took her own life. It was only when Hallie joined the Lapp family that Emma felt as if she had a mother who really cared about her. She should have been sure before now she could talk to Hallie about anything. Hallie wouldn't scold her like her own mother just did. The first chance she had she'd see if Hallie had any sensible advice for her about special friends.

&

On Saturday, John and the boys took the powered saw around the neighborhood to cut ice on the ponds. A group of farmers gathered to stack the ice chunks on their flat bed wagons to put in their ice houses. They covered each layer with sawdust and had ice from one winter to the next.

Hal folded up the ironing board just as Emma took a chocolate cake out of the oven. While the girl had Hal to herself, she wanted to confide in her about Diane's visits.

Emma set the hot cake pan on the counter. "I have something that is bothering me."

Hal turned to her. "That's not news. Do you want to talk about who is bothering you?"

"This is not about a special friend," Emma said. "In the night lately, I see someone that is dead, and she talks to me. I think I

164

am going crazy."

Hal moved close to Emma. "Who did you see?"

"My mother. Am I crazy?" Emma asked worriedly.

Hal observed Emma closely. "Where did you see her?"

"In my bedroom."

That answer took the worry from Hal's face. "Nah, you aren't crazy. You just dreamed you saw her. That's different."

Emma plopped down in a chair. "The dream seemed so real. Why did I see her?"

"You've been so upset lately you needed to," Hal said. "Did seeing your mother make you feel better?"

"Nah, she made me feel worse. Among other things, Mama chewed me out for being so choosy about picking a husband from one of my special friends. She said I was taking too much time, and I should get on with choosing," Emma stated. She could have mention her mother wasn't too happy about Hal giving away wedding gifts, but she thought she better not.

Chapter 18

In February, Hal wrapped the girls up and went to a comfort knotting frolic at Mary Mast's house. The women were putting together and knotting as many comforts as they could to give the Christian Aid Ministries.

Mary reminded Hal of a porcelain doll with ivory skin, flushed cheeks and fair hair. She was about two years older than Emma and expecting again. Her husband, Eli, brought Mary to the clinic for a checkup just to make sure she was all right. They were both thrilled when Nurse Hal said Mary was in good health. Of course, Hal said that the first time until Mary's tiny baby was born dead.

Though not a word was mentioned among the women about her pregnancy, it was so good to see the light in Mary's blue eyes when she rubbed her slightly expanding stomach. She smiled at Hal, knowing the secret they shared would turn into a job for Nurse Hal in five months. Eli and Mary longed for a healthy full term baby. Hal prayed Mary's pregnancy went all right this time, but the outcome was in God's hands.

For Valentine Day, Emma asked the pupils to bring a box lunch to give away. She put everyone's name in a drawing. She drew the first name and gave her lunch to Sarah Muhlenberg. Sarah drew the next name, and it went from there.

Matthew Stoll drew Daniel's name. When Daniel opened the box, it was empty. He was surprised Matthew didn't make a lunch and upset, because he'd go hungry. Then Daniel realized how heavy the box was and picked the piece of cardboard up that covered the bottom. It turned out to be a false bottom

Matthew placed over the lunch. All the time Daniel worked on the box, Matthew laughed.

Daniel gave a weak grin. "Very funny. I will think of something to pay you back."

Three mothers brought snacks for the party. Mary Mullet cut heart shaped puffed rice candy. Anna Bender made popcorn balls, and Beth Jacobus brought candy hearts. Emma gave the pupils valentines she bought, because she didn't have time to make them. She taped the cards to a candy bar. The pupils exchanged homemade valentines with each other and enjoyed all the good treats the mothers made.

When it was time to go home, Emma put on her black wool coat and felt something bulky in her pocket. She pulled out a small sack and found inside an apple and note. The note read, Happy Valentine Day, Teacher. You are the best. Emma was pleased and very curious which pupil gave her this surprise. She looked close at the handwriting and knew it was Matthew.

The next morning, Emma wrote on the blackboard, Thank you for the apple. It tasted so good.

Malinda raised her hand. "What is that on the blackboard?"

Emma smiled. "There is one among you that understands my message. I'll erase it, and we can begin our day."

In early March when Jake Coblentz marched into school, he went to the front and handed Emma a note. Marianne chirped from behind her brother, "You are supposed to come to our house tomorrow night for the school board meeting."

Emma read the note. "That is what it says. Tell your father I will come with my daed."

The next night, the three board members sat around Amos's kitchen table, discussing fund totals and expenses. All Emma could do as teacher was listen so she decided to make herself useful. She said quietly to Marianne, "Want to help me make coffee and hot cocoa?"

"Jah," the girl said eagerly.

"Des gute. Jake, can you get the cups. One for each of us," Emma instructed. "Marianne, you find the coffee and cocoa."

167

Emma puddled up the fire in the cookstove and set the coffee pot on the heat. She watched the milk heat and added cocoa. When the drink was hot, Emma poured two cups. Jake was in the living room, reading a book. "Marianne, take Jake his cup, and come back for yours. Be careful. The cup is hot."

Emma set coffee by her father and Enos Yutzy. When she returned with Amos's cup, she was watching her father as he discussed the new English phonetic books she asked for. Amos's hand wrapped around the cup, and his fingers laid on her hand. She flitted a look at his hand on hers and at him. He was smiling, and she felt flustered by his touch. His hand on hers wasn't an accident.

Amos said softly, "Denki, Emma, for making the drinks."

"You are wilcom," she muttered, moving her hand fast before her father and Enos saw.

Emma feared Amos was thinking how much her working in his kitchen suited him. The flustered feeling bothered her, and she wasn't sure what it was that made her feel that way. Amos's gentle touch, his warm smile or both. She knew she'd better sit on the far end of the table away from Amos and keep her head down so this sort of thing didn't happen again in front of the other directors. She'd busy herself drinking coffee. It would be better for her presence of mind if she didn't make eye contact with Amos Coblentz the rest of the night.

One morning in April, Nonni Zook, all smiles, rushed up to the desk. "Teacher, I saw a robin this morning."

"That is good news. It means spring is here," Emma replied.

After last recess, Emma said, "I am going to read a poem titled *Song of Summer* now that we are sure spring is here."

When she finished the poem about loving summer, going barefoot, insects, flowers, birds and even thunderstorms, Emma wrote on the blackboard – flora, fauna, insects, picnic and field trip. "Flora means flowers and plants. Fauna means animals. I think it is time we went on a field trip."

The children buzzed like a hive of honey bees.

"While we are on this field trip, I want you to think about the poem I read. Look around so you can tell me during class what you liked about nature that God made. Bring paper and a pencil on the trip. Bring an envelope or container to put in samples you want to show us. As for fauna, I do not want live catches. Noah and Daniel's coon was all the fauna I can stand this year. You can draw pictures of animals you find. Does anyone know of someone that has wagons we can use for this trip?"

Jake Coblentz suggested, "My daed has a wagon he can bring."

Noah offered, "I can drive our wagon."

Emma wished for another offer besides Jake's, but since she didn't get one, she told Jake to ask his father if he was willing to help out. "You have to bring lunches and a fishing pole if you like fishing," Emma told them. "Otherwise, you can explore for things to share in class."

"Where are we going?" Daniel asked.

"How does Miller's bluff sound? Roseanna Nisely said we were welcome to picnic there," Emma told them.

Jimmy Miller said, "That bluff on our farm is really pretty this time of year with the dogwood and wild plum thickets blooming. I can show everyone the timber. I go there a lot."

The day of the field trip arrived with a bounty of sunlight on the two wagons traveling to the Miller farm. The children chattered excitedly, full of spirit and laughter. Emma sat on the seat next to Noah in the Lapp wagon as he led the way. Amos drove with his two children beside him. After the wagons were parked in the shade, the children climbed out and scattered. Some toward the pond while others disappeared into the trees.

Emma walked to the edge of the bluff and looked at the countryside. She made out the Lapp farm and their neighbors. Such a fresh time of year with brown fields and green trees under a clear blue sky.

Amos came to stand beside her. "A great sight from this bluff, ain't so?"

"Jah, God paints a pretty picture," Emma said.

"That he does," Amos agreed.

The passion in his voice made Emma turn to him, but she

wished she hadn't. Amos was staring at her. Knowing she better break the man's mood, she said, "I better get busy." She hurried back to her wagon and gathered up an armload of quilts.

Amos trailed along. "Can I help?"

"Jah, take some of the quilts and help me spread them all around so the children have places to sit when they eat lunch.

Emma spread out a quilt under an oak tree where she could watch the children. She looked up at the tall man silhouetted against the bright sky as he came toward her. Amos was back for more instructions. "We might as well sit. Although, the sitting is a bit lumpy from all the acorns under the quilt."

Amos eased to the ground and stretched out on his side, resting his head on a hand. "I am surprised the squirrels did not carry them all off."

"Me, too." Emma kept an eye on the children and was fully aware Amos watched her. Since the night he arranged that date at the Weber sisters, she'd come to realize being in this man's presence rattled her, causing her to become easily confused. He threw her so off balance she was afraid she might act like a dunce in his presence. None of the boys she dated affected her like this man ten years her senior.

"I hope the children are careful. I would so hate it if one of them gets hurt today," she worried as she tried to take in all the children darting around like squirrels.

"They will be fine, having a fun time," Amos assured her.

"I know, but I worry anyway." Emma twisted her prayer cap string. She knew Amos watched her fidget and made sure not to look directly at him.

After a few minutes of silence, Amos asked, "Emma?"

She had to glance toward him. "Hmmm?"

He said softly, "With the sun shinning through the tree leaves, dappling you like it does, you sparkle prettier than dew on a new field of daises."

Now she was really rattled. She hardly knew how to respond to such a compliment. Amos's attentive manner and the softness in his voice wasn't lost on her. He spoke to her with warmth and looked intently at her. His smile melted the last of her confidence. He meant that compliment and much more.

Emma averted her eyes and prayed for the Lord to give her something appropriate to say that wouldn't hurt Amos's feelings. Preferably without stuttering like a brainless half wit. Right away, she needed some way to put this too eager man off gently until she knew how she felt. If only she could come up with a distraction to get Amos on another subject, but so far nothing was getting past that pretty compliment repeating itself in her mind. She gave him a timid smile. "No one has ever told me that before."

Amos's grin spoke volumes. "I am glad I was the first."

Emma bit her lower lip as she realized how much she liked this man. He studied her fondly, waiting for her reply.

"Emma, look what I found." Rose Yoder came on the run to show them a monarch butterfly in the palm of her hand. She was proud of her catch and wanted to be the first to show her teacher what she'd show in class.

Emma thought, *Denki, Lord, for the interruption.* "That is one of the most beautiful butterflies I have ever seen, Rose. Sit down with us, and tell me all about it."

171

Chapter 19

Mid April was the last day of school. Suddenly, Emma was wondering how the school term flew by so fast. To her it felt like a few days ago she started as a Nervous Nelly teacher. She knew the children saw the term end differently. They were very ready for summer vacation.

Two weeks before the last day, Emma asks the children to write about their memories of the year in an essay or a poem to read to the parents. The last day of school was a big deal. Mothers fixed sandwiches and dishes for the picnic lunch while they worked on breakfast meals. Children scurried through their chores, thinking about the picnic and playing baseball with the grownups.

That morning, the program started in the school. Emma spoke about how much she enjoyed her year as teacher. She thanked the parents for letting her teach and told the children she was glad she spent the school term with them. She announced the children wrote about their memories of school, and they were going to share them. She had all the children come up on the riser. She announced she'd call their names, starting with the smaller grades first. As soon as they read their story or poem, they would sit by their parents again.

Rebecca's story was short. She liked school, playing with the other children, and she liked her teacher.

Next was Marianne Coblentz. Emma paid special attention as the girl read that her favorite memory was when Teacher Emma went for a ride with her family. They stopped to see her pet kitten and Jake's colt. Their father made lemonade which was good.

Emma hoped there couldn't be anything in the story which would give the parents the wrong impression about Amos and her. She glanced at Amos. When he smiled at her, the smile had Emma hoping Jake wrote an entirely different memory to share. With all the parents watching her, she couldn't stand two references to riding with Amos Coblentz and him smiling that way at her where the other parents could see. She lucked out. Jake wrote about watching Mark Bender with his tongue stuck to the pump during the winter.

Most of the stories were memories of the recent field trip. Daniel set the audience to laughing with his story about the day the raccoon came to school and hugged Emma's legs. Though Emma wished he'd picked a different subject, she was glad everyone enjoyed the story.

Emma saved Matthew for last. She feared he didn't have many good memories of school. Through the whole term, Matthew didn't give any indication she succeeded in getting through to him. She couldn't be sure he even wrote a story, and she felt as if she failed with the boy.

Matthew's face was serious as he read. "My favorite thing about school was Teacher Emma." Matthew smiled at the surprised look on her face. "She is a good teacher. I know I have tried her patience this year. She continued to be patient and kind to me, showing her concern that I was not learning good enough. I could tell she felt bad when she had to punish me for doing the wrong things.

One of the boys asked me why I did not quit school if I could not get along with Teacher Emma. I had not thought about quitting school so I gave that idea some thought. I have been in trouble more than once and did not like Emma correcting me. It came to me why I have stayed. No matter how hard I made it for Teacher Emma she tried to understand, and she liked me anyway."

Emma paused to digest what just happened, and Amos Coblentz started clapping and cheering for Emma. That brought on the same from all the other parents and children.

Feeling completely ferhoodled, Emma held up her hand for

silence. "I must tell you I have so enjoyed working with the pupils this year. It has been a learning experience for me as well as them. For the most part I found the children a joy to be with even Matthew." She sought him out as she said, " He has been a challenge from the very start, but I did not ever consider it an option to give up on him. Next year, Matthew Stoll, we will start out with a new beginning." She winked at him and continued, "Now the board of directors will come up to hand out the graduation gifts for eighth graders.

The directors shook hands with Noah, Mark Bender and Jennie Yoder. They handed the graduates plates with their names on them, the date and school name.

After that, it was time to eat lunch. Emma sat down and leaned against the school wall with her plate. Levi Yoder sat down next to her and cradled his heaped plate on his legs.

"Looks like you are gute and hungry," Emma said, smiling at him warmly. "How have you been, Levi?"

"Gute and always hungry is recht. How about you?" Levi asked as he stopped eating to give her an intense look.

Emma giggled. "Am I hungry or gute? The answer is both. It seems like it has been awhile since we talked."

"That it has," Levi agreed. His face was unreadable as he studied Emma. It made her uncomfortable not to know what he was thinking. He blurted out, "Reckon you heard I have been dating Katie Yost?"

Emma replied, "Katie is a nice person. We have been gute friends for years."

"I think she is nice, too," Levi said before he took a bite out of his ham sandwich. "It does not bother you we are dating?"

Emma paused, wanting to make sure she said the right words. "Nah, it does not bother me. If you are happy with Katie, that is a gute thing."

"Denki." Levi smiled weakly at her.

His weak attempt at a smile left Emma wondering if he was thinking about what might have been between him and her, but no matter. Emma knew Levi needed and wanted to move on. She was glad for him.

Trying to clear the air, Emma explained. "I would not have known what to do without you to help me when I needed it. You were there as a friend when we were growing up. We have been close like brother and sister. That is not enough for a union, but it is gute memories to keep us friends forever."

Levi patted her hand. "I agree. Friends forever."

"Levi Yoder, come play a game of softball with us," yelled Noah. "It is the students against the old fellows."

"Be recht there." He chuckled. "When did I become one of the old fellows?"

"Ask Noah to explain that. I certainly do not see an old fellow beside me," Emma said, laughing.

When the parents gathered around the diamond, Emma couldn't see the game so she moved to the end of the crowd.

Amos Coblentz eased up beside her. She gave him a weak smile. "You are not playing softball with the others?"

"Nah, I consider myself too old a fellow to be on the team. Besides, I wanted to talk to you while everyone else is busy. Wondered if you were ready to give up teaching now?" Amos spoke softly, trying to talk below the crowd's cheering.

"Nah, not yet." Emma noted disappointment on Amos's face. She added, "I like teaching."

"I see you do, and you are gute at it. Just thought I would check. As a director. Just in case." Amos stumbled over the excuses and managed to come up with another reason. " So I could look for another teacher if we needed one."

"You will not need a new teacher this year." Emma uttered shortly and turned to leave.

"You will not watch the game with me?" Amos asked.

"I am helping with clean up," Emma replied, walking away.

After helping prepare supper in silence, Emma finally spoke about what she'd been thinking. "Hallie, am I ever going to find the man I am looking for?"

"You will. I know you will, and you must always think you will until that day happens," Hal told the girl.

"I am watching all my special friends move on. My feelings

must be so dulled I will not ever know who I want to marry," Emma fretted as she set the table.

"You want to know what I think. You worry too much about the future. Just live in the moment. The future will happen and to your liking. I'm sure of it," Hal advised.

As if she hadn't heard a word Hal said, Emma went on, "Maybe it is that I am too dumb to make the recht choice?"

"Nah, the time will come when you'll know which man is recht. You'll look in that man's eyes and feel the world spin beneath your feet," Hal said.

Emma remembered that feeling when she was with Eli and now how unsure she was of him. "Is that how it was for you with my daed?"

Hal paused and smiled at the memory of meeting John Lapp. "Jah, pretty much it was."

After supper and devotions, John sat down in his rocker. "Where did Emma go this time?"

"She's in the porch swing, feeling sorry for herself. She needs your fatherly advice. Go talk to her, John."

He rubbed his fingers across his eyes. "I am not gute at giving advice when it comes to special friend problems for a girl. Not sure what I can say that will help her."

"You were a special friend at least twice. Give it a try. The words will come," Hal encouraged.

"Will she want to hear I think she is trying too hard to conform her life the way she wants it. Trying that hard just makes her feel worse and more confused. She needs to realize she has her planted spot already picked out for her. She needs to let God guide her to it when he is ready," John said.

Hal smiled. " You said that perfectly. Tell her that." When John stood up, Hal said, "When you are done talking to Emma, come back and comfort me."

John's eyes sparkled. "Glad to, but any special reason?"

"I know no matter what Emma decides to do I'm going to lose her. Whether she remains a teacher or gets married, she won't be around anymore," Hal said. "I miss her being here to turn to when I need help."

"Jah. I know how you feel. Emma is growing up. From the time she was a baby until now has passed by swiftly. I am facing soon I will lose my daughter to some man. Perhaps, we can comfort each other," John said, seriously.

❦

Emma looked up as the screen door hinges squeaked and stopped the swing's motion. Her father sit down by her. He stretched his legs out and stared at the barn. "Got yourself a whole milk pail full of worries?"

"That I have," Emma said fervently. "I always thought it would be such a simple thing to pick a husband. One man would court me. I would say jah, and we would marry. I never imagined I would have so many men to choose from. What do I do now, Daed, with so many choices? How do I pick one? How do I do that without hurting all the other men's feelings?"

John scratched the side of his beard. "I must admit I have been confused by all your special friends taking turns to pick you up. It is so much different from the way I remember how dating works. I have given that some thought. Seems to me you are luckier than most girls."

Emma looked at him like he'd grown horns. "Lucky! How can you call this mess I am in lucky?"

"You have several men to pick from. Most girls do not have a choice. When you are ready to decide, you will pick the right man. I know you will, because you are a level headed person with a gute heart. As for the rest, they will find another special friend to take your place and move on. That is how it works."

"In the meantime, what do I do if they all grow tired of waiting for me to decide? I could lose all of them and not ever get married," Emma worried.

"I have faith in you making the right decision." John smiled as he stood up and put his hands in his pants pockets. "In Matthew 6:3 the scripture says do not let your left hand know what your right hand is doing."

Emma groaned. "Denki, but I am not sure I like that advice."

"I just meant keep all those men guessing until you make your pick so they stick around. The men know you are worth waiting for." John started to go back inside then he added, "The right love grows slowly and surefooted like the gait of a gute horse. That love is made of equal parts of comfort and respect. You want that kind of love so you are right to be sure before you make a choice."

"Daed, is that how you feel about Hallie?" Emma asked.

"Jah, I can tell you that for sure and certain," John said.

"Denki, Daed. I feel better now," Emma told him.

That night instead of kneeling at bedside for her evening prayer Emma knelt at the window so she could look at the sky. She split the curtains and took in the stars. A gentle, warm breeze fluffed her loose hair as she listened to the peepers sing. The song was always consistently creee-eee-eek.

When she prayed, she found herself praying that some day soon things would work out for her. She did enjoy being a teacher. More than she thought she would, but she'd always imagined herself in her own home, raising a family. What did God have in store for her? What if getting married was not God's will? She prayed "Thy will be done. I know I must leave my future in your hands."

She slipped under the covers, and her thoughts tumbled as she dozed off. Her school, the classroom and the children working at their desks were vivid in her dreams. There were smiles on the pupils faces, and she was happy teaching.

The next day, John called from the living room. "Hal and Emma, where are you? We have company."

"We're in the kitchen," Hal replied. She went to the door, drying her hands on her apron. "Wilcom, Amos Coblentz. How nice to see you."

"You too, Nurse Hal," he greeted, placing his hat on a peg.

Hal glanced back at Emma, still standing by the table. The girl took a second to smooth her prayer cap before she appeared in the doorway.

Amos's eyes glinted. "And you too, Emma."

Emma nodded, her face suddenly pale.

Hal looked from one to the other and wondered what was wrong this time.

"Amos wants to have a talk with me," John stated. "Can you bring us something to drink?"

"Of course, we can," Hal said.

Emma placed the glasses on the counter. In her haste, the glasses clanked together. One turned over and clattered against the counter. The glass rolled toward the edge, but Emma caught it. "How gute that it did not break," Emma rasped.

As Hal filled the glasses with ice tea, she whispered, "What's the matter? And don't say nothing. Something is wrong."

"I am afraid Amos is going to ask Daed if he can marry me," Emma hissed.

"Ach, nah!" Emma nodded. "Really? Today?" Hal hissed.

Emma looked beside herself. "Jah."

"What are you going to do?" Hal asked

"I do not know. At this moment, I do not want to say jah to Amos anymore than I do the other men," Emma declared.

"Calm down and wait. You don't know what Amos is here for. Not really. Maybe this visit is school board business," Hal said. "Here take the tea."

"You take the glasses," Emma urged, nervously.

"Nah, you do it. You have to keep facing Amos," Hal ordered, putting the glasses in Emma's hands. She turned the girl around and pushed her toward the doorway.

John and Amos were on the couch. Emma handed one glass to her father. As she leaned toward Amos with the other, he winked at her. The glass slid out of her limp hand, tumbled down, bounced off Amos's knee and hit the floor. A giant spout of tea and ice shot upward and splashed on all of them.

Emma didn't know which man looked more surprised, John or Amos. She apologized profusely for being so clumsy as she backed toward the kitchen. "I will get towels to soak up the mess on you and ----. I need the mop. Jah, the mop. Emma turned in the doorway and bumped into Hal. "Hallie, could you get Amos another glass of tea?" Emma pleaded.

179

After clean up, Emma took the mop and pail back out to the mudroom. Hal followed her. "Emma, what happened?"

Emma whispered, "Amos is not here on school business. If it was a school board meeting, Deacon Yutzy should be here. Shouldn't he?"

"You're probably right," Hal admitted. "But what sent you into a tizzy."

"When I started to hand Amos his tea, he winked at me," Emma groaned.

"I see," Hal said, hiding her twitching lips behind her hand.

"Do not laugh at me. I am feeling like a cornered rat, and that tom cat out there is fixing to gobble me up," Emma hissed.

"You might be wrong. I don't think Amos will be that bold. Doesn't he have to get a go between to talk to your father if he is thinking about marriage?" Hal reasoned.

Emma's eyes wavered from the living room to Hal. "Jah, he should."

"Doesn't Amos have to have your permission first, before he discusses marriage?" Hal asked.

"He should," Emma agreed. "But I am still worried."

"All recht. Only one way to find out what's going on. Listen in," Hal whispered as she slipped over by the door and leaned against the wall.

"We should not do this," Emma warned, getting behind her.

"You want to know, don't you?" Hal asked, bending her ear toward the doorway.

Emma nodded, leaning her ear toward the wall.

Amos said, "I have come across other teacher prospects for the coming year. I wanted to run the choices by you."

Puzzled, John asked, "We need choices for teacher? Emma has not said she is quitting. Was she not gute enough?"

"It is not that. Emma was a fine teacher," Amos declared.

"Gute! Other parents have told me they liked how she did her job," John defended.

Amos cleared his throat. "Emma did a very gute job, but I thought she might stop teaching."

"Really," John said. "She hasn't told me that. If she does I

180

will let you and Deacon Yutzy know right away."

In the kitchen, Hal whispered, "Amos is certainly eager to put you out of a job."

Emma frowned, wadding the sides of her apron up in her hands. "Jah, if I lose the teaching position he thinks I will marry him. I told him I wanted to teach one more year when he asked me at the school picnic. He is trying to fix it so I will lose my job."

"Your father won't let that happen. Amos will have to back off and wait until you're ready," Hal said softly in Emma's ear.

≈

The next morning, Hal shook out the last dampened pillow case in the laundry basket and slid it over the end of the ironing board. She placed her cooled sad iron on the cookstove and attached the handle to the other bottom. All the while she was keeping track of how Emma kneaded the bread dough with resounding thunks.

As soon as Hal finished ironing, she set the iron bottoms on a trivet on the shelf behind the stove and carried the folded up ironing board out to the mud room.

Emma still pounded the dough.

Hal said, "It seems like such a long time since you've hummed. Now you're working that dough over with a fury. Do you have a case of heavy duty frustration or ----?"

Emma wheeled around as she swiped at her forehead to move a curl out of her eyes, spreading flour from her hands over her face, blouse and apron. "Go ahead. Finish what you were saying."

"Just that you are extra tense this morning. I'd say you haven't been sleeping well lately so you're overly tired. Want me to put the dough in the pans for you while you rest."

Emma looked guiltily at the dough. "I can put the dough in the pans."

"Want me to grease the pans for you?"

"I did that first so I would have lard on my hands while I kneaded. You can get me a dish towel to lay over the pans if you want." Emma divided the dough between the loaf pans and set them on top the warming oven. Hal handed her the towel.

"Now, young lady, let's sit down and talk. You're keeping too many thoughts pent up. That's not gute," Hal insisted.

Emma plopped into the chair while Hal poured their coffee. The girl covered her face with her hands. "Hallie, I am so ferhoodled. I feel as if every single man in this community has sized me up for marriage. Being single ain't easy for a woman."

Hal fought back a smile as she gripped her cup. "That could be considered a compliment. After all, you are gute wife material. You've taken gute care of this home and mothered your two brothers so you have a lot of the experience that men look for in a wife. I'd say you are a lucky girl to be so popular."

"You sound like Daed. I do not feel one bit lucky," Emma complained.

"You are lucky, because you have several gute choices to pick a husband from," Hal pointed out.

Emma gave that some thought. "It is true I have choices. That is exactly what Daed said, but I am just seventeen. I like being a teacher too well to give it up now. I will want to get married some day, but I want to teach school at least one more year. I worry by the time this next year is up all the men interested in me will have found someone else. How am I ever going to choose a husband when I have so many choices, and I like them all? I can not trust my feelings."

"It isn't fair to those men to wait for you for a year to make a choice. You should pick one and let the rest look elsewhere if there is one of them you want to marry," Hal advised.

"Daed said I should keep them all guessing," Emma shared with a weak smile.

"Did he now?" Hal snorted. "That's not what he was supposed to say to you. That's a man for you."

"I have been honest with some of my special friends. I wish I could decide on one before it is too late," Emma said. "I fear they will move on, and I will end up a maidel."

"Have you ever thought about doing a pro and con list on each man?" Hal asked.

Emma wrinkled her nose. "Nah, how does that work?"

Hal wanted to get the one John and she considered the worse pick for a son-in-law out of the way first. "Maybe this will help. For instance, what do you like about Eli Yutzy?"

Emma considered. "I think my attraction to Eli is he is different from all the rest now that he is in rumspringa. Same reason the other girls in the youth group are drawn to him. My best friend, Katie Yost, just barely spoke to me for awhile. She had her eyes on Eli when he picked me to date."

"Don't worry about Katie. A nice girl like her will find another boy. There are plenty around."

"I fear she already did. Levi Yoder," Emma shared.

"Really?" Hal gasped then tried to keep them on track. "Back to Eli. What else do you like about him?"

"Eli is experimenting with the way he dresses and acts. He talks about more freedoms if he becomes English. He would move to a city, get a job and buy a car."

Hal frowned. "Would you like that kind of life?"

Emma said slowly, "I do not think so. I like living on a farm. Whether I like it or not, I would have to go where my husband does, and I used to think that was with Eli."

Hal nodded. "All recht, now what are the cons about Eli?"

"I do not like his friends. They are in rumspringa, too. They drink beer and smoke. They are too reckless."

Hal looked stern. "Does Eli drink beer when you date him?"

"Jah. I do not like his personality changes when he drinks. He angers easily when he does not understand why I say I do not like what he does. He is always trying to get me to join in rumspringa, but most of his actions are against how we have been taught to live," Emma said.

Hal set her cup down. "Yet you are still dating him."

Emma shrugged. "I accepted this last date so I can tell him I do not want to see him again."

"All recht. How about Bobby Keim?"

"He is settled on a farm with a home already. I like his family very much. He is gentle and kind. He will make a gute husband and a gute father. I know that from the way he treats Adam," Emma said in a thoughtful tone.

"Gute, now the cons," Hal encouraged.

"Bobby is looking for a woman just like Annie. I told him I am not like Annie. He does not want to hear that. If we were to marry, I know a day will come when he realizes I am Emma. He might not be happy he married me then. He does not act like he can move on. I do not want to wait for Bobby to come to grips with his loss to see if he really wants to marry me."

Hal asked, "How about Amos?"

"He is ten years older. At first thinking about that made me nervous, but I have become comfortable with him. He is handsome with a pleasant personality."

When Hal's eyebrow went up, Emma defended, "I know I should not think about the man's looks, but I can not help it. Amos took me by his farm, which he owns, and pointed out his nice home. I like his children. I can tell they like me. We would make a gute family, and I would not have to worry about starting out as a young newlywed." Emma paused to think, wanting to phrase her cons right. "Yet, Amos seems to be in too big a hurry to find a wife. His insistence worries me. So at the school picnic when he asked about my future I told him I was going to teach school again."

"And?" Hal asked.

"He looked disappointed, but does he really love me? Or, is he just looking for a mother for his children and any woman in his bed would do?"

"My goodness! You have certainly given Amos thoughtful consideration. You've figured out being financially stable when you first get married isn't everything when it comes to picking a husband. That is being sensible."

"After Amos's visit, it does not look like he is ready to give up on me yet, but the time will come when he meets a woman ready to settle down with him. He will forget me," Emma said.

"Now Levi," Hal said.

"He is a younger version of Amos. He has a ways to go before he is farming on his own, but he is honest and has a gute work ethic. He is courteous and respectful. A quiet, handsome man that will take gute care of his family." Emma wrinkled her nose up and said softly, "But Levi is predictable."

"That doesn't sound like a bad thing," Hal said, trying to defend John and her pick. "He certainly isn't like Eli, and that's a gute thing. What's wrong with being predictable?"

"Sometimes, a surprise might be nice. Ach! My problem is until lately, I've thought of Levi as a brother." Emma sighed a heavy gust. "With Levi everything has to be so serious and intense. He does not have a very gute sense of humor. His idea of a compliment was to tell me he thinks I smell like homemade bread baking."

Hal tried to look serious. "What's wrong with that?"

Emma shrugged. "Not much of a compliment. I now know the difference after the one Amos gave me."

"What did Amos say?" Hal asked eagerly.

Emma put her hands over her hot, tingling cheeks. "You are too eager. I will not say, but just know, I liked it better than being compared to fresh bread. Levi told me at the school picnic he is dating Katie. I told him that was gute."

Hal sat back in her chair. "Levi is a very gute choice. Are you sure you're all right with him moving on?"

"I like Levi an awful lot. He would make a gute husband. It was not fair for me to make him wonder while I dated other men so I suggested he ask Katie out so he would stop paying so much attention to me."

"Not too smart to help your competition get a date with one of your special friends," Hal quipped.

"Anymore bits of gute advice for me," Emma quipped dryly.

"It seems to me if you're having this much trouble picking from all these men, you aren't very taken by any of them. Particularly the ones you've tried to get to move on.

You're trying too hard. Be patient. When you find the right man to wed, it will just happen. It may not be one of the special friends you've had so far," Hal said, patting Emma's hand.

"Denki, but why does that not make me feel better?" Emma grumped. "With advise like that I might end up a maidel for the rest of my life for sure and certain."

Chapter 20

After supper, Emma was ready to leave for her ride with Eli. John noticed she didn't look all that excited about this date. When Emma was going out the door, he felt the need to caution her, "Be careful tonight, daughter."

"I will be fine, Daed," she replied with a slight smile.

"Gute evening," Eli greeted from the bottom porch step.

"Gute evening. Where are we going on this ride?" Emma asked as she scrambled into the buggy.

"Bender Creek Road. We have been invited to a hoedown in the timber."

"What is a hoedown?"

"It is a word used to talk about a party without saying party in case parents are listening," Eli said frankly.

Before they rounded a curve in the dirt road, Emma heard loud music and laughter. Once they rounded the bend, she couldn't believe the number of old cars, pickups and buggies lined up along the road.

"I am not sure I will like this party," Emma said hesitantly.

"If you do not, I will take you home right away. Come with me and see. Many from the youth singing group are here."

Emma put her hands over her cheeks. "Ach, nah!"

"Jah, see for yourself," he assured her.

They walked along a narrow path beaten down by many feet in the underbrush until they reached a clearing lit by a bonfire. Boom box speakers were hook to a car battery. Rock music blasted the clearing.

Couples sat or laid on the leafy ground. Some were nodding their heads and swaying to the music. Everyone was dressed in

186

T shirts and jeans. Many of the boys had crew cuts or shaggy hair. The English girls had spiked, unnatural shades of dyed hair. Gold rings in their nostrils and lips twinkled in the reflection of the bonfire. They had cut the end off their T shirts so their navels and small tattoos were exposed. Their hair was hanging down their backs or in pony tails.

Priscilla Tefertiller reached for a cigarette from the boy next to her and took a puff. She eyed Emma, wondering how she would react. Emma was too shocked by all she saw pay much attention to Priscilla.

Diana Kingman took a drink from Jason Fisher's beer can. He elbowed her in the side as he snatched the can back. "You get your own beer. You know where they are."

One boy turned his back to his date and spiked her pop with vodka. He handed her the can and mixed another for himself.

Emma nodded toward a group of boys she didn't know. "Who are they?"

"English friends."

One of the outsiders whispered in a Plain girl's ear. She smiled bashfully at him as he offered his hand to help her up. She followed behind him, and they disappeared into the dark underbrush.

Eli and Emma walked by one boy limply propped against a tree, passed out. The girl beside him groaned as she held her stomach. She rose to her knees, grabbed the tree to steady herself so she could get on her feet and staggered for the underbrush. Emma was sure before the night was over everyone would be passed out or sick.

She felt queasy enough to be sick about what she was seeing without consuming liquor. She froze. Her feet felt so heavy she couldn't take another step forward into this awful party.

"Come on, Emma. I will get us something to drink," Eli said, tugging on her hand.

"Nah, not me. I am not staying. It is not recht to be here. Just because others from the youth group are here does not make it recht for me. I can not do this," Emma insisted vehemently.

"Relax, Emma. Rules are made to be broken. Just give me a

chance to show you a gute time," Eli implored.

"You take me home, or I will walk," she ordered softly so the others couldn't hear.

Eli stared at her. "All recht. I told you I would if you wanted to leave." He took her elbow and headed back on the path.

The ride home was silent, but at least, Eli didn't race his horse in anger. When he pulled into the yard, Emma said, "I am sorry if I ruined your night. I just can not take part in that sort of rumspringa. It is not in me when I know it is wrong for me to do such things."

Eli smiled at her and patted her hand. "It is all recht. You must do what is recht for you. Actually, I admire you for sticking by your beliefs. Anymore, I am not sure I believe as you do. As for tonight, you did not ruin the party for me. I am going back. A party like that lasts all night."

Emma jumped from the buggy and turned to say, "I am sure it does. Do not expect me to go with you again. I will not do it. Just be careful, will you?"

"Always am," Eli said and drove away.

When Emma opened the front door, John and Hal looked up at her expectantly.

"Short night," John stated with a raised eyebrow.

"Jah, we just took a short ride," Emma said tersely and headed for the stairs. "Think I will call it a night early for a change. See you in the morning."

John looked at Hal in concern. "Eli has done something to upset my daughter again."

Hal shrugged. She didn't know what to think about Emma's short evening.

John mumbled for Hal's ears only, "Eli Yutzy is a steeforudar zu'm goul en shlop-awrich gadur und nodeelich foul. I do not know what my daughter sees in him."

Hal giggled. "John, be careful. Emma evidently doesn't see Eli like you do. A sloppy eared and naturally lazy creature might not fit her description of him."

The next afternoon, Bishop Elton Bontrager turned into the Lapp driveway. John walked to the buggy. "Wilcom, Elton. Get down. We can find you a glass of tea."

With a newspaper under his arm, Elton nodded somberly. He put his felt hat on a peg. Then the pudgy, bald headed leader of their faith followed John to the kitchen.

Hal poured the tea and put a glass in front of each man. Emma placed a plate of fresh oatmeal cookies between them.

John was uneasy about the solemn look on the bishop's redder that usual face. "What do we owe to this visit, Elton?"

"I have bad news. A Plain boy was killed in the night in a buggy race accident on Bender Creek Road," he said sadly.

Emma let a coffee cup slip from her hand and clatter on the counter. Her eyes were as large as saucers, and her skin paled.

Watching Emma closely, John asked, "Who?"

Hal moved beside Emma as the girl held her breath, waiting for the answer. *Eli probably,* went through Hal's mind. *Emma has looked troubled ever since she came home last night. No wonder Emma didn't want to be involved.*

"Jason Fisher," Elton stated.

Emma felt relieved that Eli wasn't dead, but she gripped her trembling hands together under her apron. She dreaded hearing the awful details, knowing Eli was involved.

"Sorry to hear that. What happened?" John asked.

"A group of the teens in rumspringa had a beer party on the creek road in the timber. Some of the boys decided to have a buggy race. Jason Fisher's buggy did not make the turn onto the blacktop. It rolled down that deep ditch at the intersection. Jason was thrown out. His neck was broken. Diana Kingman was in the buggy with him. The buggy landed on her. All the racers took off except one. Coony Jonah Helmuth's son, Johnny, stopped to help, and by the way, he has a cell phone now. He called 911 and cut the horse loose.

Two deputy sheriff cars arrived with the ambulance. They found Johnny trying to lift the buggy off the girl by himself. He was arrested for drunk driving and taken to jail. They rescued the Kingman girl and sent her to the hospital. I checked, and her parents told me she is in fair condition.

That wasn't all. This morning when Deacon Yutzy was in Wickenburg, he heard talk about the party at the feed mill so he bought a newspaper. He brought the news to me about the Fisher boy, and told me his son was involved in this mess so I would not find out in another way. I told him Eli would have to admit to his sins and ask for forgiveness at the next member meeting. This was a serious matter."

Hal glanced at Emma. The girl was biting her lower lip as she braced herself against the counter.

Elton went on, "The paper has all the terrible story. I am beside myself this has happened to the young people in our community. I should have listened closer to the dire warnings from Stella Strutt. God talks to them in one ear. Satan in the other. Read for yourself, John."

Emma noticed Hal scrutinizing her. She turned her back and stared out the window, waiting for her father to read the article.

Headline - Amish Teen Beer Party Busted By Sheriff Department by Reporter Phil King.

Just because they drive buggies instead of cars doesn't mean Amish kids can't get into trouble. Four were arrested and charged with illegal possession of alcohol last night after their buggy crashed directly into a deputy sheriff car. At the time, the deputy was responding to a report from another deputy on the scene of a buggy accident with a girl trapped at the edge of the lower Bender Creek Road intersection.

Amish teenagers had been drinking in their buggies on the country road and decided to have a race. Empty and full beer cans were found scattered all around the scene. All the buggies fled from the scene of the accident except one. The driver stopped to assist at the accident and was arrested.

As for the buggy versus sheriff car, according to the deputy's account, it sounds like quite the crash. One of the fleeing buggies changed lanes as the law officer approached, and smacked into the cruiser then flipped on its side. One of the buggy occupants experienced minor injuries. The deputy called for back up while he gave aide to the injured teenagers in the buggy. While he did that, several other buggies fled the scene.

As soon as an ambulance picked up the injured boy, the deputy and several other cruisers including Wickenburg's finest drove around searching for the escaped buggies. One of the police cars soon came upon a buggy in the middle of a country road, traveling slow. The siren was sounded. The buggy picked up speed. Joe Gingerich, 16, was arrested after leading police on a one-mile chase—a very slow chase, we're guessing.

The sheriff cruiser came upon another Amish teen, name not disclosed, piloting a horse and buggy when he allegedly ran a stop sign and then refused to pull over. The cruiser kept up the chase until the boy eventually lost control, overturned the buggy, and took off on foot. The deputy gave chase and tackled the boy, knocking him to the ground. As if that boy isn't already in enough trouble, police say they've also charged him with underage possession of alcohol. He's being held in jail.

According to the sheriff in an interview with this reporter, the arrests aren't over with yet. This is an on going investigation to cut down on underage drinking. As names come to light, other teens will be picked up.

That afternoon, Emma was coming downstairs when she caught Priscilla Tefertiller coming out of the kitchen.

"I just left a plate of cookies on the table for Nurse Hal," Priscilla said sheepishly, avoiding Emma's gaze.

"That is gute of you."

Priscilla shrugged with a quick glance in Emma's direction. Just enough that Emma could see her red rimmed eyes. "It was part of my Secret Pal duty."

Emma darted a look toward the kitchen and took Priscilla by the arm. "Come upstairs with me."

After they sat down on the bed, she asked, "How are you?"

"I am all right."

"You hear about the awful things that happened because of that party last night?" Emma asked.

"Jah, I heard." Tears ran down Priscilla's face. "Emma, I

wish I had not been at that beer party. I would not have been, but Eli Yutzy took me. I was so glad he wanted to date me. I would have gone anywhere with him."

Emma blustered, "You were Eli's date?"

Priscilla's face grew red. "What is so surprising about that? You do not think you are the only one he dates, do you?"

"I am very sure now that I am not the only one he dates," Emma declared. "So what went wrong?"

"Plenty. Eli disappeared from the party. I ended up with another boy. Later, I thought I saw you with Eli, but I was not sure," Priscilla said. "Things were a little foggy by then."

"Eli brought me, but he did not tell me where we were going. That is not the kind of party I wanted to be at so I had him bring me home," Emma said bluntly.

"Eli came over after the boy with me passed out. I asked him to take me home before the party broke up. I was not feeling too gute," Priscilla admitted. "Reckon it was something in my pop."

"Priscilla! The boys poured vodka in the pop!"

"Nah, is that what happened?"

Emma nodded. "Jah. Wonder how Diana Kingman is?"

"Stiff and sore, but she will be home soon. This is only the start of her problems. She is having a baby," Priscilla shared.

"Ach, nah! You are right. If the repetition she had dating Jason wasn't bad enough now she is second hand goods. I feel sorry for her," Emma said.

"Why should we feel bad for Diana? She brought this on herself," Priscilla snipped.

"How easy for you to say that now. Did you even once think last night when you mixed in with that crowd that you might wind up just like Diana, pregnant or worse yet dead like Jason?"

"Nah, I did not think. I wanted a date with Eli so bad," Priscilla groaned.

"You would be wise not to get near Eli Yutzy again. You did not know it, but you were just one of two girls he took to that party last night," Emma said.

"What?"

"Du est recht. You saw recht. I was there, and I was Eli's other date," Emma said. "Only I didn't stay."

"Out of the two of us, that makes you the smart one." Priscilla rubbed her aching head. "If this is what rumspringa is about, I do not want any more of it."

"I do not think our parents mean for us to experiment with all the English bad habits when they permit us to go through rumspringa. I keep remembering Bishop Bontrager's sermon when he said we should keep our virtue. God preserved us pure and whole, and we should not cast that aside for the lures of lust and other sins," Emma reminded Priscilla wisely.

"I remember he said once our reputations were lost we would only regain them at a dreadful cost." Priscilla said, "Too bad Diana did not heed that sermon."

Chapter 21

That night a flashlight's circling beams on the bedroom wall wasn't much of a surprise to Emma. In fact, she was awake and half expecting Eli to show up. Her dad and Hallie hadn't asked her what she knew about the party. She was glad they didn't, but she knew they would expect her to tell them sometime. Right now she had to be very quiet. She'd be in trouble if her dad knew she was going out to meet Eli. She tiptoed down the stairs and slipped out the door. A gentle rain splattered the roof as she met Eli coming around to the front.

"Thought maybe you were going to ignore the light." Eli took her arm. "We should get out of the rain."

"I should ignore you. That was some night last night. I am glad I was smart enough to come home before I got caught in that awful mess," Emma rebuked, going up the porch steps.

"I am glad you were home safe, too. I must admit the evening was not as much fun after you left," he said honestly.

Emma's voice was tight. "That is too bad. Priscilla, your other date, wasn't much more cooperative than I was, ain't so?"

"I told you Priscilla was at the party," Eli said offhandedly.

"Jah, but you did not tell me she was your other date," Emma accused.

Emma heard the surprise in Eli's voice. "What makes you think she was my date?"

"She told me so this afternoon. Priscilla has decided she wants no more evenings like last night. She will not accept another date from you for fear she will get into trouble," Emma informed him.

"I was not going to ask her again. That is why I am here. I

wanted to tell you I am leaving tonight," Eli's voice wavered.

"For gute?" Emma asked in a hushed voice.

"Jah. It will not take long for the boys, the cops arrested, to start naming others at the party. In fact, the cops are counting on that," Eli told her.

"Turn yourself in," Emma insisted.

"I fled the scene. The law will be hard on me. Ach, nah! I have made up my mind to turn English. Why I came is to ask you if you will come with me?" Eli asked hopefully.

Emma's voice softened. "What makes you think I would want do that?"

"I need you to help me do the right things in the English world. You are the only one that can make me listen. I want to take you with me," Eli said sincerely.

"Nah, Eli. A piece of me wants to go with you, but my life is here. I have a job teaching school. This is what I want. I could never be English. I would never be gute at it. You see, I believe we have to live by the Ordnung. Otherwise, everything we were raised to believe will mean nothing," Emma said with a hitch in her voice.

"All recht. This is gute bye." Eli studied her face for a reaction.

Emma closed her eyes and felt tears rolled down her cheeks as she exhaled wearily. "Will I ever see you again?"

He shook his head no. "It would not be a gute thing to come back here with the law looking for me. Besides, Daed said the bishop wants me before the next member meeting to confess my sins. My punishment might be shunning for a while or forever. Why should I stick around to find out?"

"I see." Emma took a deep breath. "Take care of yourself and try to stay out of trouble from now on."

"I'll try. Emma?" Eli stepped closer.

"Jah, what?"

"I never did get that kiss you owed me. This is my last chance." As Emma started to protest, Eli leaned over and kissed her on the cheek. He stared longingly at her for a moment as if vacillating between staying with her and leaving.

With a slight shake of his head as if to clear his mind, Eli made his decision. He walked away, fading into the gloomy darkness just like he had in all her dreams.

Emma walked down the first step and paused to say good bye in her mind to those dreams. The rain drops pattered on the roof and dripped on her enough to bring her to her senses. Her nightgown was too damp to wear back to bed. She hurried to her room, changed and slipped under the covers.

୬

The next day, Hal looked over Emma's shoulder as the girl spread peanut butter and grape jelly on bread. "Packing a picnic lunch I see."

"Jah, Adam and I are going fishing."

Hal smiled. "You always sound so excited when you talk about Adam."

"Not like it was with Eli you are thinking. Fishing with Adam is fun and relaxing. After all, Hallie, he does not want anything but friendship from me. I reckon that is what makes him a gute listener about all my special friends."

Hal gasped. "You talk to Adam about your boyfriends?"

"Jah, I told you he is a gute listener," Emma said as she wrapped the sandwiches in wax paper.

Hal took Emma by the shoulders and turned her around. "Did you ever stop to think he has to be a gute listener? He can't talk back."

"We communicate just fine. Adam says plenty with a lift of his eyebrow or a facial expression, and he always has a notepad and pencil," Emma defended.

"Taking Adam into your confidence about all your special friends might be awkward for him," suggested Hal.

"I have not noticed that Adam minds. Maybe you are recht though. I should not put Adam in the position of worrying about my problems," agreed Emma. The sound of crunching gravel sent her rushing to the window. "Adam is here."

୬

Emma and Adam peered over the bank, before they sat

196

down. The creek was running strong after the rain. Water was tumbling over rocks and forking around sticks. Emma set the worm can between them. "May not be a gute day to fish with the creek up."

Adam nodded that he agreed, and that was the last words between them for awhile. They concentrated on fishing.

Adam's forehead wrinkled up worriedly as he watched Emma. She stared at the rushing water as if she didn't see what was in front of her. He pulled out his notepad and pencil to scrawl, "Which one has upset you now?" He tapped Emma on the arm and held the pad up.

Emma looked thoughtful and opened her mouth to tell him about her night with Eli. She stopped when she recalled Hal's admonishments about confiding in Adam. Besides, what she knew about Eli just might get him in trouble with the law if it got around. "There is nothing to talk about," she replied and concentrated on her bobber.

Adam tapped her arm with the message, "That is not so."

"Ach! Adam, I should not burden you with my problems anymore. What kind of a friend have I been to always center our time together on what is wrong in my life?" She asked.

Adam wrote as his face grew pensive, "You tell me the things that worry you, because I want to know."

Emma read the note and looked in his eyes. "Hallie says I have not been considerate of your feelings. I should not tell you all my private worries."

"I want to know why you are sad." Adam pointed to what he'd written then added, "I ask so you will tell me."

Emma nodded. "Denki, for worrying about me. Adam, I do need to talk to someone. You are always the one that makes me feel better. Nothing has gone to suit me lately, and I do not know why. I upset Levi Yoder, because I turned down his dates so I suggested he ask Katie Yost to go with him. He did."

Adam wrote, "Katie is a nice person."

"That is true, and now Levi has found that out. I do not have to worry about hurting his feelings anymore. Lately, I have distanced myself from Amos Coblentz so he has not been around. After the other night, I am wondering why I ever had an interest in Eli Yutzy."

Emma went on to tell Adam about the night with Eli at the party. She ignored her bobber, floating in zigzag motion downstream. Adam poked her on the arm. The look on his face was irritation. "Do not look at me like that. I knew the minute we stepped into the clearing I was not going to enjoy the evening. I had Eli take me home recht away."

Adam wrote, "Gute. What I heard about that night was not gute."

"The beer party was not what I wanted to be involved in," Emma said as she reeled in her line. The hook was empty. She reached for the worm can without looking. Her hand touched Adam's work roughened hand resting on the can. He wrapped his fingers around her hand and studied her ruefully.

"What? Are we short of worms, and you want to make sure you get your share?" Emma teased.

Adam looked pained as he shrugged and picked out a worm to bait his hook before he held the can toward her. Emma thought there must be more he wanted to say, but with a very troubled expression, he concentrated on the water.

Suddenly, Adam leaned back and reeled in a thrashing sunfish. Its scales caught the sunlight as it flew toward him. Its tail thumped the ground, and it did a belly flop. Adam grabbed it and opened its mouth with his thumb to take out the hook.

Emma was surprised when Adam threw the fish back. He never threw away fish that size. "Why did you throw that fish back?"

Adam shrugged as he frowned at her.

"I do not like that look. Sometimes like now, you say too much without saying anything." Emma felt tension crackle between them as palpable as lightning in last night's storm, and she couldn't figure out why.

Adam's left eyebrow arched in anger.

Emma recalled Hal's words again about burdening Adam with her problems. "All recht, since I am always talking about me, you should have a turn. You are not yourself today so tell me why."

Adam wrote furiously, "I am surprised you noticed how I might feel with so much bothering you. It is a first for you."

"Of course, I noticed. Tell me what is wrong?"

Adam laid his pole on the bank. He turned to Emma and shook his head no slowly.

"If nothing is wrong, then talk to me. What do you want most out of life, Adam Keim?" Emma asked, deciding it was time to let him talk about his feelings.

Adam hesitated, wrote quickly and handed Emma the pad.

One word in large print burst from the page at her. "I used to have a dream but not anymore. What I wanted was YOU."

Emma was surprised, but she wished she hadn't shown it when she saw the hurt look on Adam's face as he reeled in his line and stood up. He motioned for her to come and jabbed his finger at the buggy before he stalked down the path.

Emma scrambled to pick up her gear and catch up. She grabbed his arm. "Wait! Do not turn your back on me. We need to talk."

Adam yanked away and kept walking. The tall grass swished angrily under his fast moving feet.

Emma spooked up a large monarch on a dry milkweed. The butterfly fluttered away as she hurried to keep up with Adam. Remembering that joyful moment with Adam months ago when they watched the butterflies, she wished she could turn back the clock. The reality hit her she'd enjoyed that moment, because she shared it with Adam. Now thoughts about many other moments with Adam raced through her mind. Moments she so carelessly took for granted at the time. "Please, Adam, you not being able to speak does not make a difference between us. You must know that. You can tell me anything. I want to know what you are thinking."

Adam vaulted into the buggy, bringing her end up higher as she struggled to get in. He wrote, "If you think my not being able to speak is what is wrong, you do not understand at all."

He jammed his notepad and pencil in his pocket, flicked the lines and headed to the Lapp farm. Before they arrived, Emma tried several times to get Adam to respond, but he shrugged off her hand and remained withdrawn.

Once he halted the buggy, he wrote, "You have never seen me. NEVER. Not who I really am."

"I do see you," declared Emma, with a sinking feeling that somehow she'd hurt Adam terribly without meaning to do it.

"Nah, I am just a fence post that listens to your problems. I hear from you about how reckless you are with yourself when you are with Eli, and how careless you are with feelings of others that care very much about you. You are not the Emma I knew. Not the one I want to know now."

Hal's words came back to create stinging tears in Emma's eyes. Adam had been a captive listener, because she didn't notice how he felt about her. "Adam, I am so sorry. I did not understand how you felt. We need to talk about this."

Adam wrote, "That is what I wanted once but not now. With so many special friends coming to your window, you do not need me. Maybe you will think you do after they all go away now that you have hurt them. Right now you do not need me."

"You are wrong. I just need time to think about this. You mean a great deal to me. Please give me some time," Emma pleaded in a cracked voice.

Adam wrote and held the pad toward her as he jiggled the leather lines impatiently in his other hand. "Get down."

Emma climbed out of the buggy and rushed to the house. From behind the door, she heard the quick step of hoof beats as Adam raced down the road.

☙

At supper, Hal noticed Emma pushed the food around on her plate. Emma's efforts at kitchen clean up wasn't going any better. The girl stared out the window in a trance while she polished a saucer.

"Emma, that saucer is dry enough," Hal said as she washed a tablespoon. "Deacon Yutzy told your dad today Eli has left the Amish community. Did you know?"

"Jah, Eli stopped by after you were asleep to say gute bye," Emma answered dully, laying the saucer on top the stack.

"Deacon Yutzy said Eli was in a lot of trouble with the law. They are looking for him," Hal said matter of factly. "Did Eli tell you where he was going?"

"Nah, and I did not ask. I want to give Eli time to get away."

"I see. Do you think he will come back?"

"Nah, he did not want to come back. He will always be in trouble with the law," Emma replied. "Besides, he is sure he would no longer have a place in the community once he went in front of the member meeting to confess."

Hal glanced at Emma out of the corner of her eyes. "I'm surprised he didn't ask you to go with him."

"He did. I do not want him now with all his problems. I told him that," Emma said honestly.

Hal tossed two forks into the rinse pan that clattered when they hit bottom. Emma's nerves were so frayed she flinched.

Hal wasn't getting to the bottom of the girl's problem with the mention of Eli. She couldn't stop until she had zeroed in on what was wrong. "How come Adam didn't come in tonight? He always does."

"He did not want to." Emma glanced at Hal before she took a fork out of the water. "I know that look, Hallie. It is your what is Emma not telling me look, and I am dying to know."

"You hit the nail on the head. I've been trying to figure out what is wrong with you all evening," Hal said sharply. "You and Adam came back early without any fish, and he went home without so much as a gute bye to John and me. It doesn't take much to see something is wrong. If it isn't Eli's trouble bothering you, maybe it is something about Adam."

Tears pricked Emma's eyes. She blinked hard to make them go away. "Adam is mad at me."

"That is hard to believe. Adam has the patience of Job where you're concerned," Hal said bluntly as she dropped another handful of silverware in the water. As she mulled that thought over, Hal gave Emma a hard look. "Or, did his patience finally wear out? Is that it?"

"I am not sure what happened, Hallie. Adam listened to me talk about Eli and Levi ----." She paused when Hal frowned at

201

her. "Ach, I know you told me not to talk about the other men in my life, but Adam asked. He seemed interested and concerned that I was upset, because Eli had taken off and Levi is dating Katie Yost. That is until I noticed he was angry. I told him if he did not want to hear my problems he should not worry about me bending his ear anymore."

Hal swiped a spoon with her cloth. "What did Adam say?"

"He picked up his fishing gear and pointed to the buggy. He did not talk all the way home. Believe me, I tried to get him to tell me what was bothering him. When he finally did, I wished I had not asked. Now I do not know what to do."

"With all your other special friends out of the picture that just leaves Adam," Hal suggested softly.

Emma's eyes widened. "What about Adam?"

"We need to do a pro and con list on him," Hal said, leveling Emma with a serious gaze.

"Ach, nah! Adam is just my friend, or he was." Emma paused to give that some thought. "In the beginning, I wanted to help Adam feel better about being with people." Again she paused. "Somehow my helping him got turned around to Adam helping me by listening to my problems. He became my best friend. He is such a kind man and fun to be with. He has a gute sense of humor."

"Uh huh."

Emma's head came up. She squinted down her nose at Hal. "What does uh huh mean?"

"That sounds like a pretty good pro list. I was thinking those very things were what attracted me to your father," Hal said.

"Ah, Hallie, nah! I just like being with Adam as a friend. He likes doing the same things I do, and he listens to me. Or, he did. He does not want anything to do with me now," she said, her voice trembling as her eyes moistened.

"What did Adam say exactly?" Hal prodded.

"Adam says I have been reckless with my life and hurt the feelings of all my special friends by just thinking about myself." Emma picked at a stain on her apron. "He can see why they lost interest in dating me."

"Is he right? Is that what you did?"

Emma gave a long trembling sigh. "In Adam's eyes it is, but I did my best to make amends. I made sure they knew I wasn't going to marry them. That is why I think the men will move on."

"Isn't that for the best if you didn't really love any of your special friends? You wouldn't have been happy married to a man you didn't love," Hal assured her.

"Recht now I am relieved my special friends are looking for love with someone else. But ----," Emma paused, teary eyed.

"Go on," Hal insisted.

"Why am I feeling bad if I did the recht thing?"

"Perhaps, there is one of those special friends you are going to miss more than the rest. You just didn't know it at the time," Hal said wisely as she headed for the back door to throw out the dish water. "Emma, think about that a minute." She came back and took Emma's dish towel to dry out the pan. "Have any idea yet which man that might be?"

"The only man I miss being with is Adam, my best friend," Emma said frankly.

"Uh huh," Hal said knowingly.

"Stop the uh huh, Hallie. He is just my friend so it is natural I miss him," Emma chided. "I will have to get over that. Adam is not coming back." Before Hal could reply, Emma left the kitchen. She rushed up the stairs, and her bedroom door shut.

~

Emma had been forlorn for days. Nothing Hal said made a difference. The girl was sure she was going to wind up an old maid. It seemed to take all her energy to get from one day to the next. The girl was barely eating and not sleeping. Hal wanted to do something to help her, but she didn't know how.

One afternoon, Hal hitched Ben to the open buggy and drove to the Mast farm to check on Mary. She wasn't there long. Mary was the picture of health.

When Hal made it back to the intersection, she stopped. She could turn toward home or drive straight ahead. That road lead to the Keim farm. She wrestled with herself and worried

203

Emma would be mad if she found out. With a flick of the reins, she drove across the road anyway.

Hal drove down the driveway past the house and barn and pulled in front of Adam's carpenter shop. She was glad to see he didn't have a customer at the moment.

When he heard the door open and shut, Adam glanced up from a chair he was sanding. He straightened and gave a quick, unemotional nod as he watched Hal come toward him.

"Gute afternoon," Hal said cheerfully.

With a suspicious look, Adam raised a questioning eyebrow.

Running her hand over the chair, Hal said, "Very nice. I came to get you to make a special gift for John. A rocker."

Adam took out his notepad. "John has a rocker."

"He does, but I want him to have a new one," Hal insisted.

Adam wrote, "How soon?"

"No hurry. Just when you get it done," Hal said.

Adam wrote, "Is the rocker for John's birthday?"

"Nah," Hal said.

"What is the special occasion? I should have the rocker built by then," Adam insisted, watching her closely.

Adam wasn't making this easy. She had to come up with a reason for the gift. Adam waited. She babbled, "Our anniversary. Wedding one. That's it. In August. Will that give you enough time?"

Adam nodded. He wrote, "Is this rocker a surprise?"

"Jah. We only have one rocker. I want to sit in it sometimes. When I want to rock the babies. When John is home he gets the rocker," Hal fumbled for an explanation. Adam stared at her with a raised eyebrow.

He wrote, "Want to tell me why you really came?"

Hal grimaced. "Oh, fudge! Am I that bad at fooling you?"

Adam suppressed a grin and nodded yes.

"All recht, you're going to consider me a butt in mom, but you have to let me talk and not try to interrupt. Promise?"

Adam shrugged.

"It's about Emma." Adam's head shot up. "You promised me you would listen." He started sanding again. "Emma's

204

miserable, and you are too. I can see that. Emma told me what you said to her. Put yourself in her place. What if you had six different girls trying to date you?"

Adam's brow wrinkled as he waved his hand sideways.

"All recht, maybe it's not a problem for a man. Emma came to realize she didn't love any of the special friends. She felt bad when they all wanted to marry her. You didn't give her a chance to tell you she told each of them she wouldn't marry them so they could move on with their lives," Hal said.

Adam mused over that thought as he started sanding a leg.

Hal wondered if she was finely getting through to him. "Jah and what's more, Emma figured out too late the man she wanted to spend time with and misses the most is you, Adam Keim." Adam stopped sanding. He was paying attention. "That just shows you were meant to be close. You two are so much alike. You enjoy the same things, think alike and could have such a gute life together. Adam you really should go talk to Emma and try to come to an understanding."

Adam gave her a troubled look. He wrote, "Are you done?"

"Jah," Hal said tersely.

He wrote, "Does Emma know you are here?"

"Of course, she doesn't. If she finds out, I'm saying I ordered a rocker for John, and I'm sticking to that story no matter who tells her different," Hal declared, feeling uneasy about Adam's question.

"Now you said what you really came for do you still want the rocker?" Adam wrote.

"Jah, I do," Hal said.

All business now, Adam wrote, "I will work on the rocker as soon as I finish this dining room set." Hal read the notepad. Adam stuck it in his pocket, turned his back and vigorously rubbed the chair.

Hal left with a helpless feeling. She failed to get through to Adam, and before Adam finished the rocker, she had to explain to John why he had to pay for it and hope he understood why she did it.

Chapter 22

At bedtime, Emma knelt at the window so she could see the heavens. She felt crushed, broken in spirit and lonely. If she'd had a dream with a chance of coming true earlier she'd been too dense and blind to see it. Now it was too late.

"God, what do I do now? Give me strength to endure what is next in my life even if it is not to my liking." She tried to continue the prayer, but her thoughts were in too much turmoil. Exhausted from fretting, she slipped into bed and let an exhausted sleep over take her.

In the middle of the night, a beam flooded Emma's bedroom. This wasn't the ordinary small flashlight beam. It was a large spotlight glow. She pattered to the window, but she couldn't make out the person below with the bright light in her eyes. She didn't have any idea who this could be. She was curious and anxious at the same time to find out. She prayed the man she should have picked all along had changed his mind and came back to her. Emma raised the window. "I am coming."

Emma's voice was loud enough to wake Hal. She slipped to the window and looked out.

"Was ist letz?" John muttered drowsily.

Hal eased back into bed and whispered gleefully as she listened to bare feet pussyfoot down the stairs. "Nothing's wrong. Go back to sleep. Everything's suddenly recht. Things are looking up for Emma, John Lapp."

John answered her with snores.

∽

Emma walked tentatively around the corner of the house, wondering who she'd find waiting for her. Behind the spotlight, she could see the dark form edge toward her. The bright light blinded Emma. She shielded her eyes with a hand. In front of the light, she saw a large hand extended palm up toward her. Her heart beat faster as in her mind's eye she instantly recognized that hand. It was the one in her dreams that kept fading away when she reached for it. This time, she prayed she wasn't dreaming as she reached out and put her hand in the palm. The fingers closed firmly around her hand. Emma felt the strong grip. It didn't fade away this time. It belonged to a man that wanted to take care of her. It was Adam's hand.

Adam set the spotlight on the ground so it illuminated both of them. His serious eyes met Emma's tearful ones.

She cried, "Ach, Adam. I have missed you so much." Her heart started to pound as she waited for his answer.

Adam gazed at her and nodded earnestly. He had missed her, too. He pulled Emma to him. He leaned toward her, placed his warm hands on her cheeks and gave her a kiss.

That moment was enough to rid Emma of her desperation and heartache. With a quick motion, Adam turned loose of Emma. He rubbed his neck as he looked at her intently.

"What is wrong now?" Emma asked.

Adam picked up the spotlight and pointed to the swing on the porch as he took her by the arm. They walked up the steps, and Adam placed the spotlight on the rod so they were both flooded in light. He sat down beside Emma and wrote. "Sorry I kissed you. I suppose you are mad at me all over again."

"Why would I be mad? As I recall, it was you that was angry with me," Emma puzzled, handing him back the notepad.

Adam wrote, "I remember you said it was very important to you to follow the rule about no personal touching before marriage so I am sorry."

"Ach," Emma said softly as she placed her hand on his chest and felt his strong heart beats. She swallowed hard, caught up in his unwavering gaze. "Please do not be sorry. If you are sorry for kissing me when I wanted you to that just might make me angry. Can you see I know now that it was you I had been waiting for all along to kiss me and to hold me? Not anyone else. I told the others that to keep them from kissing me."

In that moment that felt so right, all the heartache and desperation Emma felt of late turned to joy. She knew the feeling she had for Adam was the deep, lasting love Hal talked about. His strong arms went around her, and she saw intense devotion replace the sadness in his eyes. He kissed her once lightly then again and hugged her to him.

She looked over his shoulder at the many stars in the dark sky and held onto Adam tightly, silently thanking God for giving her this chance to be happy. Suddenly, she felt very lucky. Her dream had come true. Her prayers were answered.

The next morning, John shut off the alarm. "Did I dream a special friend came in the night to see Emma?"

"Nah, it happened." Hal kissed him on the cheek.

He rubbed his cheek. "You are too cheerful. Is there reason to be? I have been so worried. Emma looks like she does not feel gute, and now she does not have special friend dates anymore. Still she acts like she is love sick," John worried.

"Jah, she has been that," Hal said with a lilt to her voice.

"We could hardly turn around, but what there was a different man visiting Emma then suddenly none of them are at the door," John complained, slipping on his pants. "Which one of the men is it that made her feel this way?"

"All of them," Hal said simply.

John looked mystified. "All?"

"Emma was so miserable she couldn't make a choice about which special friend she wanted to be with. Finally, I couldn't stand her tormenting herself anymore so I had a talk with her. We did a pro and con test to see if that would make her have a better idea of how much she likes each man."

John twisted around on the bed and grinned at Hal. "I am curious. Did you do this pro and con test on me?"

"Nah, I didn't bother. I was in the situation of most Plain girls. I didn't have any choices but you," she said truthfully.

"Now that is wrong. You had one. What was his name?" John thought a minute than snapped his fingers. "Bill King."

"His name is Phil King," Hal said in disdain.

John chuckled.

Hal folded her arms over her chest. "Shame on you! You were teasing me. You knew his name all the time, and you know very well he wasn't any competition for you. If I had used the pro and con test for him, his pro column would have been empty and his con column full."

"Do you ever feel the need to do a pro and con on me now?" John asked, pretending to be serious.

Hal shook her finger at him. "I just might now that you brought it up, but I'd have to get a thick notepad and a new pencil with a large eraser. That way when I changed my mind about what I wrote on the pro side, I can erase and stick it on the con side. Do you want to hear what Emma said about the men or not?"

"Jah," he sighed.

"Let's see. Emma didn't care for Eli's life style."

John looked relieved. "I am glad about that. Who else?"

"Levi."

John perked up. "Levi is a gute, young man. I always thought he should marry Emma."

"Emma's father liking his choice for her husband doesn't count. She says he's like a brother. Next was Amos Coblentz."

"Him, too? Are you sure?" John asked in disbelief.

Hal looked amazed at how dense her husband had been. "John, you've seen him come pick Emma up for rides."

"Jah."

Amused, Hal said, "Why else do you think the man was trying so hard to find a new teacher for next term?"

It was as though a lamp came on in John's head. "Is that what that was about? Emma was a gute teacher. I could not figure out why he wanted her removed."

"Amos is in a rush. He's thinking about his children's need for a mother, but Emma didn't want to rush into a decision. Next is Bobby Keim. Emma thinks he's looking for Annie when he sees her. She doesn't think that will change until some entirely different woman comes along to interest him."

John's brow furrowed. "Sounds to me like there is not one of those Emma wants. Which one came to visit in the night?"

Hal smiled like the cat who ate the canary. "None of them. There is one more man."

"Ach, nah! How did I miss that one?" John asked dryly.

"Because he was recht under your nose and Emma's, too, all the time. It's Adam."

John drew a blank. "Adam who?"

"Adam Keim," Hal said impatiently.

"Him?"

Hal sat down beside John. "The idea hadn't entered Emma's mind either until I suggested it. Ah nah, she said. Adam wasn't a special friend. He's just her fishing buddy. She said Adam is a gute listener, has a gute sense of humor and her best friend."

"And what did you say?"

"I told her the way she described him was the very attributes that attracted me to her father." Hal gave John another peck on the cheek.

John grinned. "So that is what is on my pro side."

"Until you tease me about Phil King again. Then I'm hunting that pencil with the eraser," Hal threatened playfully.

"Who would have thought of Adam Keim?"

"I did. Didn't I tell you awhile back Adam had the inside track. Most of the time, the other men were trying to keep Emma interested, but it was Adam dating her," Hal boasted as she stood up and wiggled into her dress. In a soft voice she said, "Then again what I think doesn't count anymore than your ideas do when it's Emma's choice to make. Although since Emma had some time away from Adam, I think she figured out why she missed him so much. I'm guessing she's finally going to make a choice, and it will be the recht one this time. So hurry up. We have to get downstairs and see what she says."

When John and Hal came down for breakfast carrying the two girls, Emma was humming as she cooked breakfast.

"What did I tell you? Things are looking up around here," Hal whispered in John's ear as she put Redbird in a high chair.

"What makes you so sure and certain?" John asked softly as he put Beth in the other high chair.

"Emma is humming." The whispers made Emma turn around. "Would you tell us what has made you so cheerful this morning?" Hal asked, trying not to sound too eager.

"Adam came to see me last night. He is no longer mad at me," Emma said, grinning at them.

Hal hugged her. "I am so glad."

"Funny thing. I asked what made him change his mind and come to see me. Adam did not have an answer." Emma peered intently at Hal.

"I imagine he just came to his senses and decided to make peace with you. I'm sure he missed you as much as you missed him," Hal said offhandedly.

"That he did say," Emma said, turning the sausage cakes.

"This is great news, ain't so, John? Emma is teaching school again next term. She has Adam dating her which is what she wants. Now she doesn't have to worry anymore about what is happening at home. I'm handling everything just fine here. At least now I cook well enough to keep us from starving."

"That is right. I have not seen food that was inedible lately anyway," John said with a twinkle in his eyes.

"John Lapp, I don't think you ever saw anything I cooked that you couldn't eat," declared Hal.

"I did," John said, grinning from the mud room doorway.

"What was it?" Hal demanded.

"Something you threw into the pig pen," John replied.

Emma turned around fast with the spatula in her hand and dripped lard down her apron. "You found food with the pigs?"

"Jah, I did, and not even the pigs would eat that black chunky thing. They tried soaking it up in the mud wallow and that did not soften it," he said and laughed as he turned away.

Hal said, "Denki for sharing, John Lapp."

Emma yelled," Look out, Daed!"

John ducked, but too late. He felt the soft thud on the back of his head as a quilted potholder bounced off and dropped by his feet.

211

Homemade Clothes Soap Recipes

Powder

2/3 bar Fels Naptha Soap Bar
½ cup Borax
½ cup Washing Soda

Grate the Fels Naptha Soap Bar. Add Borax and Washing Soda. Mix together and store in air tight container. Use 1 to 2 tablespoon per load. Low sudsing. Can be used in HE washers.

Liquid

1/3 Fels Naptha Soap Bar
½ cup Borax
½ cup Washing Soda
2 gallons water (32 cups)

Grate the Fels Naptha Soap Bar. Heat 6 cups of water in a saucepan and add grated Fels Naptha until soap is melted. Add Borax and Washing Soda and stir until dissolved. Remove from heat. Pour 4 cups hot water into a 2 gallon bucket. Add soap mixture and stir. Add remaining water and stir. Let soap sit for about 24 hours until it gels. Use ½ cup detergent per load of laundry. Low sudsing. Can be used in HE washers.

Fay Risner lives with her husband on a central Iowa acreage. Now that she has retired from her CNA job at the local nursing home, she divides her time between writing, enjoying country life, gardening and fishing.

Risner's books, with 12 font print, are reader friendly. She writes a contemporary Amish fiction series set in Iowa, a historical mystery series with a Midwestern Iowa small town flair and Stringbean Hooper westerns. The stories pull readers into each scenes, making it hard for them to put the books down until the end. Each book leaves readers wanting another book to see what happens to the characters next.

After Risner's father had Alzheimer's, her interest in helping caregivers led her to write two books on the subject. Her work as a CNA gave her much insight and experience with this disease. She was awarded the 2004 Nurse Aide award from the Iowa Health Care Association and the 2006 Professional Caregiver Award from the North Central Iowa Alzheimer's Association. In the past, she was a volunteer speaker for the Alzheimer's Association and facilitated an Alzheimer's support group.

http:www.booksbyfaybookstore.weebly.com is Fay Risner's website where you will find her books, reviews and blog.

Nurse Hal books found in my online bookstore and signed by me. Sold at Amazon and other sites. Also on kindle and nook for ereaders.

Nurse Hal Among The Amish series

Promise is a Promise - book one
The Rainbow's End – book two
Hal's Worldly Temptations - book three
As Her Name Is So Is Redbird – book four
and
Christmas Traditions – a look at Margaret Yoder's life before her husband, Levi, died and she moved in with her son, Luke, and his family.

I'm always thrilled to receive reviews from readers and relish all of them. I'd like to share this one and encourage all of you to keep the reviews coming. I love them, and I know Nurse Hal would be pleased.

Good morning, Fay!

I am a new fan of yours! I just finished reading Book 2 in your Nurse Hal series and was wondering if you plan a third book about Hal and the Lapps. Honestly, I feel as if all of the people I've read about in the series are friends of mine, and that's thanks to the way you write. I am so curious to know what's happened to Hal and John after their camping trip in the picnic grove, and if Hal actually gets baptized, marries John, and becomes mama to the Lapp children. Guess you could say I'm not ready for that series of books to be at an end.

I pray that you'll continue your writing career; what an awesome blessing from the Lord to be able to express yourself in such a way. I'm also praying for Book 3.....and 4....and 5....